LIES AND TRUTH ON XINJIANG

Exposing the US-Led Infowar Against China

Compiled by Global Times

五洲传播出版社
China Intercontinental Press

图书在版编目（CIP）数据
关于新疆的谣言与真相 / 环球时报编．-- 北京：
五洲传播出版社，2020.2
ISBN 978-7-5085-4414-4

Ⅰ．①关… Ⅱ．①环… Ⅲ．①新闻报道－作品集－中
国－当代 Ⅳ．①I253

中国版本图书馆 CIP 数据核字 (2020) 第 025542 号

关于新疆的谣言与真相（英文）

编　　者：环球时报
出 版 人：荆孝敏
责任编辑：宋博雅
助理编辑：高倩倩
封面设计：熊晓莹
内文制作：北京优品地带文化发展有限公司
出版发行：五洲传播出版社
地　　址：北京市北三环中路 31 号生产力大楼 B 座 6 层
邮　　编：100088
发行电话：010-82005927，010-82007837
网　　址：http://www.cicc.org.cn http://www.thatsbooks.com
印　　刷：北京雅昌艺术印刷有限公司
版　　次：2020 年 2 月第 1 版第 1 次印刷
开　　本：710 毫米 ×1000 毫米　1/16
印　　张：17.75
字　　数：353 千字
定　　价：148.00 元

Foreword

All of a sudden, Xinjiang Uygur Autonomous Region in Northwest China found itself caught in the frontline of a public opinion war between China and the West, which were on two entirely different pages.

Xinjiang's governance mechanism in recent years is both legitimate and morally justifiable, as it is targeted at solving pressing problems and restoring peace and stability, which is the basis of safeguarding human rights. Terrorist attacks frequently battered Xinjiang in the earlier years, when the actual severity of the situation in the region was much more serious than what the media had revealed. The tensions transpiring in the region put lives of the locals at a greater risk than those in the rest of the country, and dealt a heavy blow to social order. Terrorism also crushed local tourism and other industries, and made human rights unattainable.

To reverse the situation, the Xinjiang society has put great efforts — and paid huge prices — in the quest for de-radicalization. Most government officials in Xinjiang were sent to villages to disburse their duties starting from the very basic level of society, something few people would be willing to do under normal circumstances. Xinjiang has endured such an unusual period.

The US and Western public opinion war against Xinjiang was based on Western human rights standards and their value system. The West does not care about the urgent problems gripping Xinjiang, and even denies the terrorist nature of the violent attacks taking place in the region. It is always easier said than done! There are even some forces that gloat over Xinjiang's turmoil and want to burden China with the crisis stemming from the region.

It is difficult to engage in a debate in such circumstances. The West blatantly distorts and smears the governance of Xinjiang in their public opinion environment, which due to their wider reach often leads to extremely negative influence.

However, what Xinjiang is now witnessing is in sharp contrast with what the West has depicted. Peace and stability have been deeply entrenched in the region. Tourism has resumed and is growing at a rapid pace. It has been made possible thanks to the success of the de-radicalization work with the vocational education and training centers at its helm.

I have stated in several articles that the high-intensity governance of Xinjiang in recent years is not an ideal situation, and the training centers are unprecedented measures designed for the specific era. Those measures were politically well-intended and have yielded good results by preventing thousands of deaths and saving the facets of Xinjiang's social fabric from crumbling like a second Chechnya. Xinjiang has seen not a single case of terrorist attack for three years, which means neither any civilian life is lost nor any terrorist killed for justice. Positive change as it is will script the real meaning of human rights.

Human rights are neither an empty slogan that the entire world can be painted with without considering specific conditions, nor a double-standard geopolitical game.

Global Times reporters and commentators have been resolutely engaged in a public opinion war, presenting the outside world with the real facts and pragmatic logic of the human rights situation in Xinjiang from the very heart of the autonomous region. They also know the outside world well and have explored for a common ground for the distinct Chinese and Western narratives.

All the articles in this book were written by Global Times staff reporters with dedication and love for the motherland and for people of all ethnic groups in Xinjiang, and with persistence trying to awaken more from Western propaganda. I must say, as I write this foreword, I can attest that we have done our part to the fullest.

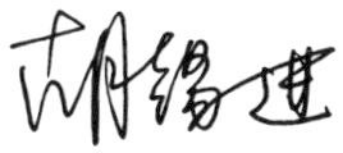

Hu Xijin

Editor-in-Chief, Global Times

CONTENTS

Reports on Xinjiang

NOTE

When interviewing people of different ethnic groups in Northwest China's Xinjiang Uygur Autonomous Region, the Global Times reporters would usually ask the interviewees the spelling of their names in Latin characters. In this book, while mentioning the names of people from different ethnic groups in Xinjiang, their preferences have been followed.

For interviewees of ethnic groups in Xinjiang, they prefer to be addressed by their first name. For example, if a girl is named Ayigul Memet, she would prefer to be called Ayigul, not Memet. Memet is her father's name; Memet Tursun is her father's full name, where Tursun refers to Ayiguli's grandfather.

REPORTS ON XINJIANG

Chapter I

SEEING WITH ONE'S OWN EYES

"What is the situation in Xinjiang right now? Is it dangerous to visit?" These are questions frequently asked by people whom have been recommended to pay a visit to Northwest China's Xinjiang Uygur Autonomous Region. The terror attacks that happened in this region had kept tourists away.

But Xinjiang is never a place that is too far away. Anyone who steps into the region, which covers one-sixth of the Chinese territory, will get the feeling this region is closely connected to the motherland. There are grassroots public servants working hard to help lift villagers out of poverty, farmers and herdsmen living along the border who voluntarily safeguard the borderline, religious figures who guide believers to unite different ethnic groups, and educators who dedicate themselves to cultivating the next generation. All people living in Xinjiang are working hard for the stability and prosperity of the region and all of China.

Xinjiang's education programs improve life chances for trainees, families

By Liu Xin in Hotan | Oct 21, 2018

Extremism would cost their chances for a better life once they go astray further, said trainees in a vocational education and training program in Hotan, Northwest China's Xinjiang Uygur Autonomous Region. They said the skills they had acquired would help in their efforts to pull themselves out of poverty.

A group of Global Times reporters visited a vocational education and training center in Hotan's Yutian County in October 2018. A sign outside the center reads, "Turn people who need jobs into people who have the necessary skills for the jobs."

Hotan is one of the four areas in southern Xinjiang that have in the past struggled to combat terrorist activities and the spread of religious extremism.

At the center, factories producing footwear, local snacks and more have been established and operating. Trainees who have performed well in courses such as the country's common language, national laws and vocational skills, as well as de-extremization education, can choose to work on the production lines, Yutian's deputy county chief Adil Abdueni told the Global Times.

Matkasim Tudi, a trainee at the center, now is also in charge of running a printing plant.

He and some other trainees raised 4.5 million yuan (about $649,400) to purchase printing machines and started their businesses in July 2018 after moving into the plant, which was built by the local government, he told the Global Times.

He said that the plant had received 3.7 million yuan in orders since July, which mainly included printing notebooks for students. It would take three to four months to finish the orders.

Workers at the plant earn about 1,500 yuan a month, plus bonuses. Most of them give the money to their families since they have free room and board.

Trainees can get up to 600 yuan in subsidies and at least two days off a week during training, a manager surnamed Yuan from a footwear plant at the center told the Global Times.

A changed and better life

Officials reached by the Global Times in Hotan said that most of the trainees had at one time been coerced, lured or pushed into terrorist or extremist activities. Xinjiang prioritizes rehabilitation in accordance with the Criminal Law, Criminal Procedure Law, Anti-Terrorism Law and other relevant national laws and regulations.

Trainees can receive free vocational training to improve their command over the country's common language, national laws and regulations and vocational skills, among others.

"I was born in a religious family and was told that I was born to be a Muslim. I had little knowledge of laws before participating in the program. Distorted doctrines spread by religious extremists are against our laws," Eli Matusun told the Global Times.

"The program was good timing for me, since we learned that extremism is the root of terrorism and violence and if we go further astray, we would become terrorists," he said.

Eli Matusun said that he hopes to learn more through the program and plans to start his own business in the future.

Matkurban, who is working at an electronic production plant, had attended a high school in Northeast China's Heilongjiang Province. But before he took the national college entrance examinations, his father — who had been influenced by extremism — asked him to drop out of school.

"He asked me to come back and learn religious doctrines and he said that he

Trainees play volleyball at the training center. (Photo: Fan Lingzhi / GT)

would not go to heaven if I didn't." Matkurban had to give up his dream of going on to medical school.

Just as he was at a loss in life, he joined the program. "I am interested in electronic production and want to learn more here," he said. "It's like being back in school."

The factories have also arranged dormitories for married trainees.

Rukeyam Abdukadir, who now works at a plant with her husband, said she can now dress however she likes and has improved standing in her family. Coming from a religious family, she had been forbidden from wearing anything except robes. She was also forbidden from working and even watching TV.

"I am the person who manages the family money now," she said.

The irresponsible reports made by some Western media outlets about the training program were "inconsistent with what really happened in Xinjiang," Adil Abdueni said.

"I was born in Yutian and I knew that influenced by religious extremism, many young people here did not go to school after finishing their primary schooling. They were easily harmed by religious extremism and finally went astray and ended up in stirring up terrorist attacks."

After joining vocational education and training programs, they can earn their own living and contribute to society, Abdueni said.

Xinjiang women gain respect and self-recognition

By Liu Xin in Kashi | Oct 24, 2018

The ongoing de-extremism efforts in Northwest China's Xinjiang Uygur Autonomous Region and the launch of vocational education and training centers

Three female dancers in the night market in Hotan (Photo: Fan Lingzhi / GT)

have helped reduce discrimination against women, and by playing a more active role in family and society, they have gained self-respect.

With the promotion of vocational skills, national laws and regulations and de-extremism education, more residents and trainees in Xinjiang begin to realize that women should not be treated as the "personal possessions" of their husbands, according to officials reached by the Global Times in Xinjiang.

Some husbands influenced by extremism would forbid their wives from working, force them to wear robes and cover their faces, or even beat their wives. Instead of obeying laws and regulations, they used distorted extremist doctrines to guide their life, the Global Times learned from a training center in Kashi.

Many female trainees at vocational education and training centers in Hotan and Kashi shared with the Global Times their stories of living a depressing life as victims of extremism.

Gulbahar Arken, a 24-year-old trainee from the training center in Kashi, was forced, when she was 15, by her father to "marry" an illegal imam, who was 40 years older.

"I was his 7th wife ... At that time, I was too young to get registered with the man in the local civil affairs bureau."

"My father, who is influenced by extremism, said that by marrying this man, I can go to heaven," Gulbahar said.

She said she was beaten by the man with the handle of a shovel and was forced to learn distorted religious extremism doctrines. She tried to run away several times but failed, with her father sending her back to the man.

Gulbahar finally managed to "get divorced" from the man after the man said "Talaq" three times to her. But her life seemed destroyed.

Triple Talaq or Islamic instant divorce means when "Talaq" is repeated three times by the husband in a Muslim family, then the couple will be formally divorced.

"The best time of my life has gone miserably and I did not and would never

Women chat on a street corner in Kashi on October 23, 2018. (Photo: Fan Lingzhi/GT)

understand why my father did this to me," Gulbahar said.

However, the influence of extremism to Gulbahar did not end with her "marriage." She still dressed in robes and lived by distorted doctrines but also asked others to do so — the victim of extremism become the crime's defender.

Gulbahar said she likes life in the center and is trying to make up by learning vocational skills, which she missed in her previous life.

Removing restrictions

The practice of men asking women to wear only robes has been stopped and the situation of banning them from working has also changed.

Patigul Abaydulla, 26, is now working with her husband in a vocational education and training center in Hotan.

She told the Global Times on October 22 that she had to cover herself thoroughly with a veil and robe at the request of her husband, who was influenced

A woman works in a workshop near her village in Xinjiang. (Photo: Fan Lingzhi / GT)

by extremism. The only income for the family of four members was her husband's earnings as a farmer and as a part-time driver.

She said that her husband has changed a lot after coming to the training center. "He has become considerate and has started to respect my parents ... and I now earn at least 1,500 yuan a month. Family life is getting better," she said.

"It is painful for women to cover our beauty ... why should we do this?" Madina Akbar, 21, who was once pressured by peers to wear a robe, told the Global Times.

Madina said she was once called a heretic when she wore short sleeves and a skirt when shopping in a bazaar in Urumqi in 2015.

Live for herself

Extremists also forbid the use of condoms but few of them would take care of the children, local people said.

The Global Times learned that girls in Xinjiang, especially in rural areas, usually get married at an early age and some would lie about their age to get registered with the local civil affairs bureaus.

"Compared with girls in other places, especially in the metropolis, the youth of many girls here is too short. They would soon be bound to the family and children and have little consideration of themselves," Madina told the Global Times.

Many trainees at the centers told the Global Times that they could find jobs and make money using the vocational skills they have acquired, which help them find renewed value in life, gain self-recognition and earn family respect.

Male trainees reached by the Global Times also said that they respect women and admire their contributions to the family.

For women who choose to stay at home to take care of the family, their lives have also been enriched.

Li Fang, director of the women's association in Xinjiang who is stationed in Naizhen Town in Kashi, told the Global Times that they have evening schools at the residential communities for women and started women's associations in villages to communicate with them.

"Mothers play a crucial role in the families and their mental state and educational level would have a greater influence on their children's development," Li said.

She noted that more women are joining the evening school to learn Putonghua, which also helps enhance their children's proficiency in it.

Efforts to eliminate extremism in Xinjiang change local lives for the better

By Fan Lingzhi and Liu Xin in Kashi | Oct 27, 2018

What happened to trainees before they joined the vocational training and education programs in Northwest China's Xinjiang Uygur Autonomous Region? How did they change after joining the program?

Stories of trainees in Kashi, a city in southern Xinjiang, show how extremism has haunted this place and destroyed people's lives, and what has happened since the local government took various measures on eliminating extremism.

Going astray

According to the regulations on eliminating extremism in Xinjiang, which took effect in April 2017, 15 behaviors were listed as extreme. These include expanding the concept of halal beyond traditional dietary rules; imposing extreme restrictions on normal social interactions and personal behavior and thought; interfering with the social life of others; wearing or forcing women to wear a burka; and covering one's face with a veil.

Trainees at a training center in Kashi all violated these regulations.

The Global Times learned from the training center that trainees here usually wrote their personal stories of "being influenced by extremism" and shared them with others.

Jurat Memet said he was duped into attending a terrorist training camp.

He was born in Kashi in 1968 to parents who were well-educated and worked for a local transportation department. "My family's financial situation was good ... The residential community where I lived is home to many peoples, including Han, Uygur, Uzbek ... We lived in harmony and there was no difference between us."

"Our Han neighbors usually went door to door offering us fried snacks during the Spring Festival and we would give them New Year greetings. The neighbors gave us a handful of candy when we went to their homes," he recalled.

He graduated from university in 1988 and worked as a teacher in Kashi. In the 1990s he quit the job to do business, at a time when many people in Xinjiang went into business to earn quick money.

After going to Kyrgyzstan on a business trip, Jurat started to wander around, seeking more opportunities.

"I had grand plans but didn't try very hard," he said.

A man from Urumqi told Jurat that if he gave the man $3,000 he would take him to Cyprus, where the "chances of getting rich were everywhere."

But when they got to Turkey, Jurat was asked to hand over another $7,000 if he wanted to reach to Cyprus. He realized it was a con and decided to take his chances in Turkey.

During his stay in Turkey, Jurat met Tursun, who started to spread extremist and separatist ideas.

The man's nonsense included the claim that Uygur people are born to be Muslim. Jurat recalled with scorn that "shamefully, I bought into this bullshit … Before meeting him I never prayed, but later I noticed that if I didn't, they would isolate me. Living in this environment, you would unconsciously be influenced by extremism."

One day, Tursun told Jurat that he could bring him to Pakistan to "do big business." Jurat believed him and agreed.

"The man who led the group to Pakistan told us that he knew our background information very well and the only way to betray him was to die," Jurat said, noting that they were given an alias on their way to Pakistan.

Their destination was a high mountain. "There were tents every 200 to 300 meters and people who lived there seemed from all over the world. There were

Asians, black people ... they seemed to know little about each other," Jurat said.

He remembered seeing a flag with words "Army of Allah."

They were trained to use guns, make explosives, and assassinate people. They were also told to "kill heretics in the light of Allah."

Jurat said they could only eat peanuts, which were bought by people down the hill and hid in a certain spot.

Three months later, a man, who was funding the training camp, came to see "where his money was used." Trainees were later deployed to different places after the man left that day.

Jurat was asked to go back to Turkey. "A month later, they asked me to make a vow of loyalty to the 'East Turkistan Islamic Movement' organization and return to China and wait for my mission," Jurat said.

He was arrested by China's public security bureau soon after returning to China and sentenced to seven years in prison for attending a terrorist training camp, a violation of Chinese law.

"My family left me behind and my life become dark ... I complained every day and prayed to get rich which ended with nothing," said Jurat about his life after he was released from prison.

He was then sent to a training center in 2017. He said that living in the training center finally allowed him to get out from under the influence of extremism.

"I now think that it was lucky for me to get punished by laws when I first came back from Turkey ... otherwise I would not understand how I violated the laws and the result could have been a disaster."

"I realize that the deep reason for my mistake was not resisting the influence of extremism and I had not realized it violated national laws and regulations," Jurat said.

"I hope that my story will help others, and prevent them from being poisoned by extremism," he said, noting that he really missed the harmonious life of his childhood.

From victim to defender

Many other trainees shared their stories of becoming victims of extremism.

Melye Mugul was born into an extremist family and her grandmother demanded she learn distorted doctrines after graduating from high school.

She married a man in an Arabic country who, in Melye's words, has "abnormally extremist thought."

Melye was required to wear burka and cover her face even at home and was forbidden from going outdoors alone. Her husband even banned her parents from visiting her.

Melye became depressed after her husband forbade her from crying at her grandmother's funeral. She was called a heretic after visiting her father who was ill.

She finally divorced the man and returned to China.

Melye had not realized the harm of extremism and began to spread extremism. She thought she had "earned respect" from others for once having lived in Arabic countries and began to stop others from drinking or smoking.

Melye wore robes and covered her face with a veil. She told people about her previous life but turned her past into wonderful stories.

"I knew clearly that women there are like men's slaves … Many people are acting wrong in the name of religion … Life there was not as good as in our country, but I still tempted others to go there … Many families have broken up after listening to what I said," she said.

Dawutjiang Tursun's life was destroyed after he was influenced by extremism when he was 19 years old. He refused help from his boss because he thought the boss was a "heretic."

After quitting his job, Dawutjiang just stayed at home, lived by extremism doctrine and asked others to do the same.

Without any income for the family, his wife sometimes complained about him. He started to beat his wife because "a wife is affiliated to a husband and should absolutely obey him."

Abdueni Toxti, deputy head of the training center in Kashi, told the Global Times that extremism harms people's life in every aspect, and it can lead to terrorist attacks and violence.

Shohrat Zakir, chairman of the government of the Xinjiang Uygur Autonomous Region, said in an interview with the Xinhua News Agency that "Countering terrorism and extremism is still a long-standing, complicated and serious issue and requires us to be on high alert."

"In particular, the four prefectures in southern Xinjiang were threatened by terrorism and seriously influenced by the spread of religious extremism in the past," said Zakir.

He said that some residents there have a limited command of the country's

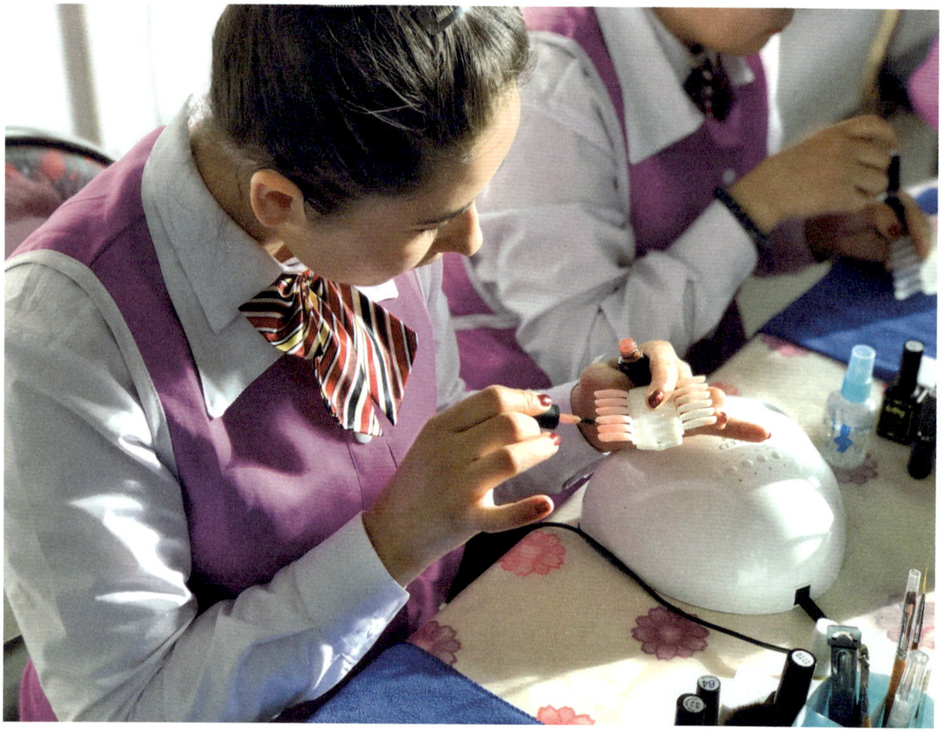

A trainee learns manicures in a vocational education and training center in Northwest China's Xinjiang Uygur Autonomous Region. (Photo: Liu Xin/GT)

national language and a limited sense and knowledge of the law. They often have difficulty finding employment due to limited vocational skills. This has made them vulnerable to coercion from terrorists and extremists.

Promoted situation

Xinjiang's de-extremism efforts and the launching of vocational education and training institutions have made some achievements.

According to data from the tourism bureau in the city of Kashi, more than 4.1 million tourists visited Kashi from January to September in 2018. They have brought revenues of more than 2.81 billion yuan ($400 million) to the city.

An owner of a hat shop in the scenic spot in the ancient section of the city told the Global Times that his business is much better with the increasing number of visitors to Kashi.

The Global Times saw visitors, performers and local residents dancing together in front of the scenic spot during a welcoming ceremony.

Life for trainees who have finished the program has also improved.

Abdunebi Abdurexit returned home from the training center in mid-October of 2018. He told the Global Times that his proficiency in the Chinese language, knowledge of national laws and regulations and vocational skills have been greatly enhanced.

He is working as a driver for a local telecommunication company. "I hope to work better and bring a better life to my family," he said.

Other family members can also see he has changed. His wife said that "he used to act like a male chauvinist and never cared about house duties. Now he gets up early every morning and helps with the housework," she said.

The employment of women has also improved.

Li Huijun, CEO of a garment factory in Kaishi, told the Global Times that she has witnessed the efforts to eliminate extremism.

"When we first came here, many employees could not speak Putonghua (Mandarin), which made it difficult to communicate with them. Many women's husbands forbade them from working here and beat them when they returned home from the factory," Li said.

After receiving education on counter extremism, the national common language, vocational training and national laws and regulations, the employees have changed.

They have become more competitive and have higher demands from life. "If they earned 5,000 yuan last month but only 4,000 yuan this month, they feel dissatisfied with themselves."

"They can use the money they have earned to buy the clothes they like. They can provide better medical treatment for their parents. Some senior employees have received shares in the company. They run the company like it's their own," Li said.

1.12 million officials paired with local households in Xinjiang

By Liu Xin | Jan 4, 2019

The moment Yan Xuning said goodbye to Abdunebi Abdurexit's family in Qianjin Village and stepped out of their house, he was ambushed by the warm hug of two little Uygur girls, who told him they just finished school.

As the Party chief of Nazerbag, Kashi, Northwest China's Xinjiang Uygur Autonomous Region, Yan goes to the village frequently and the two little girls are his friends who often talk to him about their school.

Yan is among hundreds of thousands of officials in Xinjiang deployed to pair with local families.

With the aim of enhancing ethnic unity and facilitating poverty alleviation, Xinjiang has launched a campaign to encourage officials from government departments to station in villages and undertake activities among different ethnic groups since October 2016.

By the end of 2018, more than 1.12 million officials and government employees in Xinjiang have paired with 1.69 million local households as "relatives."

Officials stationed in villages are working hard and many of them don't get to rest even during holidays and festivals. Their efforts have paid off as their work has been recognized by residents, and poverty alleviation has received a boost, some Xinjiang officials reached by the Global Times said on January 4, 2019.

However, those efforts and achievements are ignored by some Western media outlets, who accused Beijing of forcing Uygur people in Xinjiang to "forsake their religion" and labeled local governments' efforts to improve residents' professional skills as "mass persecution" of Uygur people.

Pairing with ethnic groups and deploying officials to villages are part of Xinjiang's de-extremism efforts, an official from Xinjiang's publicity department, who requested anonymity, told the Global Times.

It is strange that the West only criticizes Xinjiang without giving useful advice, he said.

The region is seeking its own solution to eradicate extremism. Though there may be problems, it will figure them out and fix them in a timely manner, said the official.

Shohrat Zakir, chairman of the regional government of Xinjiang, said in an October interview with the Xinhua News Agency that Xinjiang set up vocational training and education centers for "people influenced by terrorism and extremism."

"Officials stationed in villages would also take care of families when some members are sentenced for taking part in extremist activities or are admitted to vocational training and education centers for being influenced by extremism," said

A child and his father in Aksu Prefecture in Xinjiang (Photo: Shan Jie / GT)

the anonymous official from the publicity department of Xinjiang.

Close connection

"Leaders at all levels should set an example … in pairing with local families and pay visits," Chen Quanguo, Party chief of Xinjiang, was quoted in a release from the United Front Work Department (UFWD) of the Communist Party of China (CPC) Central Committee on January 3, 2019.

Li Fang, who is the director of the women association of Xinjiang and was chosen to head the working team stationed in Qianjin in February 2017, has worked in the village for nearly two years.

Door-to-door visits and discussing methods to reduce poverty with villagers are Li's daily work.

"Officials deployed in villages or those paired with local families are responsible for promoting policies of the government, especially those for improving health

Young people in Aksu Prefecture of Xinjiang dance in a night club. (Photo: Fan Lingzhi / GT)

service and social insurance," said the anonymous official from Xinjiang's publicity department.

Promoting knowledge of laws and regulations as well as measures for poverty alleviation are the focus of their work, the official said, noting that many villagers living in remote areas are not well educated and have little knowledge of life away from home.

Great wall of steel

Officials and government employees would pay at least one visit to their paired families every two months and be there for five days at a time, according to the release from the UFWD.

Li told the Global Times that officials of the working team have paired with 34 households in the Qianjin Village. They live, eat and work with these families and organize various activities.

Li said that as part of the activities, children from the village have been organized to visit Urumqi, encouraged to take part in calligraphy and drawing contests and sent to a summer camp.

These activities have strengthened relations between officials and the villagers, Li said.

Kemu Tursun, a resident of Qianjin, said that with the help of officials stationed in the village, she applied for a position at a public welfare program and began to breed flowers to sell. She now has a monthly income of 1,800 yuan ($262).

Aside from deploying officials to villages, officials from the central government, as well as those from local governments in other regions, are encouraged to pair with local families in Xinjiang and pay visits.

According to data from the UFWD, a total of 4,063 officials coming from other regions have paired with 4,568 residents in Xinjiang.

Shenzhen has deployed several groups of officials to Xinjiang and launched 53 programs to help with poverty alleviation work. It helped build a base on producing fruits in Paxiang, a village in southwest Kashi, to help residents earn more, the Guangming Daily reported.

By the end of August 2018, the yearly income of every household in Paxiang had increased from 2,650 yuan to over 5,000 yuan.

"With the help of officials stationed in villages, women influenced by extremism and restricted within their homes now work in factories; farmers who knew little about the internet have started their own online businesses; young people who had nothing to do and idled about have now learned to fix machines; residents in Xinjiang have become more active in work and have a better life, which became a driving force to reduce poverty," read the release from the United Front Work Department.

Xinjiang is cultivating an active force to safeguard social stability, enhance ethnic unity and oppose separatism … All the ethnic groups are holding together closely like pomegranate seeds … to build a great wall of steel, said the UFWD release.

Putonghua school in southern Xinjiang becomes model for ethnic unity

By Shan Jie in Aksu | Jan 30, 2019

"To be honest, my dream is to go to Tsinghua University," Gulzeba Kurban, 11 years old, declared confidently in front of a dozen visitors.

The small girl with short hair and wearing glasses was in a navy blue Chinese style cotton uniform, looking smart, calm and confident.

Kurban Niyaz, headmaster of the school, plays the waist drum in the classroom. (Photo: Courtesy of Niu Haiyan)

She is a sixth grade student at the Standard Spoken and Written Chinese Language Primary School in Qianjin Township, Wushi County, Aksu Prefecture of Northwest China's Xinjiang Uygur Autonomous Region.

"Even though I'm good at literature, I will choose to learn chemistry or physics in university," Gulzeba said in fluent and clear Putonghua in one of the school's activity rooms. The room featured a small wooden desk in the ancient Chinese style and posters with information about the country's history and customs.

Looking outside the window brings views of boundless barley fields. It is winter, so there were just a few goats wandering around the bare field.

Gulzeba went to Beijing last summer for a school summer camp. Now she has a clear path for her future in mind — first, get admission to a junior high school in a big city in Xinjiang, then attend high school in an eastern city. After graduating from Tsinghua University, she wants to go for further education abroad.

Gulzeba said she wants to come back to her hometown after study to work in the field of education, just like her headmaster, whom she respects greatly.

In August 2003, Kurban Niyaz, the headmaster, founded the school with his own savings after seeing the development gap between his hometown and some eastern provinces.

Despite doubts, criticisms and difficulties, he has never stopped running and leading the school over the past 16 years.

Many of his students have had their lives changed through education. The first students entered universities in Shanghai and Tianjin in 2016. One of them was admitted by Tsinghua University with the highest score in Aksu.

On December 18, 2018 at the conference marking the 40th anniversary of China's reform and opening-up, Kurban was awarded a reform pioneer medal together with Alibaba co-founder Jack Ma Yun, Baidu co-founder Li Yanhong and former basketball star Yao Ming. In Beijing, he was received twice by China's top leaders.

Students read a text in Putonghua at the Standard Spoken and Written Chinese Language Primary School in Qianjin Township, Wushi County, Aksu Prefecture of Northwest China's Xinjiang Uygur Autonomous Region. (Photo: Fan Lingzhi / GT)

"I will not forget my original goal and task to allow more children to enjoy high-quality and fair education," Kurban said.

Quick learners

Qianjin Town is one and a half hours' drive from Aksu City. The Standard Spoken and Written Chinese Language Primary School of Qianjin Township is located next to a road in a quiet village.

In the center of the campus stands a three-meter-high sculpture of Confucius. The school features courses in Putonghua.

Even though many children could only speak Uygur before entering first grade, they were able to use Putonghua to express their basic needs in as little as two weeks thanks to the methods Kurban used. "Children can learn 50 new words a day," he said.

After six years of studying here, Gulzeba's Putonghua has become as good as that of any student in Beijing. She and her schoolmates often serve as interpreters for local residents who cannot speak Putonghua.

Apart from studying language, Gulzeba also learned to play the *erhu*, a traditional instrument, sing Peking Opera and recite a number of Chinese classics.

Six years ago, Gulzeba's parents, both police officers in Xinjiang, decided to send her to boarding school, as they were very busy at work.

This summer, Gulzeba will take her first major step on her plan for the future — the entrance exam for junior high school.

If students get a certain score, they are able to study in schools in one of Xinjiang's major cities under a policy launched in 2004 to support outstanding students from ethnic or poverty-stricken regions. Afterwards, they will have the chance to study in quality high schools around China, which means more opportunities to enter one of the country's top universities.

As a top five student in class, she is confident about the exam.

The school now has 639 students, and more than 90 percent were ethnic minority students from poverty-stricken families.

The fee for one semester is 1,000 yuan ($148.5), a cost that some families still cannot afford. "I secretly remit the tuition fees of many poor students," Kurban said. "But I won't tell you how many."

Wushi is a national-level poverty-stricken county. Rural children here lack family education, not to mention personal manners and good habits. In the past decade, local people have lived under a heavy religious environment.

"I have been to university, so I want to provide a good educational environment for local children," Kurban said. "I really hope that through education, our children can walk out of their restricted space into the wider world, changing their lives through knowledge."

He noted that the "language barrier used to hinder Uygurs from leaving the region."

"Should Uygurs only do Uygur dance and play Uygur instruments in Xinjiang? Ethnic groups need to be tolerant ... If you don't know the standard Chinese language or the beauty of Chinese culture, you can never step out and show your own talent on a bigger stage," he continued.

Finding the key

In Qianjin, 99.5 percent of residents are Uygurs. Kurban was born here, a remote township in a national-level poverty-stricken county in the west end of China bordering Kyrgyzstan.

He grew up in Yingawati Village by Taushgan Darya, opposite the Fourth Regiment of the First Division under Xinjiang Production and Construction Corps.

"My dream used to be becoming a carpenter. But then I saw the different food, costumes and vehicles in the Fourth Regiment, and understood that there was a world outside," Kurban told the Global Times.

He then decided to become the first university student from Qianjin.

In 1982, Kurban entered Xinjiang University, majoring in standard Chinese language and became a teacher at Aksu Vocational and Technical College in 1986.

In 1999, he entered the world of business just as reform and opening-up was in full swing in China and soon earned a fortune. "I could have earned more, but I wanted to do something meaningful for my hometown."

He decided to found a school in the township, teaching standard spoken and written Chinese. "Language is the key to the wider world and further roads," he believes.

"The Passion"

In 2003, Kurban invested 600,000 yuan in building the school, using a piece of land provided by the township government. He also recruited several Han teachers, including Li Yonghong, a teacher from the Fourth Regiment, who later became Kurban's most trusted working partner.

Most of the residents in the township cannot speak Putonghua, nor could they understand Kurban's intentions. Some even suspected that Kurban was trying to deceive the government in order to get land.

To recruit students, Kurban and the teachers went to villagers' homes to promote the school, and used small toys and picture books to attract children, something the residents of less-developed villages had never seen before.

Finally, more than 80 children registered at Kurban's school and became the first students there.

But it was extremely difficult over the years, Li, now the vice headmaster of the school, told the Global Times. Many of the children often cried as they could not speak any Putonghua initially. There were lice and fleas in the bedding, which also infected the teachers. Many teachers could not stand the environment and left.

Moreover, some extremists tried to deter Kurban from running the school and damaged the property from time to time. For instance, they took away the school's plaque or set fire to the kitchen.

But Kurban never faltered and believes he is on the right road. "In the hardest times, I like watching *The Passion of the Christ*. It helps me."

In 2010, the first graduates of Kurban's school took the admission exams for junior high school.

"I didn't know if my method worked or not. I had planned to escape," he said. However, to Kurban's surprise, 32 students out of 38 passed the exam, a result that had never been achieved in Aksu before.

After that, some parents were prepared to camp for a whole month outside the school to secure a place for their children.

In June 2016, the school moved into a new campus with the support of 16.5

million yuan of funds from Xinjiang's education department. The Aksu government also gave 760,000 yuan to the school in financial support annually.

National pioneer

On December 12, 2018, Kurban answered an official invitation asking him to attend the grand conference on reform and opening-up. He and his wife were then received by China's top leaders in Beijing twice. "It was like a dream," he said.

"The pupils at Qianjin school all have ideals and are also well-mannered and polite. They are grateful as well," Amina Yakexi at Aksu's education bureau told the Global Times. The school's focus is on practicing multi-cultural education and joining mainstream culture, and teaching students about national unity.

Now the region is promoting Kurban's methods, and he has been delivering speeches around Xinjiang.

"I have been on the right road by founding the standard Chinese language school and practicing ethnic unity," he said.

This winter holiday, he told his students to watch a Chinese movie every day. He also encouraged them to learn about Chinese celebrities.

He always tells the students, just like a drop of water can exist forever by running into the ocean, an ethnic group needs to blend into the big family of the country for continuous development. "One of the Uygur people's greatest achievements in history is to become a member of the Chinese family."

Xinjiang deploys officials in villages to help with poverty alleviation

By Liu Xin in Aksu | Feb 18, 2019

"Edible fungus grown from a bacteria stick needs to be cultivated in the shade of other trees … If the water we use has too much alkali, it will damage the fungus's quality," Wang Xin said, while checking the sprinkling irrigation system in a greenhouse.

Although he can usually be seen in farmland or greenhouses in Yusitunke Ayikule Village of Awati County in Aksu Prefecture of Northwest China's Xinjiang Uygur Autonomous Region, Wang is not a farmer or an agro-technician, but an official from the health commission of Aksu.

A law school graduate and former police officer, Wang is now working as the

Women from Tuowanke Maigaiti village learn to make knitted goods at a training workshop on February 16, 2019. This skill can earn 1,500 yuan to 2,000 yuan a month. (Photo: Fan Lingzhi / GT)

head of a six-member working group that was deployed to Yusitunke Village in January 2018. Before working in the village, he was stationed in five counties and villages in Aksu.

Since 2014, more than 43,700 officials in Xinjiang have been deployed in five batches to over 1,000 villages in Aksu.

Their tasks include collecting information on local economic and social conditions and people's needs, promoting the central government and Party's favorable policies on benefiting residents, strengthening grass-roots level Party organizations, mediating disputes between residents, and in particular helping with poverty alleviation work and promoting ethnic unity.

Human touch

The village where Wang works was registered as a deeply poverty-stricken village in 2017. Sixty-eight of the total 329 households in the village were registered as poor families.

In order to get a better understanding of the reasons behind their poverty, members of the working group usually cycle or walk when they visit local residents.

"By walking or cycling, we can stop at any time to say hello to villagers … We use our legs and bicycles to measure every inch of the country road," Wang said.

In response to villagers' requests, the working group applied for the national poverty alleviation fund and repaired a 5.7-kilometer cement road. The project offered temporary work to local residents, helping them earn a total of 129,000 yuan ($19,046) in 2018.

Since the village economy is mainly dependent on agriculture, the working group encourages local residents to plant vegetables, including tomatoes as well as edible fungus.

They invited agro-technicians from Urumqi to give lectures to local farmers, cultivate the vegetables in their seeding stage, harvest vegetables with villagers and help contact buyers.

The efforts of the working group and local villagers paid off, as they saw a bumper harvest in 2018.

According to data from the working group, 47 households that planted tomatoes in 2018 have earned more than 73,246 yuan. A total of 140 tons of tomatoes were completely sold.

"None of our tomatoes was unsellable! Even our sliced and dried tomatoes were sold out," Wang said.

The village has also planted 3.82 hectares of wheat, more than 20 hectares of cotton and 9.25 hectares of fruit trees, which will benefit 58 poverty-stricken households. Tuerhong Emeti, 41, a villager in Yusitunke Ayikule, whose family was registered as poor and who previously worked as a mason, happily took photos with the big white radishes and other vegetables he planted.

His income as a mason was unstable — sometimes earning 200 yuan in a day and sometimes nothing for a week. Now, he can earn at least 1,500 yuan a month planting vegetables and growing edible fungus. He also has another income from working at a local seasoning products factory.

According to China's poverty criteria, which were updated in 2011, a farmer is recognized as poor if his or her yearly disposable income is less than 2,300 yuan. According to this standard, Emeti has been lifted from poverty.

Another major mission for working groups in villages is fighting against extremism, something the southern parts of Xinjiang have been more susceptible to.

Ayikule is one typical example. In contrast to its poetic name — which means "moon lake" — the place has been plagued by extremism. Rumors were spread saying that pills distributed to villagers to prevent poliomyelitis were actually contraceptive medicines. Impoverished people often do not dare pick up their subsistence allowances because of threats from extremists, according to local officials.

Ajirhyim Emeti, 37, a single mother of three children in Tuowanke Maigaiti Village, opens a shop selling cakes after receiving training. (Photo: Fan Lingzhi/GT)

Local working groups stationed in villages have made great efforts to eliminate the influence of extremism, including promoting national laws and regulations.

Tackling extremism

The Xinjiang regional government has also deployed officials from subordinate departments to these villages.

These officials are usually appointed as head of the working groups stationed at national-level poverty-stricken villages, or those that suffer from extremism. They usually make full use of their resources in certain fields to carry out their work in villages.

Officials from the Executive Leadership Academy and the Organization Department of the Xinjiang regional government were deployed to Tuowanke Maigaiti Village in Wushi County.

Under the guidance of the working group, Tuowanke Maigaiti Village has built 24 kilometers of road, 32 kilometers of canals and 10 kilometers of protective forest. It also helped bring investment and funds to build a primary school, houses for villagers, libraries, entertainment rooms, shops and public toilets near residential communities.

Working groups stationed in villages also take on the responsibility of solving residents' problems in daily life, including domestic disputes, quarrels with neighbors, shanty town transformation projects or applications for public rental housing.

Officials from the public complaints and proposals bureau in Xinjiang were deployed to Kalasa Village of Wensu County in Aksu five years ago. The working group has nicknamed their office in the village the "Pomegranate Seed Workshop" and aims to get residents of different ethnic groups to bond together.

Located in the outskirts of the city, Kalasa Village has a relatively large floating population and more disputes between residents. For example, many villagers used to hand in complaints to higher departments on problems of unpaid wages or land contract disputes.

Departments and institutions affiliated to the regional government in Xinjiang have stationed 70,000 officials in villages every year for the past five years.

Striving for unity

Officials stationed in villages frequently find themselves busy the whole day.

Wang usually begins work at 7:30 am even though working hours in Xinjiang usually begin at 10:00 am. Before 8:00 am, he needs to think about ways to help poverty-stricken households sell six tons of tomatoes in a day and plans out a program to grow edible fungus. At around 9:00 am, he needs to arrange the day's work with other officials.

Between 2:00 pm to 5:00 pm, he talks to residents to help solve their problems in their daily lives. He usually spends at least three hours visiting villagers in the afternoon and sometimes holds night class on Putonghua and national laws with the villagers.

For other members of the working group, when the whole village goes to sleep, they still need to work till around 2:00 am, inputting their whole day's work, especially the ways they solved villagers' problems, into their computers.

Their dedication to work means less time for their families.

Wu Min is a deputy director of the human resources department from the cadre school in Xinjiang, and now works as a member of the working group stationed in Tuowanke Maigaiti Village, Qianjin County.

Working groups in villages are using their sweat and tears to close the gap with local residents. These efforts are paying off, as more villagers recognize their work and take an active part in it, especially on poverty alleviation, according to Wang.

Media group from Indonesia and Malaysia given full picture of Xinjiang's de-extremism measures

By Liu Xin in Hotan | Feb 28, 2019

A media group from Indonesia and Malaysia visited Northwest China's Xinjiang Uygur Autonomous Region in February, 2019. During the trip, they came to various re-education centers and mosques and got a full picture of the region's counter-terrorism and de-extremism measures as well as religious protection policies.

A total of 11 reporters from the two countries started the trip in Urumqi on February 22, 2019 and visited the Kizilsu Kirgiz Autonomous Prefecture, Kashi and Hotan in the following days.

They visited vocational training centers in different places and talked to trainees

A reporter from Indonesia takes pictures with residents in a village in Atux of the Kizilsu Kirgiz Autonomous Prefecture, Northwest China's Xinjiang Uygur Autonomous Region. (Photo: Liu Xin/GT)

about how they came to the centers, their study life there, when they would graduate and their families' attitude toward the centers.

Nuramina Tursun, 24, from a training center in Kashi, shared her story with reporters.

Tursun said that she came across some videos which promoted terrorism and extremism when browsing overseas websites.

"After that I usually searched for videos on overseas websites which promoted jihad and other extremism and terrorism ideas. Gradually, I changed into another person," she said.

"I began sending messages to my friends, asking them not to have any contact with non-Muslims ... I quarreled with my friends who spoke to non-Muslims in the street and I even beat my brother's friends when they were invited to the house ... Deep in my heart, it was like I had killed heretics a thousand times," Tursun said.

Tursun's changes worried her family members and they sought help from a village official.

"The village official introduced me to the national laws and regulations, as well as behavior of being influenced by extremism, and I found that my previous behavior violated the laws. So I applied to go to the center," Tursun said.

She said that she now realized that if she had not come to the center, she might have become a terrorist under the influence of extremism, which would not only destroy herself but the whole family.

Paher Tursun, 36, a trainee in a training center in Shule County, told reporters from the group that he went to the center because he sent videos which promote terrorism and extremism to friends.

"I am not a Muslim but I used to send extremist videos to my friends. One of my friends reported my situation to the police who later talked to me about my violation of laws," Paher Tursun said, noting that he is now grateful for his friends stopping him from going further astray.

According to China's Anti-Terrorism Law, enacted in 2016, it is illegal to watch and spread video and audio which promotes terrorism.

Xinjiang has also issued a regional regulation on de-extremism which lists 16 behaviors as extremism, including promoting extremism, forcing others to believe in a certain religion as well as downloading and spreading video and audio which has extremism contents.

Mijti Mermoti, principal of the training center in Kashi, told reporters that "establishing training centers in Kashi could prevent extremist and terrorist activities before they happen and it also avoids these trainees becoming the victim of extremism and terrorism."

Life in the centers

When talking about his previous life under extremism, Memeti Aili Erken's eyes became red with tears. Being influenced by pan-Islamism, he refused to send his two children to school and when his wife argued with him, he beat her.

Erken has changed a lot now and is learning knowledge on fixing electric facilities in the Shule training center and he started to share housework and take care of the children when coming home every week.

"My wife is happy to see my changes and my family is in harmony now. I am studying hard in the center to get graduation early and want to find a job to earn a better life for my family," he said.

Reporters from the group also paid attention to the trainees' daily life in these

Memeti Aili Erken learns to fix electric facilities in the Shule training center in Xinjiang. (Photo: Liu Xin/GT)

centers.

Nuramina Tursun told reporters that aside from learning the national standard language, national laws and regulations, she also continued her childhood interest in drawing by taking the clothes design classes. The notebook placed on her table has her hand-drawn sketches of some clothes.

She said that she can leave the center once she passes the language and law tests as well as having enough vocational skills for employment.

Paher Tursun wants to expand his online business of selling second-hand cars by using the e-commerce knowledge acquired in the center.

In response to Indonesian reporter Zulfiani Lubis' question on whether the trainees can do religious practice in the centers, Paher Tursun told her that according to China's laws, nobody should do religious practice in non-religious areas, including in schools.

The media group visited dormitories, canteens and entertainment rooms in different centers.

Rahimy Bin A Rahim from Malaysia told the Global Times that before visiting the training centers, he learned from other media that trainees were mistreated, but he saw in these centers that they are in good health and have the freedom to do what they want.

Yohana Margaretha from Indonesia said that she was impressed by many of the trainees' stories and the facilities in these centers are good.

"I believe that the Chinese government has offered good conditions for the trainees to learn and live in these centers," she said.

Exchanging experiences

Extremism and terrorism also pose threats to Indonesia and Malaysia, and the two countries are also exploring ways on de-extremism, reporters from the foreign media group said.

Asmaliza Binti Mansor from Malaysia told the Global Times that in facing terrorism and extremism, every country has the right to take their own measures.

"Offering vocational skills to people is a good way, especially for young people who have been influenced by extremism, to have a new start," she said.

Nugroho Fery Yudho from Indonesia told the Global Times that some terrorists in Indonesia committed suicide bombing and the most distressing part was that they even forced their wives and children to do so.

"We have religious groups come to lecture believers, especially the youth, to make sure that they have the right understanding on religion," he said.

He noted that the government is also exploring ways to prevent extremism in its early stage.

"I admire the Chinese government's courage to explore its own way on de-extremism … Some countries rely on international organizations or other countries for de-extremism, which seemed to achieve little," Nugroho Fery Yudho said.

Echoing Yudho, Yohana Margaretha said that the most important measure of counter-terrorism is to prevent terrorism before terrorist attacks happen.

"China has made its efforts with de-extremism. The Chinese government as well as our government should adapt to new ways of dealing with terrorism and extremism as they might as well change with the times," she said.

The media group also visited many mosques during their trip in Xinjiang, including the Eidgah Mosque in Kashi, two villages in Shule County and Hotan respectively.

Many reporters expressed their surprise and admiration for the local governments' efforts in updating the infrastructure in the mosques.

Border patrol officers keep Xinjiang secure

By Liu Xin and Fan Lingzhi in Aksu | Apr 29, 2019

Farmers and herdsmen have been deployed as civilian border guards in Aksu Prefecture, Northwest China's Xinjiang Uygur Autonomous Region to work with local police officers to patrol border areas to stop any suspected terrorists from either leaving or sneaking into Chinese territory.

Aksu shares a 263.8 kilometers of border with Kazakhstan and Kyrgyzstan, and the total area designated as border area measures 16,700 square kilometers, according to a release from the publicity department of Aksu Prefecture.

Located in the southern part of Xinjiang, Aksu has long been the frontline in the fight against terrorism and extremism.

"Aksu has prioritized safeguarding the stability of border areas ... and has

Border guards ride horses in a drill in Laohutai Village, Baicheng County in Aksu Prefecture, Northwest China's Xinjiang Uygur Autonomous Region. (Photo: Fan Lingzhi/GT)

formed a system that relies on people and technology," reads the release.

Local line of defense

Organizing local herdsmen and farmers to act as border guards is one strategy to stop any illegal cross-border incidents as these local people are familiar with the environment in the area, officials from the department on border security in Aksu said.

Tuohuti Tilaixi, 54, from the Kirgiz ethnic group in Yamansu Village of Wushi County is a third generation border guard in his family.

Every day, he walks more than 30 kilometers along China's border with Kyrgyzstan to make sure no suspicious person has been there. He usually takes a nan bread and water for lunch. In winter, when the snow is too heavy to walk, Tuohuti patrols on horseback.

"My father taught me what I should pay attention to during patrol — to observe suspicious footprints on the ground, especially in winter, and to talk to strangers and listen to their accents," Tuohuti said.

Such long walks and horse rides have made Tuohuti's hands and feet swell. The wind and sunshine in the mountains that are 2,000 meters above sea level have weathered his wrinkled face.

He began this life when he was 19, following in his father and grandfather's footsteps.

In 1962, Tuohuti's grandfather helped local police stop a man who tried to cross the border to Kyrgyzstan. As a teenager, Tuohuti's father followed his father to herd sheep in the mountainous border area and helped local police stop those who wanted to escape or steal into China's Xinjiang.

By the end of 1985, his grandfather had retired. His father stopped patrolling one year before he passed away.

Tuohuti says he wants to patrol the area until his last breath. "I was born and

Tuohuti Tilaixi, 54, from Kirgiz ethnic group in Yamansu Village of Wushi County is the third generation of border guards in his family. (Photo: Fan Lingzhi / GT)

grew up in the border land. It is my responsibility to safeguard it. As long as I stick to my duties, the area will be safe, and so will the country," he said.

Tuohuti's son and daughter-in-law have taken on the family tradition and now work as the fourth generation of border guards in the family.

Like Tuohuti, there are several thousand border guards in Wushi and Wensu counties in Aksu Prefecture. Most are farmers and herdsmen from the Uygur and Kirgiz ethnic groups. Wushi and Wensu share 137.2 kilometers and 126.6 kilometers of border with China's neighboring countries.

Border guards usually work in three shifts — one shift for the usual patrol, one to train and one to rest. The training includes China's border policies, relevant laws and regulations, information collecting and the procedures after they find suspects, Shu Yabang, an official from the border security department in Wensu County, told the Global Times.

Border guards reached by the Global Times in Wensu and Wushi are all very cautious and have a strong sense of confidentiality, especially when asked about details of their daily work.

"If we could not shut up, and we told people details about the mountain passes to neighboring countries or neglect suspicious situations we spot, how could we ensure border security?" Tuohuti asked.

Shu said that every border guard is equipped with a telescope, an electric baton and a cellphone. Those who patrol mountain areas are given subsidies to buy a motorcycle or a horse.

If border guards spot suspicious people or activities, they are suggested to talk or follow them and report the situation to the local border security station.

"Protecting their safety is the priority," Shu said.

Border guards have been given a monthly subsidy since 2004 and the money has increased from 600 yuan to at least 2,000 yuan ($297) a month to improve their living situation.

Local governments in Wensu and Wushi have also built houses in the border area for border guards. Staples such as rice, flour, cooking oil and water are delivered to the houses regularly. Coal is offered for heating, Shu said.

"When my grandfather patrolled the border area, he lived in a partly underground cave at night, and he had nothing but damp firewood to burn to warm himself," Tuohuti said, noting that his life as a border guard has greatly improved.

Thanks to the work of the border guards, border security departments in Aksu have seized several suspected terrorists who tried to escape or get into China's territory through the four mountain passes to Kyrgyzstan since 1959, Wang Fuli, a police officer from Ying'ate border police station in Wushi County, told the Global Times.

A border guard practices with his horse in Aksu Prefecture of Xinjiang. (Photo: Fan Lingzhi / GT)

Solid border wall

Aside from the border guards, police officers and auxiliary police officers in border police stations form another line of defense to safeguard border security in Northwest China.

Border soldiers and officers in Xinjiang have become members of the frontier police assigned to entry-and-exit check stations. These soldiers, who used to belong to the Xinjiang Public Security Frontier Corps, became police officers of the region's general exit-and-entry frontier inspection station in January 2019, China News Service reported.

The change is part of a reform announced by the Central Committee of the Communist Party of China in March 2018.

Alikam Aniwar, 35, now works in Pochengzi border police station in Bozidun Village in Wensu County.

The station is right at a vital communication point of two branches of a main road — one heads to the China-Kazakhstan border and the other to Xiate pass, which connects Wensu County in Aksu in southern Xinjiang and Zhaosu County in northern Xinjiang's Ili Kazak Autonomous Prefecture. Xiate pass is the shortest route between northern and southern Xinjiang.

Checking the passing vehicles and people are important duties of Alikam and his colleagues. Other duties include regular drills, border patrols and dealing with tourist emergencies.

Serving in the army since 2006 and working in the frontline on safeguarding border security for years, Alikam has dealt with several cases of terrorists who wanted to escape or sneak into the territory.

In January 2012, Alikam and his colleagues received reports from civil border guards about five strangers who appeared in the mountains carrying long knives.

Since most police officers were away for the Spring Festival holidays, Alikam, accompanied by seven other officers, went to check out the situation.

They fired blank shots to warn the suspects, after which there was a confrontation. With the help of 20 officers who came to reinforce them, they seized the group.

"They had several bags of eggs and nan bread. They finally confessed that they had taken part in the terror attacks in Urumqi on July 5, 2009. They came here and wanted to illegally cross the border and go to Afghanistan and Syria. They wanted to plan 'something big' when they returned to Xinjiang," Alikam said.

Illegal cross-border incidents are rare these days as Xinjiang's regional government has strengthened efforts on border security. However, the workload for security stations in border areas has not decreased.

Gu Dongxin, a 27-year-old police officer who came to work in Pochengzi border security station in January 2019, told the Global Times that he usually drives with two to three police officers to check several security points along the border.

The furthest one is 4,000 meters above sea level.

"The sand road is bumpy with many cliffs in the mountains. I still need to patrol with a senior police officer because I'm not very familiar with the situation in the area," Gu told the Global Times.

Aside from the weekly checks on security points, Gu and his colleagues also need to join a monthly large-scale check on the whole border area with civilian border guards and staff from border security departments, especially in sparsely populated areas.

Despite the hard work of the police officers and hundreds of civilian border guards, they are still shorthanded, Wang Fuli from Ying'ate border police station said.

Take Ying'ate border police station as an example. Ying'ate border police station is responsible for safeguarding a large border area with some mountain passes connecting adjacent countries, Wang said.

To ensure no terrorist escapes from or enters into Chinese territory, the border police station has deployed electronic radar monitoring system in key areas, which can help trace quickly moving targets and send back alarm signals, Wang said.

Ying'ate police station also uses patrol dogs.

"Dogs have better noses than people and they sometimes are more alert than us. We also encourage five to seven civilian border guards as a group to raise a dog, which protects them and their sheep from wolves," Alimujiang Abulaiti, a police officer from Ying'ate station, told the Global Times.

He noted that on one night in February, 2019, before a civilian border guard was aware of the situation, his dog stopped several drunken men who tried to cross the warning line.

Dedicated to the job

No issue is too small when it concerns border security — the sentiment was the same from almost every police officer reached by the Global Times. While dedicating themselves to serving the motherland, many of them are unable to fulfill their family duties by being a good spouse or a responsible parent.

On a message board at Ying'ate border police station, a police officer wrote that he wishes to bring his fiancée to Xinjiang and have their own home. Another wrote that he wishes the best and good health to his family.

The Pochengzi station in Wensu where Gu lives is surrounded by mountains and all the officers work and live in the same three-story building.

It takes at least two hours to get to the county town. But Gu, who was born in Meizhou, South China's Guangdong Province and had served in the army in Guangxi Zhuang Autonomous Region for eight years, does not think life is boring.

"Before applying for the job here, I have prepared myself mentally. I used to learn about violent terrorist attacks in Xinjiang and I really wanted to make my own contribution to change the situation," Gu said.

Gu noted that his parents supported his decision.

However, for Alikam from the Ying'ate station, who has been married for 10 years, it is not easy to balance life and work.

"I have four to five days as holidays a month and that's when I can go back home to meet with my wife and two children. But sometimes, when we have to deal with some urgent situations, there's no time to see them," Alikam said.

His wife complained when they were first married as the burden of taking care of their parents and children mostly fell on her.

But she gradually understood Alikam and supported his work to keep the family and other people safe and sound.

For Alimujiang, safeguarding the border area is not only to serve the country. It means more.

A soldier, who taught Alimujiang almost everything when he first joined the army, was killed when two terrorists drove an explosive-laden car into a group of soldiers in Kashi in August 2008.

Sixteen people died and 16 were injured in the incident, the Xinhua News Agency reported.

"He was more like a teacher or parent to me. I didn't even have the chance to share the happiness of being enrolled in the police academy with him," he said with tears in his eyes.

"Some terrorists have destroyed the image of our people and only by removing them can we experience better development. It is every Chinese person's responsibility to safeguard the country, no matter which ethnic group he or she is from," Alimujiang said.

He wants his son to be a soldier in the future to make his contribution to the country.

Thanks to the contributions of civilian border guards and police officers, China's Northwest border line has remained safe with few terrorists succeeding in illegally crossing it in recent years, which has contributed to the country's and the world's anti-terrorist efforts, experts said.

"One important characteristic of global terrorist activities now is that domestic and overseas terrorists conspire and conduct acts of terror together. Terrorists who have returned after training with international terror groups pose a greater threat to a country's security, especially after the Islamic State has been scattered," Li Wei, a Beijing-based anti-terrorism expert, told the Global Times.

Strengthening the security along the border in Northwest China's Xinjiang not only prevents the infiltration of terrorism and the return of terrorists, it also secures domestic stability and contributes to Central Asia as well as the global anti-terror efforts, Li told the Global Times.

Stability benefits Xinjiang tourism, business

By Liu Xin and Fan Lingzhi in Aksu | May 24, 2019

The simultaneous kickoff of the cultural and tourism festival and the 2019 Taklimakan Rally in Jinlan square of Aksu Prefecture, Northwest China's Xinjiang Uygur Autonomous Region has been a boon to Adili Reheman's (pseudonym) business.

Adili sold handmade scarves, souvenirs and wine, which is made from grape in a traditional local way, in a stand near Jinlan square. Before the opening ceremonies, he could only make 200 yuan ($29) a day, but he made more than 1,000 yuan on the opening day.

Adili said he opens a temporary stand at big events, and also has a shop near the airport, which sells special local products.

Villagers use mobile stalls to sell food, beverage and other products in Tagelake Village, Wensu County, Aksu. (Photo: Yang Ruoyu / GT)

An aerial view of part of the 2019 Taklimakan Rally, the largest, longest and most difficult car race in Asia. This year's race started in Aksu, Northwest China's Xinjiang Uygur Autonomous Region on May 19, 2019. (Photo: Yang Ruoyu / GT)

Two drivers share a light moment before the Taklimakan Rally on May 20, 2019. (Photo: Yang Ruoyu / GT)

"I can earn more than 50,000 yuan a year compared to 10,000 yuan three years ago," he told the Global Times.

While Adili was busy doing business near Jinlan square, more than a hundred racing drivers were waiting for the start of the 2019 Taklimakan Rally.

The increasing income of Adili and the lively scenes of the Taklimakan Rally were the culmination of the gradually booming tourism industry in Aksu and in southern Xinjiang, an area once plagued by terrorism and extremism.

Open to the world

This year's Taklimakan Rally, the largest, longest and most difficult car rally in Asia, started in Aksu on May 19, 2019. Drivers from 58 teams will navigate through nine stages covering 5,000 kilometers, passing Gobi deserts and Danxia landform areas before finishing in Hotan.

"Drivers and co-drivers need to pass through the Taklimakan Desert, enduring the high temperature and rocky roads. They also need to deal with emergencies. Even a small screw spike could influence their performance," Sun Kai, a member of the RZOIL Team, told the Global Times.

An aerial view of a scenic spot in Tagelake Village of Wensu County in Aksu. (Photo: Yang Ruoyu/GT)

Song Chuan, a senior counselor of the Taklimakan Rally, who has been working for the rally for 10 years, told the Global Times that "The landforms in Aksu — deserts, Gobi, riverbed, and canyon land — are perfect to hold a car rally. There are many depopulated zones where the racing stages could pass."

"Xinjiang is a place like heaven, and holding a car rally here fits many drives' dreams of being tested by the extremes to pursue a hero dream," Song said.

Song said that the rally could help boost Aksu's tourism.

The race is only one part of Aksu's tourism development. The local government has organized nine events, including a cultural and tourism festival, food fair, local products fair and public welfare program for students to promote local tourism, according to a release from Aksu's publicity department.

"We want to combine culture and sports events, and tours in scenic spots to repackage the image of the place," Chang Yuxuan, head of the Party committee in Aksu, told the Global Times.

Stable for development

Data from the publicity department shows the prefecture received nearly 2.84 million trips in the first four months of 2019, with an increase of 46.7 percent from the same period in 2018, which brought in 1.65 billion yuan in tourist revenue. More than 9.75 million trips are expected in 2019 with total revenue expected to reach 5.6 billion yuan.

The surge in tourist number in Aksu and other places in Xinjiang is one of the benefits of a stable social environment, Zhang Hui, vice president of Duolang and Qiuci Tourism Development Ltd, told the Global Times.

Many residents and officials share Zhang's opinion.

Luo Yansen, 38, is the head of a civil rescue team in Alar, a city near Aksu. He and his team came to Aksu to work as volunteers for the 2019 Taklimakan Rally.

"The rally has been held in Xinjiang several times but this is the largest ever,"

Luo told the Global Times, noting that no big events were held years ago when the security situation "was not that good" in Xinjiang.

Luo used to run a hotel in Alar from 2009 to 2012. But the situation was so bad that he had to close the hotel.

"The security situation has improved in recent years and we have seen more big events in Xinjiang. I told many friends outside Xinjiang concerned about security that they can walk with a million in cash in their pocket without worrying about their safety here," Luo said.

Many places, especially the southern parts of Xinjiang had been suffering from terrorism and extremism for a long time, which greatly affected local residents' safety, property and social development, according to a white paper on *The Fight Against Terrorism and Extremism and Human Rights Protection in Xinjiang*, which was released by the State Council Information Office.

Xinjiang has taken various measures to fight terrorism and extremism in recent years and there have been no violent attacks in the region for more than two years, according to Xinjiang officials reached by the Global Times.

Christian Zweifei from Germany and Simon Ton from Singapore came to Aksu for the first time and were impressed by the security situation.

They work for a German company producing lubricating oil, which sponsored the RZOIL Team for the 2019 Taklimakan Rally. They came to the rally to test their products as well as to cheer the team.

Zweifei told the Global Times that before coming to Xinjiang, his friends in Germany told him "it is not a safe place," but the situation is quite the opposite. He saw police officers patrol the streets.

Ton said that what he saw in Aksu was "different from what he read from the news" and local residents of different ethnic groups are friendly and live normal lives.

Talking about the stable social environment, Sun said that the Dakar Rally used

A local villager sells grilled meat in Tagelake Village, Wensu County, Aksu, Northwest China's Xinjiang Uygur Autonomous Region. (Photo: Yang Ruoyu / GT)

to be moved to South America from Africa due to the threat of terrorism in Africa. "But this would never happen in Xinjiang," Sun said.

Aside from holding big events, stable situation and tourism developments in Xinjiang have also brought benefits to local residents.

"People now feel safe to go square dancing every day or join some events. Local residents' horizons have broadened and their lives are enriched with more big events being held here," Luo said.

Luo hopes to reopen his hotel one day.

Better plan for better future

With the stable environment and the promising development of tourism, Aksu is working to better manage local tourism resources and encouraging more residents to take part.

Tagelake Village in Wensu County is located in a rangeland in a mountainous area. The long stretch of grassland and the view of the mountain snow far away make it a scenic spot. The good tourism season lasts from May to September in 2019.

To integrate the tourism resources, the village has set up a cooperative to encourage residents with yurts, horses and rangeland to join, Liu Xiang, head of the working team stationed in Tagelake, told the Global Times.

Liu said the village worked with tourism companies to make plans for tourism development. "We plan to plant different flowers at different months to attract tourists, and divide the scenic spot into a horse-riding area, an entertainment area and a section for agritainment, and to bring in more animals like yaks," Liu said.

To improve the services in the scenic spot, the village has invited experts from the restaurant and catering association of Aksu to train local villagers, according to Liu.

He added that developing local tourism relies on changing people's minds and this is the reason why the village is organizing different training for free for villagers.

Takelage Village received more than 100,000 visits in 2018 and is expected to welcome more tourists this year, as Liu said that more than 5,000 tourists came to the spot in the first week of May 2019, which was not the prime season.

The average yearly income of villagers in Takelage also increased in recent years from 3,000 yuan to 9,000 yuan in 2018.

"Xinjiang is a very beautiful place with friendly people. We welcome more tourists to see the development here with their own eyes," Liu said.

Xinjiang's Kizil Caves showcase history of exchanges between East and West

By Liu Xin in Aksu | Jun 4, 2019

After driving east from downtown Baicheng and passing continuous stretches of desert and yardang landforms for more than an hour, a yellow cliff with several hundred caves carved into it eventually emerge. It is the Kizil Cave-Temple Complex, which was built between the 3rd and 8th centuries and is believed to be the earliest Buddhist cave complex in China.

The Kizil Caves site is associated with the ancient Buddhist kingdom of Kucha [Qiuci in Chinese], located in the ancient Silk Road. The cave complex lies in present-day Baicheng County of Aksu Prefecture, Northwest China's Xinjiang Uygur Autonomous Region.

The statue of Kumarajiva in the Kizil Cave-Temple Complex in Baicheng, Aksu Prefecture of Xinjiang Uygur Autonomous Region (Photo: Liu Xin / GT)

There are 339 caves at the site with a total of 4,000 square meters of wall paintings and some colorful clay sculptures within them. All these caves were carved into the cliff of a mountain extending two kilometers from east to west.

During the thousand years after their completion, the caves witnessed the rise and fall of Buddhism and the conflicts that took place between Buddhism and Islam for nearly two centuries. They are also proof of the ancient Silk Road and the civilization of Qiuci, Xu Yongming, head of the Qiuci Research Institute in Xinjiang, said at a seminar on the Kizil Caves in October 2015.

"The early caves at the site showed the history of Buddhism being introduced from India to Central Asia, the Western Regions and the Central Plain. The wall paintings inside the caves verify the exchanges between the West and the East. Paintings from Syria showed these artistic exchanges. Calligraphy works and wall paintings in the caves contain rich information and show the lifestyle and traditions of the Qiuci Kindgom," Xu said.

An aerial view of the Kizil Caves site (Photo: Yang Ruoyu/GT)

Historical proof

Palida Pulati has been working at the Kizil Caves site as a tour guide for more than a year, and has seen more domestic and overseas tourists arriving in recent months. She usually starts her tours from a square at the foot of the cliff, where the statue of Kumarajiva stands.

Kumarajiva was a Buddhist monk, scholar and translator from the Kingdom of Kucha who lived from 344 to 413. He is most well known for his translation of Buddhist texts written in Sanskrit to Chinese. Through his efforts, more than 300 Buddhist classics were translated into Chinese, the first time in Chinese history that foreign classics were translated on such a large scale.

Palida said that the statue was built to commemorate Kumarajiva's contributions. After telling tourists about the life of Kumarajiva, including his experience living in Chang'an at that time, Palida then guides tourists up to the cliffs into these caves.

Many of the caves in the Kizil site have a central pillar design that allows pilgrims to walk around a central column. A large vaulted chamber is located in front of the column and a smaller rear chamber behind it, with two tunnel-like corridors on the sides linking these spaces.

Statues of Buddha were erected in the front chamber, but none of these sculptures survived at the site, Palida told the Global Times.

The wall paintings inside the caves are the most valuable cultural relics here. They not only tell stories of Buddha doing good deeds, but also of local residents' lives, animals and scenes of nature.

Unlike other Buddhist caves in China, where stories were engraved on a series of pictures, painters in the Kizil Caves usually completed a complex story on one diamond-shaped picture. For example, a picture in Cave No. 17 shows the image of a camel, two men with hats and a man with his arms up.

Palida explained that this wall painting tells the story of 500 merchants who became accidentally trapped in a dark valley. After growing increasingly anxious

A wall painting inside the Kizil Caves site (Photo: Liu Xin/GT)

about being robbed in the dark, the head of the merchants wrapped his two arms in felt, dipped them in oil and lit them. He raised his arms high to guide the group in the darkness. After seven days and nights of walking, the group finally got out of the valley.

"If you look closely at these figures' clothes, you can see that they are wearing white hats and robes with turned-down collars. These are clothes worn by Sogdians, who usually lived in West Asia and played an important part in the trade route of the Silk Road," Palida said.

Some of the pictures include images of the gods of the Sun and Moon from Greek mythology.

"These elements show the close exchanges between the Central Plain and countries along the Silk Road," Palida told the Global Times.

More evidence of the busy cultural exchanges come from the materials used to make these wall paintings.

The wall paintings inside the caves usually have four colors — white, black, green and blue. The blue color was made from lasurite, a mineral which was produced in Afghanistan. This was also used for many cultural relics in Egypt and Europe, according to Palida.

A wall painting inside the Kizil Caves site (Photo: Liu Xin/GT)

Great losses

While these wall paintings recorded scenes of prosperity along the Silk Road, they also suffered from clashes between different religions and damage by foreign explorers.

Many faces of the figures on the wall paintings were destroyed by Muslim residents and some caves were blackened from the smoke of fires built by herdsmen who rested there, Palida said.

According to Xu, Islam reached the Pamirs in around the 10th century, which triggered a clash between Buddhism and Islam that lasted nearly 200 years.

According to an introduction in the Aksu Museum on the evolution of religion in Xinjiang, in the middle of the 10th century, after Islam was accepted by the Qara Khanids dynasty, the rulers launched a religious war lasting more than 40 years to force the people to convert to Islam.

"By the middle of the 14th century, people in Kucha, Shaya, Wensu and other places were forced to believe in Islam by means such as war. By the early 16th

A wall painting inside a cave that was half cut out but not removed by foreign explorers. (Photo: Liu Xin/GT)

century, Xinjiang had formed a pattern in which many religions, mainly Islam, coexisted and continued until now," Niger Tusun, from the Aksu Museum, told the Global Times.

However, not all the Buddhist elements from the caves have disappeared.

Images of honeysuckle, which were widely used in Buddhist ornaments, were found in some caves. "These flower images have been printed on the hats of the Uygur and Kazak ethnic groups," Palida said.

More wall paintings in the Kizil Caves were removed by foreign explorers, including Sir Marc Aurel Stein, a Hungarian-born British archaeologist, and Albert Von Le Coq from Germany.

In 1906, the German expedition team of Albert Von Le Coq explored the Kizil Caves in Xinjiang and removed about 500 square meters of murals. Most of the fragments removed are now at the Museum of Asian Art in Berlin. Some fragments have been found in museums in Russia, Japan, Korea and US, according to Palida.

Under protection

Palida usually takes tour groups to Cave No. 10, which does not have any wall paintings or sculptures inside, only some words engraved by Han Leran, a Chinese artist born in 1898.

Han wrote on the wall, "I read about Von Le Coq and Sir Aurel Stein on their archaeological expedition in the Western Regions and began to learn that there were rich cultural relics here … It's a pity that most of the wall paintings were damaged by these teams, which was a great loss."

Palida said that Han died in a plane crash travelling from Urumqi to Lanzhou in 1947, and many first-hand materials he collected on the Kizil Caves were destroyed in the accident.

The Kizil Caves site did not have any protection until the founding of the People's Republic of China in 1949. More professional protection work of the Kizil Cave-Temple started in 1961 when it was listed in the first batch of State Protected Historical Sites. In June 2014, it was included in the World Heritage list.

Equipment to monitor humidity and air quality, as well as cameras have been installed in every cave to carry out preservation work.

Tourists are divided into small groups of no more than 10 people, and take turns to enter the caves, which have been opened to the public. They are prohibited from bringing recording equipment or using flash.

In order to allow more tourists to admire the beauty of the caves without causing damage to them, advanced technology has been used to duplicate some of the caves.

Replicas of Cave No. 17 and No. 38 have been exhibited in Aksu Museum, where tourists can see these colorful wall paintings up close and take pictures of them.

The value of the cave site has also been recognized by a growing number of scholars and visitors.

According to data from the publicity department of Aksu Prefecture, the cave site has received nearly 1 million tourists since 1992. And in the past three years, the number of tourists reached more than 200,000, with more than 10,000 of them coming from overseas.

Baicheng County plans to turn the Kizil Cave site into a national scenic spot in 2020, and make it a highlight for local tourism development.

Scan QR code to watch the video

Xinjiang sees better religious facility: Hatifu

By Fan Lingzhi in Hotan | Jul 4, 2019

Northwest China's Xinjiang Uygur Autonomous Region has taken multiple measures to fight terrorism and extremism, which have helped bring development and prosperity to the region.

However, some Western media have attacked China's Xinjiang policies, accusing the central and regional governments of "suppressing religious freedom."

Despite the exaggerated reports and even "fake news" of some Western media, people who live in Xinjiang are in a much better position to speak about the situation.

The Global Times on July 3, 2019 conducted an exclusive interview with

Wubuliaishan Tursunyaz, a 53-year-old Hatifu, or religious teacher, at the Jiamai Mosque in Hotan, southern Xinjiang. Hotan used to be plagued by extremism and was once the main battlefield of de-radicalization.

Wubuliaishan has been working as a Hatifu for more than 27 years.

Jiamai Mosque, which is located in Naerbage Street in Hotan, was built in 1848. It is the largest mosque in Hotan.

Wubuliaishan was buying a dutar for his 7-year-old grandson at a shop near the Jiamai Mosque when the Global Times reporter reached him on July 3, 2019.

Dutar is a musical instrument played by many ethnic groups in Xinjiang, including Uygurs.

Wubuliaishan said he intended to cultivate his grandson's interest in music. He smiled whenever he talked with people, and seemed satisfied with his life. But 10 years ago, he was living in fear.

Wubuliaishan recalled that extremism was once rampant in Hotan. Few residents knew national laws and regulations, which made them susceptible to brainwashing by illegal imams with distorted Islamic doctrines.

Illegal imams also attacked and threatened religious people who expressed support and love for the country, he said.

"One typical example of residents being influenced by extremism at that time was that local women had a very low social status. Many people thought that 'women could only rely on men' and women were banned from working outside," he told the Global Times.

Some villagers thought it was useless for girls to go to college. Instead, they were eager to get their underaged daughters married, Wubuliaishan said, noting that only one or two girls could get the chance to go to college in a village, but their parents still prevented them from going.

"To be honest, I felt useless and guilty with the situation at that time," Wubuliaishan said.

As a Hatifu, he used to persuade these parents who prevented their daughters from going to college. Luckily, three girls finally got the precious opportunity to go to college.

"They still keep in touch with me and treat me like their father. I always tell them that they should thank the government for its de-radicalization efforts, which help give women an equal chance."

To fight terrorism and extremism, the regional government in Xinjiang passed the *Regulations of Xinjiang Uygur Autonomous Region on De-radicalization* in March 2017. It states that no one should prevent their children from receiving an education or interfering with the implementation of China's education system.

"I feel better now," Wubuliaishan said with a smile, noting that Xinjiang's de-radicalization efforts have also enhanced local residents' legal awareness.

"Local residents will turn to working groups in villages and local governments

Wubuliaishan Tursunyaz, a 53-year-old Hatifu, or religious teacher, at the Jiamai Mosque in Hotan, Northwest China's Xinjiang Uygur Autonomous Region poses for a picture. (Photo: Liu Xin / GT)

to help them with their legal problems. I think it is good," he said.

Protecting legal activities

Some Western media always criticize China's Xinjiang policies, alleging that they would "suppress residents' religious freedom." However, by abiding by related laws and regulations, Xinjiang has respected people's religious freedom and protected legal religious activities.

Wubuliaishan told the Global Times that more than 50 residents come to the mosque to pray every day. More than 800 religious residents come to the mosque to listen to his sermon every Friday.

"I always promote the unity of different ethnic groups. I tell religious residents to do good things. Recently, I lectured on the harm caused by drugs, telling them to stay away from drugs," said Wubuliaishan.

Aside from ramping up efforts on de-radicalization, Xinjiang has also taken greater efforts to improve facilities at religious sites.

Wubuliaishan said that there was only dry latrine in the mosque before, which was not sanitary.

But now, the facilities in the mosque have been improved.

The Global Times reporter saw air conditioners at the mosque. Books on religion, technology and laws are offered in the mosque's reading room. Bathing equipment and toilets have also been installed.

According to a white paper released by the State Council Information Office in March 2019, mosques in Xinjiang have been equipped with running water, electricity, natural gas, radio and television facilities, and libraries.

All this has greatly improved the conditions of venues for religious activities and better satisfied the reasonable requests of believers.

Wubuliaishan told the Global Times that religious teachers like him could get a 1,800 yuan ($262) monthly allowance from the government. As the instructor of religious affairs, he had led several groups for Hajj.

"I was there to help believers solve their accommodation and communication problems. The government arranges instructors to help them accomplish the Hajj. This shows the government's respect for people's religious needs," he said.

Safety guaranteed

In response to some Western media criticism of Xinjiang's religious freedom situation, Wubuliaishan said angrily that "What they said is nonsense!"

Three facts can prove they are terribly wrong: the government has taken good care of religious teachers and imams; their social status has improved; and more importantly, their safety has been secured, according to Wubuliaishan.

According to the white paper, many religious leaders were assassinated by terrorists. For example, 74-year-old Senior Mullah Juma Tayier, who was vice president of the Xinjiang Islamic Association and imam of the Id Kah Mosque in Kashi, was killed by three terrorists on July 30, 2014.

As religious leaders, they need to guide believers to do good things, promote the unity of different ethnic groups and promote social harmony, he said.

"If my health permits, I would like to devote my life to my role. I also hope my grandson grows up soon and becomes someone useful to the country and society," he said.

Xinjiang residents hail improved livelihood, stability a decade after Urumqi riot

By Liu Xin in Urumqi and Fan Lingzhi in Hotan | Jul 5, 2019

As one of the main roads that run through the downtown district of Urumqi, capital city of Northwest China's Xinjiang Uygur Autonomous Region, Jiefangnan Road sees cars and thousands of passersby every day.

The doors to shops along the road are wide open with their owners standing outside to solicit customers. Some elderly sit by the road, chatting and laughing. Naughty boys playing around make faces at their parents after being scolded.

A glimpse of what is happening along Jiefangnan Road may give visitors a view of the local residents' peaceful and abundant life. However, it was a totally different scene on Jiefangnan Road ten years ago.

"Buses were turned upside down on the roads. Cars were smashed and set on fire. I never saw this in my life," Yili, a 28-year-old man from the Kirgiz ethnic group who lives in Urumqi, recalled his experience on July 5, 2009.

Yili told the Global Times that he happened to see three men with knives and bricks in their hands. He saw blood on the knives and was terrified. That was the worst time in his life.

On July 5, 2009, terrorists and rioters gathered along Jiefangnan Road and Heping Road. They smashed shops, turned buses and cars upside down and set them on fire. They beat and attacked people in the area, according to witnesses reached by the Global Times.

The riot, which was engineered by the "East Turkistan" terrorists inside and outside China, caused 197 deaths and injured 1,700. A total of 331 stores and 1,325 vehicles were smashed and burned, and many public facilities were damaged, according to a white paper released by the State Council Information Office in

Children look at nan, a traditional food in Xinjiang, displayed in a shop in Urumqi. (Photo: Cui Meng/GT)

March 2019.

"Terrorist and extremist forces in Xinjiang, driven by the goal of separatism, engaged in sabotage activities. This badly undermined local stability and brought enormous suffering to all ethnic groups in the region," according to the white paper.

Fighting terrorism and extremism to safeguard social stability has become a consensus of all ethnic groups living in Xinjiang. Security has been greatly improved in the past 10 years, especially since the regional government took multiple measures on counter-terrorism and de-radicalization, experts said.

Better-off life

In recent years, the regional government in Xinjiang has taken measures on counter-terrorism and de-radicalization in accordance with laws, including launching vocational education and training centers to help people guilty of minor crimes and those who have been influenced by terrorism and extremism.

Focus has also been put on improving people's living standards.

Hotan is located in southern Xinjiang. It used to be plagued by extremism and was once the main battlefield of de-radicalization, as well as poverty alleviation.

The lack of arable land, slow infrastructure construction, and frequent drought and bad weather conditions have led many people in Hotan to live a poverty-stricken life.

Take Ayidingkule Village in Hotan as an example. The village has 2,076 residents while the arable land is 710 *mu* (47 hectares), which means per capita arable land is 0.35 *mu*, according to Yang Jinping, head of the working team stationed in the village.

"Lack of arable land is the main reason for poverty in the village. Having less labor force and vocational skills also worsens the situation," Yang told the Global Times.

To lead the village out of poverty, Yang and the working team decided to develop some industries. But instead of running a garment plant like many other places have done in Hotan, they began to produce beverage bottles.

With the 730,000 yuan ($106,157) in poverty-alleviation funds, the village built a plant. A total of 14 poverty-stricken residents work in the plant and they can earn at least 1,500 yuan a month, with some as much as 3,700 yuan.

Rehaitebage Village has a plant which manufactures brooms. Working in the plant for a year, Marmunisha Aihamaittuohuti earned more than 30,000 yuan while previously she was a housewife with no earnings at all.

"I used to ask my husband for money. But now I can also earn money, and my husband has begun to help with the housework," she said.

Rehaitebage Village is also working on building a night food fair. People from poor households can join in running the snack stands for free and they can cooperate with villagers, who are better at cooking, according to Kaderdan Abulimit, head of the working team in Rehaitebage Village.

Infrastructure in almost every village in Hotan has been improved with new solar street lamps.

Aside from helping enhance villagers' income, the working team in Ayidingkule Village also pays attention to improving residents' living environment. A total of 120 trash cans have been installed in the village with 10 people hired to clean public areas. They get 800 yuan a month.

"The average yearly income of the villagers has reached 10,070 yuan, compared to 4,000 yuan a decade ago," Yang said.

Increasing villagers' income is one aspect of enhancing their living standards. Work on education and medical treatment also needs to be done.

Wuernishahan Talip lives in Ayidingkule Village. She is 79 years old and has cardiac disease.

Luckily, 95 percent of her medical fees are paid by the government and she can get 2,000 yuan a year in allowances. Doctors in the village would give her a regular check-up and help her replace the overdue medicine, Wuernishahan said with tears in her eyes.

Poverty is one reason why villagers easily get influenced by extremism. They used to know little about laws and turned to illegal imams for help, said Kaderdan, head of the working team in Rehaitebage Village.

By working hard to shorten the distance between villagers and help them in their daily lives, village officials have helped improve the situation, with more villagers willing to share their worries with them, Kaderdan said.

Xinjiang has added 1.4 million new urban jobs and transferred 8.3 million surplus rural laborers for employment from 2016 to 2018. It has expanded the nine-year compulsory education and provided free three-year preschool education in urban and rural areas in southern Xinjiang. It also provides insurance for serious illnesses and full coverage of centralized treatment for 15 serious illnesses, according

A young man sells traditional handmade candy in a bazaar in Aksu Prefecture, Xinjiang. (Photo: Fan Lingzhi/GT)

to the white paper in March 2019.

As people's standard of living improves, the public provides greater support to the government's counter-terrorism, de-radicalization and stability-maintenance effort.

A safe place to visit

There have been no violent attacks in Xinjiang for nearly three years, which is a great achievement for the region's current policies.

Xie Fen, who runs a shop selling special local products in the Grand Bazaar in Urumqi, told the Global Times that businesses were affected for more than two years after 2009 as fewer tourists came to Xinjiang over security concerns.

"But security has been greatly changed in recent years. People of different ethnic groups live happily together. We now have more tourists coming to Xinjiang,"

Xie said.

During the peak summer season, thousands of tourists come to the Grand Bazaar every day. They walk in the pedestrian zone, with snack stands along the two sides offering delicious special local food, including nan and roast lamb. Or they can go into one of the clothing or carpet shops for a closer look at the lives of different ethnic groups.

A tourist surnamed Song told the Global Times that his family came from Beijing to Xinjiang for a holiday. "Urumqi is a very safe place! We are attracted by Xinjiang's natural landscape and local traditions. I would like to recommend this place to people who have never been here."

The stable situation in Xinjiang not only attracted domestic visitors but also those from other countries.

Hiroshi Konno, a Japanese tourist, said he had stayed in Kashi in southern Xinjiang for two days and he was attracted by the unique architecture.

"When I was in Japan, I always heard negative news about Xinjiang from the media. But it turns out that these reports were unreliable. Only those who come to Xinjiang can know what is really happening here," he said.

According to data from the Xinhua News Agency, Kashi received nearly 1.24 million tourist trips from January to April in 2019, with an increase of 30.8 percent from the previous year, hitting a historic high.

Abulikemu Ahoti has been selling honey for ten years in Kashi, a place that has become a popular spot for tourists in recent years.

Abulikemu told the Global Times that more tourists come to Kashi now and he earns at least 3,000 yuan a day. He also gets acquainted with tourists who buy his honey several times.

Memeti Yiming's shop of traditional musical instruments of ethnic groups in Xinjiang has also been doing brisk business. He said he sold 2,000 hand-made drums within a few minutes in one day.

The Global Times reporter saw on July 5, 2019 that most of the residents in Kashi live a leisurely and comfortable life — the elderly sit in a teahouse near the Id Kah Mosque and chat, while children play around trees.

People who live in Xinjiang are best qualified to say whether they are happy or not. For the past 10 years, residents of all ethnic groups have been working together to make sure what happened in 2009 doesn't happen again, and are working together for a better future, residents in Xinjiang said.

Scan QR code to watch the video

Efforts of police contribute to over 30 months' peace in Xinjiang

By Fan Lingzhi in Hotan and Liu Xin in Urumqi | Jul 7, 2019

Editor's note

Northwest China's Xinjiang Uygur Autonomous Region has taken great efforts to fight against terrorism and extremism. There have been no violent attacks in the region for nearly three years.

The current peace in the region has not occurred independently. People of all ethnic groups, police officers and officials at all levels in Xinjiang have made their own contributions to safeguarding the region's stability.

Police officers in Xinjiang work on the frontline of the fight against terrorism. According to data from China's Central Television, from 2013 to 2016 a total of 127 police officers in Xinjiang sacrificed their lives in the line of duty.

Here are the stories of some police officers from Hotan and Aksu in southern Xinjiang, places which used to be plagued by terrorism and extremism. To protect these individuals from terrorist retaliation, their identities have been replaced with pseudonyms.

"I have been to the food fair frequently but never eat there."

Ayiguli Kurban: I joined the Public Security Bureau in Hotan in 2011 and now I am responsible for patrolling the Hotan night food fair every day from sunset to late at night. I may be the person who has spent the most time at the night food fair, but I never eat there. We have rules that we cannot make calls, chat or eat when we are on duty.

I have a son who is too young to go to school, but I have little time for him. Sometimes, when he cries to see me, his grandparents bring him to the night food fair. We can see each other from a distance.

The night food fair is famous among the many tourists who come here. I sometimes see children get lost in the food fair, and I make efforts to return them safely to their parents. The situation always makes me think how my heart would be broken if it were my son who were lost.

"If the answer is no, please stay silent."

Li Jian: I am Li Jian from the Public Security Bureau of Hotan. I was with the SWAT team for two years and dealt with several anti-terrorism operations.

What struck me most was a violent event, which happened in the summer of

2013. An illegal imam instigated a group of terrorists to take actions in Hotan. They carried hacking knives, bludgeons and stones to smash and burn shops and hurt innocent residents.

After receiving the information, I called for an "immediate assemble" which means all SWAT team members should gather and be ready to start off to the scene within one minute.

When we arrived there, we ordered the terrorists to drop their weapons through a loud speaker, but the terrorists outnumbered us and refused to listen. They began to attack our cars. Under these circumstances, we decided to take action. All of them were arrested, including those who tried to run away.

I will always remember what happened on that day: A terrorist held a hacking knife two meters away from me. This was the first time that I encountered a terrorist within such a short distance and this was the first time I saw their atrocity.

Although we had watched videos of mobs' ruthless ways of conducting violence, their madness was still beyond imagination when I was put into that scenario. It is an unforgettable moment when you face death.

During the action, my partner and I were positioned back-to-back and shouted loudly to let the other know we were alive. After the operation, I found my hands were trembling. I did my research after the incident. Within five meters, cold weapons including knives have a greater advantage than guns as they can cause larger wounds. People who hold guns are in danger if they miss the first shot.

I never told my parents about what really happened that day. After a long time, I told them that it was not a big deal and that we outnumbered the terrorists, but the truth was that we were almost surrounded by them. At the time, we did not have the chance to feel terrified.

Another time, we tried to arrest a terrorist who was hiding in a bath center. We persuaded him to surrender but after he came out, he stabbed one of our men with a knife.

The police officer fell bleeding. In a narrow lane, we finally captured the terrorist. Our man was rushed to hospital for treatment. Fortunately, he survived.

We voluntarily stood guard for him that night in hospital, in the fear that the terrorists might return to take revenge.

I have seen life and death pass before my eyes far too many times, and know how important stability is to a country. There have been no violent attacks in Xinjiang for more than 30 months now, a result that is attributed to the contributions of people of all local ethnic groups and police officers.

Despite this, we can never slack off but will try harder. We want the region to stay peaceful for 40 months, 50 months and forever.

Why can't we be relaxed? According to our analysis, terrorist forces outside China have never ceased their infiltration into China's Xinjiang. They usually conduct violent attacks in Xinjiang by remotely commanding domestic terrorists. They release videos on the internet which promote terrorism. They never stop when they have the chance.

Some anti-China forces have not ceased slandering China's Xinjiang policies and its police officers under the excuse of "freedom and human rights."

I would very much like to ask them three questions: Have you ever seen innocent people be killed in front of you? Have you seen people who you work with every day fall and bleed? Have you ever been challenged by a hacking knife? If your answer to these questions is "no," please stay silent.

"He was more like a teacher or a parent to me."

Alimu Abudu: I am 35 years old and now work in a border police station in Aksu Prefecture. I was called to assemble on July 5, 2009. We held shields and tried to separate people in violent attacks.

When we returned after that day, a comrade suddenly pointed at my arm and asked, "What happened?" Only then did I realize my left arm was soaked in blood.

I had been hurt by someone using a knife during the day but I had been too busy to notice. The incident left me with a scar on my arm that I see every day. It is still painful for me to say this: A soldier who I had been a friend with since I first joined the army died in a terrorist attack in 2008. He was one of the soldiers who were killed.

They were taking a morning run in Kashi in August 2008 when two terrorists drove an explosives-laden car into them. Sixteen people died and 16 were injured in the incident.

He was like a teacher or a parent to me. He taught me everything since my first day in the army: from how to stand at attention to learning Putonghua. I didn't even have the chance to share my happiness with him of being accepted by the police academy. I miss him.

Terrorists have tarnished the image of our people and only by removing them can we see a better tomorrow. It is every Chinese person's responsibility to safeguard the country, no matter which ethnic group he or she is from.

I want my boy to become a soldier too. I want him to grow up like a true man and make his contributions to the country.

Chapter II

REFUTING RUMORS

Oppression, disappearances and concentration camps — these harrowing words and phrases have been spotted in many Western media reports on Xinjiang. It seems each of their Xinjiang reports contains these words and sometimes just changes the name of interviewees to accuse China in their stories.

They often make fake news only to be refuted. They spread rumors in the news before being disproven by those at the center of such rumors. Many Western media reports on Xinjiang, which have been guided by ideology and bias rather than professionalism, seem to enter into this loop. It is pathetic to see that they never get bored. The Global Times reporters reached out to people at the center of rumors propagated by some Western media. It turns out that truth can never be covered by lies.

Anti-terrorism efforts stressed in white paper on Xinjiang

By Liu Xin | Mar 18, 2019

Northwest China's Xinjiang Uygur Autonomous Region government has prioritized preventive anti-terrorism and taken multiple measures, including setting up training centers and improving residents' livelihoods, to protect people from the harm of terrorism and extremism, according to a white paper released on March 18, 2019.

The paper, titled *The Fight Against Terrorism and Extremism and Human Rights Protection in Xinjiang*, was released by the State Council Information Office.

It stresses that Xinjiang has been an inseparable part of Chinese territory, tells the origin and development of terrorism and extremism in Xinjiang and the current anti-terrorism and de-extremism measures.

Terrorist and extremist forces in Xinjiang, driven by the goal of separatism, have engaged in damaging activities, which have severely undermined local stability and greatly harmed the lives, security and property of local residents, according to the paper.

"Terrorism and extremism jeopardize human rights and sustainable development as they propagate intolerance between different religions, cultures and societies, challenge human justice and dignity, and do great harm to peace and security," the paper reads.

It points out that echoing the UN resolutions on "addressing the conditions conductive to the spread of terrorism" and "preventing and combating terrorism," China's Xinjiang has taken measures — harshly cracking down on terrorist crimes while at the same time improving people's livelihoods, strengthening education on laws, setting up vocational education and training centers in accordance with laws and other measures.

Preventative efforts

"How to prevent terrorist activities before they happen remains the biggest problem for the international community, as no punishment after a terrorist attack could make up for the huge casualties and loss of property," Li Wei, a Beijing-based anti-terrorism expert, told the Global Times.

Establishing vocational education and training centers is one of the preventative measures.

The white paper says that Xinjiang has included de-extremism education in its daily courses in training centers.

By learning national laws and regulations, ethnic policies and religious knowledge, trainees can realize that religious extremism totally deviates from religious doctrines.

They can understand the essence and harm of terrorism and extremism and finally get rid of their control and influence, according to the white paper.

Li also said Xinjiang's ongoing de-extremism measures have proved effective as they help protect local residents' right to life and development, which are basic human rights.

And "by giving people who have been influenced by extremism a new chance in the training centers, their human rights have also been protected," Li said.

Xu Jianying, a research fellow at the Chinese Academy of Social Sciences' Research Center for Chinese Borderland History and Geography, noted that Xinjiang's de-extremism measures, drawn from previous experience, fit the local situation.

For example, Xinjiang combines de-extremism efforts with measures to improve residents' livelihoods.

By offering vocational training in the centers, residents could find a job after graduation, enhance life and consolidate the anti-terrorism foundation, according to Xu.

There has been no terrorist attack in Xinjiang for more than two years, which is an achievement brought about by de-extremism efforts in the region, according to Xinjiang officials reached by the Global Times.

"Xinjiang's ongoing measures can offer some experience to the international community on combating extremism. However, hindered by long-term bias, some Western countries will not acknowledge Xinjiang's achievements," Li said.

"The West has adopted double standards on, for example, defining terrorist attacks: What happened in their own countries are terrorist attacks but similar cases in developing countries, including China, are protests against local government policies on ethnic groups," Li noted, saying the double standards would affect global efforts to combat terrorism.

Kashi residents chat with each other. (Photo: Fan Lingzhi / GT)

"There is no doubt that Xinjiang's fight against terrorism and extremism is an important component of the global struggle, and has made an important contribution to the latter," reads the white paper. It also called for countries to abandon double standards.

Many foreign diplomats and media have been invited to visit Xinjiang and they were impressed by the achievements of the region's de-extremism.

Nugroho Fery Yudho, a reporter from Indonesia, told the Global Times during his visit to Xinjiang in February, 2019 that "I admire the Chinese government's courage to explore its own way on de-extremism ... Some countries rely on international organizations or other countries for de-extremism, which seemed to achieve little."

Facts on Xinjiang

The white paper also lists incomplete data and cases of thousands of terrorist attacks, launched by separatists, terrorist and extremist forces in Xinjiang, which killed a large number of innocent people and hundreds of police officers and caused immeasurable damage to property.

Terrorists and extremists in Xinjiang also killed people from the religious field.

The white paper notes that on November 6, 1997, a terrorist group under the command of the "East Turkistan" organization stationed abroad shot and killed Senior Mullah Younusi Sidike, member of the China Islamic Association, president of Aksu Islamic Association and imam of the Great Mosque of Baicheng County, on his way to the mosque for worship.

On July 30, 2014, the 74-year-old Senior Mullah Juma Tayier, vice president of Xinjiang Islamic Association and imam of the Id Kah Mosque, was brutally killed by three terrorists on his way home after morning Fajr prayer.

The data, rarely released to the public out of concern at causing panic, has been gradually opened to domestic and overseas media recently, to show the world the previous suffering of Xinjiang from terrorism and extremism, an official from the Xinjiang publicity department told the Global Times.

"These facts showed clearly why we are making efforts at eradicating extremism in Xinjiang currently," he said.

Since 2014, Xinjiang has destroyed 1,588 violent and terrorist gangs, arrested 12,995 terrorists, seized 2,052 explosive devices, punished 30,645 people for 4,858 illegal religious activities, and confiscated 345,229 copies of illegal religious materials, according to the white paper.

While seeking the way of de-extremism, Xinjiang has insisted on not linking terrorism to a certain place, religion or ethnic group.

Mijuti Mehmoti, principal of a training center in Kashi, told the Global Times that Xinjiang's current de-extremism measures, including the training centers, are not targeting a certain ethnic group or religion but to help those being influenced by extremism.

Xinjiang fully respects and safeguards residents' rights including freedom of religion, protects legal religious activities and meets the demands of religious groups, according to the white paper.

It fights terrorism and crimes which spread hatred among different ethnic groups and split the country under the disguise of religion, reads the white paper.

The white paper also notes that Xinjiang's anti-terrorism and de-extremism measures are implemented in accordance with national laws and regulations.

Aside from abiding by the national law systems on counter-terrorism, Xinjiang has also put forward regional regulations including regulations on managing religious affairs and regional de-extremism regulations, to offer legislative authority on cracking down on terrorism and extremism.

The untold truth about Xinjiang in Western media

By Xie Wenting and Bai Yunyi | Mar 20, 2019

Editor's note

Misleading headlines, groundless accusations, obscure interviewees, double standards are not hard to spot in many articles covering China's Xinjiang Uygur Autonomous Region in Western media outlets.

Recent months have seen an intensive outburst of such reports which have tainted China's anti-terrorism efforts in the region by adopting tactics including using words with a negative connotation, providing incomplete information and

Residents chat with neighbors about their daily life on February 15, 2019 in Yusitunke Ayikule Village of Awati County in Aksu Prefecture in Northwest China's Xinjiang Uygur Autonomous Region. (Photo: Liu Xin / GT)

stirring readers' emotions.

Global Times reporters Xie Wenting and Bai Yunyi researched Xinjiang reported in the Western media and interviewed American YouTuber Nathan Rich, Kurbanjan Samat, a Uygur photographer and director who shoots stories about people from Xinjiang, and Erkin Öncan, a Turkish journalist focused on Xinjiang reporting.

Fabricating "truth"

"For me, you haven't seen things like this since the 1930s," said Michael Kozak, head of the US State Department's human rights and democracy bureau, at a news briefing on March 13, 2019 about China's treatment of Muslims in Xinjiang.

"Rounding up, in some estimations ... in the millions of people, putting them into camps, and torturing them, abusing them, and trying to basically erase their culture and their religion and so on from their DNA. It's just remarkably awful," Kozak said, according to a Reuters report.

The use of the pejorative word "camp" for a "vocational education and training center" was not only evident in Kozak's speech, but is also frequently used in Western media reports.

"The use of the word 'camp' or 'concentration camp' has a negative connotation in English, which directly invokes imagery of Nazis and Nazism," said Nathan Rich, a US citizen who is also a technical executive at a Beijing-based company.

Rich gained fame in China last month when he released a video slamming a report by The New York Times about China's medical system.

The video has garnered tens of millions of views on social media platforms.

For Rich, himself a Jew, drawing parallels between Nazism and the Chinese government is "totally insane."

"It's very strange — it's just an overt attempt to use suggestive propaganda,"

Rich said.

"Nazis murdered Jews who had done nothing wrong, but in Xinjiang, the regional government only tries to limit the actions of those who have committed crimes or are suspected of terrorism," he said.

Shohrat Zakir, chairman of the Xinjiang regional government, said on the sidelines of this year's two sessions in Beijing that Xinjiang is a victim of terrorism and extremism and the vocational education and training centers aim to fundamentally eliminate the environment for terrorism and extremism.

"It is not targeting specific ethnic groups or specific religions. Instead, it is targeting the three forces of violent terrorist crimes, extremism and separatism," he said.

Besides deliberately choosing negative words, some Western media reports just simply resorted to lies.

On January 21, 2019, CNN issued a report in which it interviewed Mihrigul Tursun, who alleged her son had died at Urumqi children's hospital in Xinjiang in 2015. "I will tell them everything," Tursun said in the CNN report. "I will tell them the Chinese government killed their brother."

Tursun also claimed that she witnessed the death of nine Uygur women when she was detained in Urumqi's prison.

This report was slammed by Hua Chunying, Chinese Foreign Ministry spokesperson, who provided concrete evidence.

Hua said that Tursun's son was sent to Urumqi children's hospital in January, May and November 2016 with pneumonia, hydrocephalus and other illnesses.

The official record showed Tursun and her husband took the child out of China in April 2018.

According to Hua, on April 21, 2017, Mihrigul was taken into custody by the public security bureau of Qiemo County on suspicion of inciting ethnic hatred and discrimination. She was released 20 days later after being found to have infectious disease out of humanitarian consideration.

Mihrigul had never been detained by police in Urumqi, neither had she been jailed or put into any vocational education and training center, Hua said.

While Western news agencies extensively rely on sources from websites and social accounts run by "East Turkestan" terrorists, Kurbanjan Samat, a Uygur photographer and documentary director, told the Global Times that the authenticity of these materials was questionable.

Kurbanjan has seen how his works were "transformed" by "East Turkestan" terrorists with fake captions added to fool the public.

Kurbanjan once shot a series of photos about a small village in Xinjiang's Hotan in 2006 and 2007. The village is off the beaten path even for locals in Hotan due to inconvenient transportation. "I simply recorded the life and culture of the local people back then. The village later had a good development," he said.

To his surprise, he later found out that some of his photos were deliberately chosen by "East Turkestan" terrorists and were used in their accounts with texts such as "how miserably people in Xinjiang live under the governance of the Chinese government."

This was "a complete distortion of facts," he said.

Erkin Öncan, a Turkish journalist, told the Global Times many Western news agencies' reports about Xinjiang are based on the allegations of NGOs that are run by "East Turkestan" terrorists and funded by the West.

Öncan has focused on Xinjiang for many years and he also traces jihadist movements in Turkey, Syria and Afghanistan.

Public data showed that the Uygur Human Rights Project and World Uygur Congress, citing sources in Western reports, receive funds from the National Endowment for Democracy (NED). NED is also known as a "shadow CIA."

"I realized the Western media's provocative and misleading attitude when I started to compare the news about Xinjiang. I saw their reports about the region were written with no source and based on unreliable things," Öncan said.

What these Western media outlets are doing isn't caring about Muslims' life in China, but "a political agenda of the Western countries against China," he added.

Double standards

Rich said many Western media framed reports in a sensational way to mislead readers.

He provided examples, such as "sweeping campaign to detain and indoctrinate Muslims," and "China's Xinjiang experience demonstrates the peril of large-scale anti-Muslim policies" in Western media.

Rich said this totally "doesn't make sense." In cities including Beijing and Xi'an where he has been, Muslims live a peaceful life.

Also, as he pointed out, the Chinese government's governance in Xinjiang has never been about hatred toward Muslims and what the government is trying to do is to stamp out terrorism in the region.

According to Rich, the malicious accusations against China's anti-terrorism efforts in Xinjiang reflect double standards, given that the US has led the war on terrorism for many years.

Following the September 11 attacks, the US has led a war on terrorism in Afghanistan and other nations, striking and bombing them, which continues to cause a significant number of civilian deaths, Rich said.

"To wage a war on terrorism which is not in your country is different from waging a war on terror in your country. If Americans woke up tomorrow and found that, for example, Libya had just suddenly appeared in the middle of Texas, what would be the solution to the inevitable terrorism that would happen?"

The best way, he said, might be to declare "martial law," limit certain people's travel and investigate where this terrorism comes from.

Kurbanjan pointed out that the biggest "double standards" in the Western media's Xinjiang coverage is that they only reported the so-called "results," but they failed to tap into the underlying reasons, background and process.

Kurbanjan cited his own experience in Hotan as an example.

Hotan was once plagued with separatism and extremist ideology, where all women were required to wear back clothes, headscarves and face veils.

But his mother didn't want to wear the veil to cover her face. His sister was also unwilling to wear a headscarf and insisted on going to school.

"Because of this, my family was isolated and scolded by other people. We had to live an almost isolated life for 20 years. But the Western media won't tell you this," he said.

Selective reporting materials are also reflected in Mihrigul Tursun's case. Most Western media turned a blind eye to China's evidence.

Rich told the Global Times that "If you try to understand China's actions while assuming they are 'anti-Muslim,' as portrayed by some Western media, many things don't add up. It doesn't make sense."

Due to anti-terrorism efforts in the region, the local economy is on the rise in the past few years and more women are freed from domestic violence and free to control their own life.

Even in the photo coverage, many Western media tend to shoot police and police cars on Xinjiang streets to reflect their angle of suppression and strict supervision.

But what they do not mention is that these are security measures taken after a serious of terrorist tragedies and they help ensure a peaceful environment.

The Western media also like to photograph pedestrians with their heads down to create a depressing atmosphere.

But in fact, on the streets and in the squares of Xinjiang, relaxed and light-hearted citizens are everywhere but unable to enter the lens of Western media.

"With using fancy language, with police or Muslim photos, they are trying to create an image," said Öncan.

Discourse hegemony

Another notable characteristic of the Western media's Xinjiang reports is their discourse hegemony.

They place themselves at the commanding heights of "human rights" and do not allow doubts or critical voices to exist.

In a previous interview with the Global Times, many foreigners told reporters that they did not dare to make any positive comments on China's governance in Xinjiang, as it would quickly incur suspicions and even attacks.

Öncan said he tried to argue with Western journalists about their biased reports.

But when he brought this up with Western journalists, he only got the same answers all the time.

"In every stage of China's governance, they claim China as an 'oppressive' country, but this allegation is their main excuse for fabricating false news. With doing this, they thought that they can write whatever they want, and when the proof has been asked for, they answer 'We don't have it. Because as an oppressive country, China has closed itself to the outside world for searching into the allegations,'" he said.

But China has already invited politicians and journalists from other countries to the region, Öncan said.

The regional government has organized tours for diplomats and media delegates from other countries to visit Xinjiang.

Some journalists have published articles which credited the regional government's work but these words weren't seen in the Western media.

For defending China's policy in Xinjiang, Öncan is threatened by "East Turkestan" terrorists and other people holding different opinions in Turkey.

"When they couldn't answer the facts about Xinjiang, they choose to accuse me of 'being a spy' and try to discredit me. They even claimed that my name was also given by Chinese authorities, because Erkin is also a Uygur name. They are also trying to link my journalism activities with an intelligence agency," he said.

Öncan said he has received threats like "Wherever he appears, his head should be separated from his body."

Kurbanjan also revealed to the Global Times that when he was working overseas, he was tracked and his personal safety was threatened by people who disagree with his Xinjiang views.

One time in the US, as he finished talking to his interviewee from Xinjiang, three young men carrying baseball bats approached, threatening to beat him.

Öncan told the Global Times that he doesn't worry about his personal safety.

"Because I know that the truth always wins," he said.

White paper clarifies historical facts of Xinjiang

By Bai Yunyi and Liu Xin | Jul 21, 2019

The State Council Information Office released a white paper on July 21, 2019 to clarify historical issues about the Xinjiang Uygur Autonomous Region, including that the Northwest China region has never been "East Turkistan" and Uygurs are not descendants of the Turks, two false ideas promoted and distorted by separatist groups and some Western media.

Chinese experts said that important historical facts on Xinjiang are matters of principle. Clarifying the history of ethnic groups, cultures and religions in the region is important to unifying different ethnic groups, maintaining stability and development.

The white paper *Historical Matters Concerning Xinjiang* clarifies seven major questions: Xinjiang has long been an inseparable part of Chinese territory. Xinjiang has never been "East Turkistan." Ethnic groups in Xinjiang are part of the Chinese

How did Uyghur ethnic group form in history?

In Sui and Tang dynasties:

Ouigour people,
Main ancestors of Uyghurs

They lived on Mongolian Plateau. Historically, Ouigour people united with some Tiele tribes to resist oppression and slavery of the Turks.

In 788, Ouigour ruler wrote to Tang emperor to change the name into "Uighur."

In 840, Uighur Khanate was defeated by the Kyrgyz people. Some of the Uighurs moved inland to live with the Han people, the rest were divided into three sub-groups:

- One moved to the Turpan Basin and the present-day Jimsar region, founded the Uighur Kingdom of Gaochang
- One moved to the Hexi Corridor, merged with local ethnic groups to become the Yugurs
- One moved to the west of Pamir, joined the Karluk and Yagma peoples in founding the Kara-Khanid Khanate

They merged with the Han people in the Turpan Basin and the Yanqi, Qiuci, Khotan, Shule, and other peoples in the Tarim Basin to form the main body of the modern Uyghur ethnic group.

In Yuan and Ming dynasties:

Ethnic groups in Xinjiang further merged; the Mongols were fused with the Uighurs.

In 1934:

Xinjiang issued government order to stipulate the standard Chinese name for Uyghurs.

GLOBAL TIMES

Source: Xinhua Photo: VCG
Editor and Graphic: Globaltimes.cn

nation. The Uygur ethnic group formed through a long process of migration and integration. Xinjiang ethnic cultures are part of Chinese civilization. Multiple religions have long coexisted in Xinjiang. Islam is neither the indigenous nor the sole belief system of the Uygurs.

Terrorists and extremist forces, backed by certain people in the West, have been beating the drum for separatist activities by distorting, fabricating and falsifying the history of Xinjiang, Chinese experts told the Global Times in response to the white paper on July 21, 2019.

Separatists seek to split Xinjiang from Chinese culture and history, but history and truth cannot be falsified, experts said.

"The seven issues listed in the white paper are important ones related to religion, ethnic groups, culture and history of the Xinjiang region, which have also been distorted by Western media and 'East Turkistan' separatists. The white paper was published to clarify misperceptions on these issues," Xu Jianying, a research fellow at the Institute of China's Borderlands of Chinese Academy of Social Sciences in Beijing, told the Global Times.

The paper is based on abundant, informative, accurate and solid research on the region's history, culture and religion, Xu said.

It represents the views of academic circles in China and by refuting previous false theories on Xinjiang, it will also help Xinjiang's unity, stability and future develop-ment, he asserted.

Cao Qianfa, a research fellow who participated in drafting the white paper, told the Global Times that "the white paper is the first time for China to proactively introduce the history, religions and cultures of Xinjiang spontaneously and systematically."

"It is a powerful counterattack to US' offensive toward China using Xinjiang question as an excuse," said Cao.

Not Turks

The new white paper clarifies that never in Chinese history has Xinjiang been referred to as "East Turkistan," and there has never been any state known as "East Turkistan."

From the 18th century to the first half of the 19th century, as the West made a distinction between the various Turkic languages, some foreign scholars and writers coined the term "Turkistan" to refer to the region south of the Tianshan Mountains and north of Afghanistan, which roughly covered the area from southern Xinjiang to Central Asia.

They called the two areas on either side of the Pamirs "West Turkistan" and "East Turkistan," according to the white paper.

"Separatists in and outside China politicized the geographical concept and used 'East Turkistan' to distort the history of Xinjiang and the Uygur ethnic group," said Li Wei, a counter-terrorism expert at the China Institute of Contemporary International Relations.

"They attempted to split the country. Now these distorted theories have been refuted in the newly issued white paper."

Li said that what the white paper says on the history of how the Uygur ethnic group formed and became an important part of the Chinese nation is a forceful refutation of separatists' absurd theories on Xinjiang.

The white paper also denies what separatists inside and outside the region usually claim — as their language is Turkic, Uygurs are descendants of the Turks.

The Uygur ethnic group came into being through a long process of migration and integration. It is part of the Chinese nation, the paper says.

Scholars in Xinjiang also reached a consensus on this view.

Yasheng Sidike, mayor and deputy Communist Party of China (CPC) chief of Urumqi, wrote an article published in the *Urumqi Evening Post* on August 20, 2018 saying, "The Uygur people are members of the Chinese family, not descendants of

Xinjiang Has Never Been "East Turkistan"

GLOBAL TIMES Source: White Paper
Editors and graphics: Globaltimes.cn

the Turks, let alone anything to do with Turkish people."

Fallacies that claim "'East Turkistan is our country' and 'Uygur as natives of Xinjiang' are ridiculous, ignorant and condemnable," the article said.

The white paper also offers a detailed timeline proving that Xinjiang is an inseparable part of Chinese territory — from the place being called Western Regions in ancient times and having close contact with the Central Plains to the Xinjiang

Uygur Autonomous Region being established in 1955.

"Xinjiang has been a multi-ethnic region since ancient times. A large amount of cultural relics were found in ruins of the two ancient cities in the current Xinhe County of Aksu Prefecture, which include seals with standard Chinese written on them that show the Central Plains' rule over the place in the Han Dynasty," Muchi Yundengjiacuo, dean of the School on Ethnic and Religious Studies at Northwest University of Political Science and Law, told the Global Times.

These relics, which showed close exchanges and ties between Xinjiang and the Central Plains, have been displayed in the Museum of the Xinjiang Uygur Autonomous Region.

The World Uygur Congress and other separatist groups keep spreading rumors that the Han and other ethnic groups including Hui and Kazak were "foreign groups" coming to Xinjiang, which is groundless and has no historical basis. Muchi said.

The truth is that they want to instigate isolation and hatred. The last thing they want to see is people of different ethnic groups unite and live in harmony in Xinjiang, he asserted.

"Working together for a prosperous and better future has become the consensus of people living in Xinjiang. They are aware that without unity among different ethnic groups and social stability, there will be no development of each ethnic group," Muchi said.

Multi-religious region

Xinjiang has long been a region of multiple religions, the white paper says. The history of Xinjiang shows that many religions have long coexisted there, with one or two predominant.

The region's religious structure was characterized by blending and coexistence. Islam is neither an indigenous nor the sole belief system of the Uygur people, the paper says.

Cultural relics in Xinjiang could prove the changing religions in the history of Xinjiang. For example, the Kizil Cave-Temple Complex in Aksu Prefecture, built between the 3rd and 8th centuries, is believed to be the earliest Buddhist cave in China.

According to an introduction in the Aksu Museum on the evolution of religion in Xinjiang, in the middle of the 10th century after Islam was accepted by the Karahan Khanate, the rulers launched a religious war lasting more than 40 years to force the people to convert to Islam.

Palida Pulati, a tour guide of the Kizil Cave site, told the Global Times that many faces of the figures on the wall paintings were destroyed by Muslim residents, which showed the clash between Buddhism and Islam around the 10th century.

"By the middle of the 14th century, people in Kucha, Shaya, Wensu and other places were forced to believe in Islam by means such as war. By the early 16th century, Xinjiang had formed a pattern in which many religions, mainly Islam, coexisted and continued until now," Niger Tusun, from the Aksu Museum, told the Global Times.

The white paper released on July 21, 2019 says that "in the process of accepting Islam, the ancestors of the Uygurs and Kazaks integrated it with local faith and traditions, while absorbing the cultures of other ethnic groups in the region and from inland areas."

For example, images of honeysuckle, widely used in Buddhist ornaments, were found in some caves in Aksu.

These flowers have been painted on the hats of the Uygur and Kazak ethnic groups, which can be widely seen today.

Xinjiang white paper justifies vocational education and training centers

By Liu Xin and Bai Yunyi | Aug 16, 2019

China on August 16, 2019 released a white paper on vocational education and training in Northwest China's Xinjiang Uygur Autonomous Region, clarifying the legal basis for the training centers and declaring a key victory against terrorism and extremism through these centers.

The white paper includes six parts — urgent need for education and training, law-based education and training, content of education and training, protection of trainees' basic rights, remarkable results in education and training, and experience in countering extremism.

A trainee in a training center in Kashi, Northwest China's Xinjiang Uygur Autonomous Region, takes an apparel design class in February. (Photo: Liu Xin/GT)

A media group from Indonesia and Malaysia talks to trainees in an education and vocational training center in Hotan, Northwest China's Xinjiang Uygur Autonomous Region in February. (Photo: Liu Xin/GT)

The release marks the third white paper on Xinjiang this year. China released a white paper, *The Fight Against Terrorism and Extremism and Human Rights Protection in Xinjiang*, on March 18 and another white paper, *Historical Matters Concerning Xinjiang*, on July 21.

"China released the white papers to provide a full picture to the international community on its Xinjiang policies amid attempts by some Western media and anti-China forces to use the issue to stir trouble and contain China," Qian Jinyu, executive dean of the Human Rights Institution of Northwest University of Political Science and Law in Shaanxi Province, told the Global Times.

The white papers reveal the spirit of innovation, and that the rule of law has been fully implemented in China's policies in Xinjiang, Qian said.

Xu Jianying, a research fellow at the Institute of China's Borderlands of the Chinese Academy of Social Sciences, told the Global Times that one of the key points in the white paper is the legal basis for organizing the training centers. The Chinese government, for the first time, gives an open and comprehensive explanation on the legal basis of the training centers, which will further promote China's policies in Xinjiang.

"The white paper also shows China's responsible attitude toward its work in counter-terrorism and de-radicalization," Xu said.

Legal basis

Terrorism and extremism have long existed in Xinjiang. Incomplete statistics show that from 1990 to the end of 2016, separatists, religious extremists and terrorists plotted and launched thousands of terrorist attacks, including bombings, assassinations, arson and riots, killing large numbers of innocent people and hundreds of police officers and caused immeasurable damage to property.

Education and training in Xinjiang is practiced in line with the requirements of the rule of law in China. It also reflects the ideas and principles of counter-terrorism and de-radicalization as practiced by the international community, the white paper says.

It lists the legal basis — including the *Counter-Terrorism Law of the People's Republic of China* (PRC), the *Measures of the Xinjiang Uygur Autonomous Region on Implementing the Counter-Terrorism Law of the PRC* and the *Regulations of the Xinjiang Uygur Autonomous Region on De-radicalization.*

The white paper clarifies the three categories of trainees at the centers and explained the legal procedures of how the centers are run.

The trainees at the centers fall under three categories:

— Those who were incited, coerced or induced into participating in terrorist or extremist activities, or people who participated in terrorist or extremist activities in circumstances that were not serious enough to constitute a crime.

— Those who were incited, coerced or induced into participating in terrorist or extremist activities, or people who participated in terrorist or extremist activities that posed a real danger but did not cause actual harm, whose subjective culpability was not deep, who acknowledged their offenses and were contrite about their past actions, and thus do not need to be sentenced or can be exempted from punishment, and who have demonstrated the willingness to receive training.

— Those who were convicted and received prison sentences for terrorist or extremist crimes, and after serving their sentences, have been assessed as still posing a potential threat to society, and who have been ordered by people's courts to be educated at the centers in accordance with the law.

Qian noted the importance of educating women on laws, as many married female trainees have little knowledge of their basic rights.

"Some men in Xinjiang used to divorce their wives after they said 'Talaq' three times to the wife [Triple Talaq, a type of instant divorce in Islam]. Women were beaten by their husbands. After learning about the law, they know their rights are protected in marriage," Qian said.

The training centers also help these women improve the economic status of their families. With the vocational skills they have learned, they can earn respect from their husbands, Qian said.

Refuting rumors

For a long time, Western media and anti-China forces have hyped China's human rights "violations," "mistreating" trainees at the centers, and even "depriving" them of using their own ethnic language.

Xu told the Global Times that the white paper also addresses concerns from the international community.

As extremism has been effectively contained in Xinjiang, and no terrorist incidents have occurred in Xinjiang for nearly three years since the education and training started, the white paper offers facts about Xinjiang which would help the world better understand the policies, analysts said.

The vocational education and training centers provide trainees with residential vocational training free of charge, and issue certificates of completion when they reach the expected criteria. After graduating, the trainees can choose their own jobs, or employment can be arranged for them with the assistance of relevant authorities, the paper says.

The white paper also reiterates that the basic rights of the trainees have been protected and the training center programs are aimed to help trainees to break free from ideas of terrorism and religious extremism and that it has never targeted any specific region, ethnic group or religion.

Under the premise of respecting ethnic groups' rights to use their own ethnic spoken and written languages, lectures on standard Chinese have been given to trainees to help them learn about science and technology, acquire vocational skills, seek work in other locations, communicate with other ethnic groups, and adapt better to modern living.

The training centers fully respect and protect the customs and habits of trainees hailing from different ethnic groups as well as their right to use their own language. Rules at the centers, curriculum and menus use local ethnic languages and standard Chinese.

The white paper also notes the trainees' freedom of religious belief has always been respected.

According to China's laws, no religious activity should be organized outside religious institutions and venues. The centers practice separation of education and religion in management, which means trainees should not organize or take part in religious activities at the centers, but they can choose whether to legally do so at home, the white paper said.

The UN's *Plan of Action to Prevent Violent Extremism* says poverty, unemployment, lack of job opportunities, low education levels and violent extremist groups using religion, differences between ethnic groups, and other reasons have helped create violent extremism.

The plan also suggests broadening responses, engaging earlier, and addressing the influences of violent extremism to counter terrorism. Preventive measures are also needed to complement the countering of violent extremism.

Great achievements

The training centers have helped rescue people from extremism, safeguarding the fundamental interests of all ethnic groups.

Thanks to these preventive measures, Xinjiang has experienced changes in its social environment. A healthy atmosphere is spreading, while evil influences declining. As the infiltration of religious extremism has been curbed, public order and security have returned, where equality, solidarity and harmony among ethnic groups and religions have prevailed, and people are enjoying peace and stability, the paper says.

Through measures such as vocational education and training, Xinjiang has achieved key victories in countering terrorism and extremism, which deserves the understanding and respect of the international community, it says.

Since December 2018, nearly 1,000 people have visited Xinjiang. They include foreign diplomats to China, UN officials, Geneva-based senior diplomats of various countries, as well as more than 40 groups (or delegations) of people from political parties, civil society organizations, news media, and religious organizations of various countries, the paper says.

A number of foreign journalists who have conducted interviews at the education and training centers have published stories that reflect the true role of the centers and express their understanding, approval and support for the education and training programs in Xinjiang.

Some countries and organizations or individuals apply double standards in their approach to terrorism and extremism, which will in effect shield and incite terrorism and extremism, it says.

Scan QR code to watch the video

Pompeo slammed for lying that Xinjiang woman was sent to training center, forcibly sterilized

By Fan Lingzhi | Oct 13, 2019

The elder brother of Zumrat Dawut on October 13, 2019 slammed US Secretary of State Mike Pompeo for making up lies, saying his sister has never been sent to a vocational education and training center in Northwest China's Xinjiang Uygur Autonomous Region or forcibly sterilized.

Abdulhelil Dawut on October 13, 2019 posted a Uygur language video to "tell the truth to the world" on Chinese short video platform Kuaishou.

"This is an outright lie," he says in a video of Pompeo's speech in the Vatican earlier in October 2019.

"My sister Zumrat Dawut has never been to any vocational education and training center and has never been forced to get sterilized," he said.

He said her sister once went to hospital to have an operation for myoma of uterus.

"I think Mr. Pompeo, as the US Secretary of State should have based his words on facts; stop using my sister Zumrat Dawut to make up lies and disturbing our otherwise quiet life."

US-based Breitbart News reported on October 3, 2019 that at a symposium in the Vatican on October 2, 2019, Pompeo said Zumrat Dawut "was shackled, interrogated, and taken to an internment camp where she was forced to recite Chinese propaganda and beaten for giving an ailing fellow prisoner her food. She was injected with unknown drugs."

Pompeo said he got to know Dawut's story during a conference in New York in September 2019, VOA reported.

The Chicago Tribune reported on September 28, 2019 that Zumrat Dawut was "even sterilized."

"Using the so-called victim to testify [against China] is actually finding someone to talk nonsense," Lü Xiang, an expert on US study at the Chinese Academy of Social Sciences in Beijing, told the Global Times on October 13, 2019.

"This is the US' typical tactic, like supporting the cults in the past. The CIA has been doing this for decades," he said.

"Pompeo is secretary of state, but he makes up lies on public occasions, which shows that he is a typical opportunist," Lü said.

"Pompeo once said that work at the CIA was about deception. He seems to take the work style there to his position as secretary of state."

The Chinese foreign minister has reiterated on many occasions that "Xinjiang affairs are purely China's internal affairs. No country has any right to interfere. The so-called human rights issue in Xinjiang claimed by the US is actually non-existent."

"Any restriction imposed by the US on Chinese entities and individuals over

Xinjiang, no matter what pretext, constitutes a grave violation of basic norms governing international relations and a flagrant interference in China's internal affairs. China is firmly opposed to that," Geng Shuang, the spokesperson of the Chinese Ministry of Foreign Affairs, said at a press conference on October 9, 2019.

Scan QR code to watch the video

Relatives of so-called Uygur activists slam Pompeo's detention claim

By Liu Xin and Fan Lingzhi in Yining | Nov 17, 2019

Northwest China's Xinjiang Uygur Autonomous Region released a statement on November 9, 2019 refuting US Secretary of State Mike Pompeo's remarks that claimed the so-called Uygur activists' family members are detained in Xinjiang.

Pompeo issued a statement on November 5, 2019, titled "Harassment of the Family Members of Uygur Activists and Survivors in Xinjiang, China," claiming that family members of the so-called activists Furkhat Jawdat, Alapat Arkin, Zumrat Dawut have been subject to harassment, imprisonment, and arbitrary detention.

The Xinjiang statement said what Pompeo stated "is simply not the case." The fact is the relatives of the names mentioned live and work normally in Xinjiang, and they are ashamed of the scum among their families.

The Global Times reporters visited the relatives of Furkhat Jawdat, Alapat Arkin, Zumrat Dawut in Urumqi and Yining and recognized that what Pompeo said is not consistent with the truth. No family members of the three people have been mistreated and they lead a normal life with numerous assistance from the residential community.

No more lies

Zumrat attracted Pompeo's attention for her accusation that she made overseas against the Chinese government's Xinjiang policy. The Global Times reporters learned from Xinjiang authorities that before going abroad, Zumrat, 37, lived in Urumqi. She married a Pakistani national in November 2013. On January 3, 2019 the couple together with their three children went to Pakistan and later to the US.

Abduhelil Dawut, one of Zumrat Dawut's elder brothers, plays with his son in their home in Urumqi, Xinjiang. (Photo: Fan Lingzhi/GT)

The November 5 statement was not the first time Pompeo mentioned about Zumrat.

On October 2, 2019, Pompeo said in a meeting in Vatican that he listened to Zumrat's story and learned that she was summoned to the public security bureau in Xinjiang in April 2019 and was sent to a "concentration camp." Pompeo claimed that during her stay there, she was injected with some drugs.

A report on the *Chicago Tribune* on September 28, 2019 noted that Zumrat was forcefully sterilized.

Abduhelil Dawut, one of Zumrat's elder brothers spoke through a video about a month back to quash the rumors, saying "these are outright lies." In the video urging Pompeo to stop disturbing their peaceful lives, he said, "Respect the facts and do not make use of my sister Zumrat Dawut to make up lies."

The Global Times reporter visited Abduhelil, who lives in Urumqi. Abduhelil and his wife now work for a residential community in the city. The interior of their house and the cleanliness suggests that residents live a good life there.

Abduhelil told the Global Times his sister has never been to a vocational education and training center and "when delivering the third child, she was found to have fibroid and later had a surgery."

Abduhelil released a video on October 13, 2019 to refute Pompeo's remarks on her sister. Zumrat recently wrote on an overseas social media platform that the Chinese government spread rumors on her uterus being removed. However, no one has mentioned about anything on this.

The whole family was against Zumrat's marriage but Zumrat "was stubborn."

The relations between Zumrat and the other family members were "strained" after that. Abduhelil said, "She treated our father well when she was in a good mood, but when my father said something she did not like, she would slam the door and refrain from speaking to him for a year."

In 2018, Zumrat, her husband and the three children went to Pakistan and never came back. She finally went to the US without informing the family members, including their father.

Their father died of a heart disease last month. Abduhelil had a video chat with Zumrat and "I told her to stop spreading rumors and retract the lies she peddled online previously. She cried and said yes. But later, she continued peddling lies online."

Pompeo claimed that Zumrat's father, who was reportedly "detained and interrogated multiple times by Chinese authorities in Xinjiang in recent years, recently passed away under unknown circumstances."

However, Abduhelil told the Global Times that their father lived a normal life with them, and had neither been "interrogated" nor "detained."

After suffering from serious heart diseases, he died at the age of 80 at a hospital in October 2019 after medical treatment was exhausted. While he stayed at hospital, his relatives looked after him.

The death certificate of Zumrat's father mentioned the cause of death as "coronary heart disease."

Erkin Dawut is one of Zumrat's elder brothers. He was the one who signed his father's death certificate. He thought his father's physical conditions worsened partly because he missed Zumrat very much.

Erkin did not want to talk to Zumrat since "she always uttered lies since childhood."

"She is the youngest one among us. She was my father's favorite. My father grieved as she left without telling him," he told the Global Times.

Erkin was visibly in tears, as he recalled their father. "I keep my father's phone number and hope that he could call me like before," he said.

Not to be manipulated

Pompeo also mentioned about Furkhat Jawdat and Alapat Arkin, claiming that

Alapat's mother was also put in the "concentration camp" since 2017 and his father was imprisoned in March 2018.

After meeting with Pompeo on Mar 26, 2019, Furkhat Jawdat claimed his mother was moved to a prison from a vocational education and training center.

The Global Times reporters learned from authorities in Xinjiang that Alapat and Furkhat were born in Yining. Alapat went to the US in 2015 and then joined the infamous violent terrorist and separatist organization "World Uygur Congress."

Furkhat went to the US in 2011 and later became a member of the "World Uygur Congress." Furkhat's father, brother and two sisters have obtained green cards in the US.

The Global Times reporters met with Alapat's mother who currently lives with Alapat's grandmother in Yining.

Gulnar Talat, Alapat's mother, told the Global Times that she lives a normal life and is not under detention. She plans to get medical treatment in Urumqi.

She said she wants to tell Alapat that "you should not be influenced by your father or take part in something bad. You should not be manipulated by others."

"Do not believe those who have ulterior motives. We live a good life. You were born and grew up in China. Thanks to the development of the country, you have the opportunity to study overseas. Hope you can study hard in the US and come back to contribute to the country."

The Global Times reporters learned that Alapat's father Erkin Tursun is in prison for inciting hatred and discrimination among different ethnic groups and covering up criminals.

Alapat's deeds worried his relatives. Alapat's uncle Asat Talat hoped to tell his nephew that his father was imprisoned for breaching the laws. "You should neither believe in rumors nor spread it. We sent you abroad to study and to honor the country. Not for something bad," Asat said.

Pompeo also noted about Furkhat's mother in his November 5 statement. Apart from Alapat, Furkhat's father, a younger brother and his two sisters, all live in the US now.

His mother failed to obtain her visa and now lives in their house in Yining.

Munawar Tursun, the mother, told the Global Times that she talks to her son almost every day. She pointed to a TV set in their house that her son bought online and was delivered to the house days earlier.

Furkhat did not admit that he is a member of the "World Uygur Congress." But he defended the organization on overseas social media and participated in its activities.

Munawar told the Global Times that she knows nothing about what her son has done overseas and persuaded him not to get involved in any illegal activities. "I told him, if he wants me to go abroad, it must be via legal means and that he must not engage in illegal activities."

Munawar believes Rebiya Kadeer, a separatist from Xinjiang, is a scum among the Uygurs.

Furkhat claimed that the Chinese government harasses Muslim families in Xinjiang and they went abroad to seek asylum.

However, according to Munawar, Furkhat's father went to work in the US in 2006 and the children went to the US one after another within the next five years.

Furkhat's uncle Enwar Tursun told the Global Times that he used to be against all the children going to the US since Furkhat had good academic records and would have had a better future if he stayed in China and he can also take good care of his mother.

"Furkhat, you are a smart boy. What you are doing is wrong. You will regret it!" Enwar said, insisting that the "World Uygur Congress" is a separatist organization. "As for Pompeo, I think he took advantage of my nephew, which is ignominious."

Receiving help

In order to rally support from the overseas separatist groups, Zumrat, Alapat, and Furkhat distorted the truth and played victims. Separatists from China's Xinjiang share a common interest in hyping Xinjiang issues. "Detention" or "oppression" are the words usually mentioned by them.

The Global Times reporters did not find any oppression or detention of their relatives. Instead, family members of these so-called Uygur activists are taken good care by the local residential communities.

Alapat's mother Gulnar Talat told the Global Times that she was in hospital in Urumqi due to some ailment in her spine. Colleagues and head of the kindergarten where Gulnar works for, visited her and donated 2,000 yuan toward her treatment.

The Yining educational bureau also allowed her to take a long vacation so that she could fully recover.

Furkhat's mother Munawar has become "the relative" of Zhang Liping, secretary of the residential community, who has taken a good care of Munawar.

Munawar has no job or earnings aside from the governmental subsidiaries.

In September 2019, there was something wrong with the water pipes in Munawar's house. Munawar also owed 500 yuan in water fees. Zhang paid that amount herself to help Munawar with the water fees.

"My monthly salary is around 3,000 yuan. I treat her as my family member and would not hesitate to help her," Zhang told the Global Times.

Zhang lost her 25-year-old son in 2017, while Munawar's children are far away in the US. The common emotion of parental love toward their children brings Zhang and Munawar together.

Zhang said she once saw Munawar shed tears while talking about her son. She comforted her by sharing the sorrow of losing her son.

"I often say to Munawar that I envy her because she can see her children via video chat. But I can only see the tomb of my son," Zhang said.

"There are many senior residents in my residential community. They comforted me and helped me get over my pang. As grassroots public servants, we need to devote our heart in helping the residents. The senior residents here also like me and greet me whenever we meet. This makes me happy," Zhang said.

Scan QR code to watch the video

Exclusive: Xinjiang spokesperson dismisses Western reports

By Liu Xin and Fan Lingzhi | Dec 3, 2019

Editor's note

Correspondents of Global Times recently interviewed the spokesperson of the People's Government of Xinjiang Uygur Autonomous Region, speaking about the ICIJ's organization of multiple foreign media outlets to fabricate and distort reports about Xinjiang. The spokesperson stated that the reports published by the ICIJ and other foreign media are nothing but distortions and concoctions to smear Xinjiang's vocational education and training centers, and its counter-terrorism and de-radicalization work, and that we are resolutely opposed to such reports.

Question: Recently, the ICIJ (International Consortium of Investigative Journalists) published an article about Xinjiang, illustrating the "personal experiences" of multiple victims including Mirigul Tursun and Shaylagul Sawutbay. They said that they were harshly mistreated in the "concentration camp," some "detainees" were hung on a wall and they were allowed no more than two minutes to use the bathroom, and at least nine female detainees died due to the terrible environment and medical conditions. Is what they said true?

Answer: In August 2019, the State Council Information Office of the People's Republic of China issued a white paper, *Vocational Education and Training in Xinjiang*. It gave a thorough introduction to the education and training centers in Xinjiang. I'd like to stress again that the education and training centers in Xinjiang are school in nature, set up according to law. They were never the so-called "concentration camps" at all. Clinics are available in all the centers and professional doctors are there to provide 24-hour free medical service to trainees. Minor ailments are treated at the clinic. In the case of major and acute illnesses, trainees will be sent to hospital. The alleged nine female deaths are pure fabrications.

The spokesperson of the Foreign Ministry of China has clarified Mirigul Tursun's lies many times. And I'd like to tell you the truth once again. Mirigul Tursun, a Uygur, was a resident of Qiemo County, Xinjiang. She was arrested by the police of Qiemo County on April 21, 2017, on the charges of instigating ethnic hatred and ethnic discrimination. During that time, as she had contracted syphilis and other infectious diseases, the Public Security Bureau of Qiemo County revoked the compulsory measures on her on May 10, 2017, due to humanitarian considerations. Mirigul was totally free in China apart from those 20 days of criminal detention. According to relevant records, from 2010 to 2017, she travelled 11 times between China and countries including Egypt, the United Arab Emirates, Thailand and Turkey. Mirigul has never been locked up by the police of Urumqi, nor has she been put into prison or studied in any vocational education and training center. Mirigul Tursun lied that her younger brother was abused, resulting in his death, in the training center. After hearing her lies, her younger brother Akber Tursun said, "My sister always tells lies. She also said she had seen other people dead, besides me."

Shaylagul Sawutbay, a female, Chinese citizen and Kazak ethnic, became the head of the central kindergarten in Chahanwusong Town, Zhaosu County, Yili Prefecture, Xinjiang, in April 2016. In March 2018, she was dismissed by the local educational authority and relocated as a teacher to a primary school in Chahanwusong Town, Zhaosu County, Yili Prefecture, because of her incompetency for her previous post and infringing on other teachers' interests by seeking performance bonuses through cheating. She is a suspect of fraud, and 249,000 yuan is still unrecovered from her. She has never worked in any vocational education and training center, and had never been imprisoned before she illegally went abroad. Where on earth did she see "trainees being hung on walls" or "restricted to use the toilet within two minutes"? To avoid legal punishment, she travelled to Kazakhstan and acquired refugee status by cheating, making up many lies about Xinjiang, which is despicable.

Question: The New York Times called Xinjiang vocational education and training centers "internment camps," and alleged that students returning home during summer vacation could not see their family members. What is your comment on this?

Answer: Xinjiang set up the vocational education and training centers according to law, and they are schools in nature. The New York Times mistakenly called them "internment camps," which is totally irresponsible.

The vocational education and training centers are schools in nature, and use boarding management. The trainees can go home and ask for leave at any time. The trainees have the freedom of communication. Trainees' relatives are totally aware of the education and training that they receive. Their families can call and have video-chat with them, and visit them at the centers.

The vocational education and training program in Xinjiang has achieved good results since its implementation, and has received positive comments from the international community. Since the end of 2018, more than 70 delegations of over 1,000 people from 91 countries and regions have visited Xinjiang, including senior UN officials, foreign envoys to China, delegates of international organizations, permanent representatives of different countries to the UN office at Geneva, journalists of foreign media and leaders of religious groups. Through field trips, many of them have seen the truth and come to understand that it is a necessary, legal and reasonable effort to carry out the vocational education and training in Xinjiang. They have all expressed that the terrorist activities which occurred in the region were brutal, inhumane and outrageous, and that the vocational education and training program has made important contributions to international efforts to fight terrorism and extremism, and generated valuable experience that is of great reference value.

Question: In a recent Xinjiang-related report from The New York Times, the July 5 riot was called an ethnic resistance suppressed by the government. What is your comment on this?

Answer: There has long been a final verdict on the July 5 riot in Urumqi, and many mainstream foreign media reported the facts of the incident 10 years ago. In the riot, the "East Turkistan" forces at home and abroad colluded with each other in organizing, plotting and committing serious violent crimes — beating, smashing, looting and arson, killing 197 people including Uygurs, injuring more than 1,700, and causing immeasurable property loss. Until today, many families have not yet come out of the shadows as the trauma still lingers.

Instead of condemning the heinous and inhumane violent terrorist activity, The New York Times glorifies it as an "ethnic resistance." This is a typical representation of double standards on counterterrorism and de-radicalization. It violates basic professional ethics and human conscience, and is despised by all good and just people. According to the logic of The New York Times, aren't the September 11 attacks also an ethnic resistance, suppressed by the US government?

Question: The New York Times report said families of trainees at the vocational education and training centers are discriminated against. Can you tell us the truth?

Answer: Government at all levels in Xinjiang treat the trainees' families equally as other people, and help them solve problems with employment, medical services, education and poverty alleviation over time. They enjoy equal policies in their basic living allowance, free health examinations, endowment insurance, medical insurance, and accident and injury insurance. Children of the trainees can equally enjoy 12 years of free education, and those in the four prefectures in southern Xinjiang can enjoy 15 years of free education. All candidates from their families who are admitted to college can enroll successfully, and those from in-need families receive government subsidies and can be employed normally after graduation just like other students.

Children in Xinjiang Uygur Autonomous Region (Photo: Cui Meng / GT)

For example, Reziwanguli Alimu from Cele County, Hotan Prefecture, studied at a vocational education and training center. Not only were her family members not discriminated against, but the local government also subsidized her family when they were building an anti-quake house, and her mother received a basic living allowance according to the government policies. Another example: while Abulaiti Aimaiti from Yingjisha County, Kashi Prefecture, received vocational education and training at a center, his daughter was recruited as a teacher by a primary school in the county without any discrimination or influence after her college graduation.

Question: Earlier this year, Olsi Jazexhi, a journalist from Albania, visited Xinjiang and said that he saw with his own eyes that Xinjiang was carrying out a massive genocide, and that the vocational education and training centers were an Alcatraz prison in the middle of the desert. What is your comment on this?

Answer: From August 17 to 23, 2019, Olsi Jazexhi made a field visit to Changji, Aksu and Kashi in Xinjiang with more than 20 foreign media representatives from 16 countries such as Russia and Turkey. Despite the fact that Olsi Jazexhi said during his visit that the studying and living conditions in the vocational education and training centers were very good, he ignored the facts and spread false information to the public when he returned home. The videos he published do not contain any pictures or recordings of interviews in Xinjiang. He is talking entirely on his own. This kind of behavior seriously violates the basic professional ethics of journalism, and the intention is evil.

In fact, all other members from the foreign media delegation who had visited the same places reported the opposite of what Olsi Jazexhi did. For example, Dimitri Yevgeny, a political commentator and China specialist from RIA Novosti, said in an interview — which I will directly quote — that, "I have seen that this is a school, it's a way to combat terrorism. We are combating terrorism in Russia, and we have a lot to learn from China. We need to cooperate and face the challenge together. The measures China took can be examples for other countries." The chief editor of Mongolian newspaper Ben Menghetula said in an interview that, "Before I came to Xinjiang, China, I heard some media reports said that the Chinese government had gathered lots of young people in concentration-camp-like places, brainwashed them and did not allow them to go out, so on and so forth. But after I came to the vocational education and training center and saw it with my own eyes, I realized that it was all ill-intentioned propaganda made by the Western media." Rustam Atovulloev, an expert of human rights in Uzbekistan, said that "China has always protected the rights of people who believed in Islam and the development of Islam as well. The statistics shared by the Chinese government indicate that at present, there are 24,300 mosques and the Muslim population has reached 11.3 million in Xinjiang."

Since the end of 2018, nearly 1,000 people from more than 90 countries and regions have visited Xinjiang. They have all recognized that the comprehensive de-radicalization measures adopted by the Xinjiang authorities, such as offering the vocational education and training programs, have made an important contribution to international efforts to fight against terrorism and extremism, and accumulated valuable experience of significant reference value. The vicious deeds carried out by Olsi Jazexhi will not succeed.

Question: It is reported that Wang Songlian, a researcher from the Human Rights Watch, claimed that Xinjiang has carried out massive monitoring over Muslim ethnic minorities. An expert from Hong Kong named Shi Jianyu also said that holding a foreign passport would make you suspect. Is this true?

Answer: Since the end of 2018, nearly 1,000 people from more than 90 countries and regions have visited Xinjiang, including foreign diplomatic envoys to China, officials from international organizations and representatives from the media. They have seen that people in Xinjiang are living happy and fulfilling lives with political stability, economic vitality, and social harmony. But Wang Songlian has never been to Xinjiang. What he said was vicious speculation.

Similarly, Shi Jianyu made irresponsible remarks, saying that holding a foreign passport makes you suspect in Xinjiang. Xinjiang is an open area. In 2018, the region registered more than 150 million trips by domestic and international tourists. Among them, 2.4 million were international visitors, witnessing a year-on-year growth of 10.78 percent. They came to Xinjiang with great interest and returned with satisfaction, thinking highly of Xinjiang.

Question: According to the report, more and more evidence shows that there has been forced labor in the vocational education and training centers in Xinjiang. What is your response?

Answer: The vocational education and training centers in Xinjiang provide various courses to the trainees, such as the standard spoken and written Chinese language, knowledge of laws and regulations, vocational training programs and de-radicalization courses. To remedy a lack of occupational skills and employment difficulties, vocational skills-training programs are offered. The education and training centers regard vocational skills as an important step to improving the trainees' ability to find jobs. Based on local demand and employment conditions, the courses may include food processing, typesetting and printing, hairdressing and beauty services, interior design and decoration, livestock breeding, horticulture, therapeutic massage, household services, handicrafts, flower arrangement, rug weaving, painting, performing arts such as music and dance, and so on. Eligible trainees can pick up more than one skill if they wish. The courses are delivered in two categories: theoretical studies taught in classrooms and actual skills practiced in workshops. Practical training is conducted after trainees have mastered the theories to improve their skills, and no actual products are made. Hence, the so-called forced labor does not exist at all. Most of the trainees have enhanced their employment abilities through the education and skills-training programs.

After completing their training programs, trainees are free to find jobs on their own, or gain employment with the assistance of relevant authorities. Many trainees have gone on to find employment in factories or enterprises, and some have even started their own businesses. Some of them have chosen to continue their studies in local secondary and higher vocational schools in order to prepare themselves better for the future. Qualified trainees who find employment in enterprises sign contracts of labor as formal staff and have their salaries paid according to the Labor Law and Labor Contract Law of the People's Republic of China. But production activities performed for their employers and the products sold by these factories and enterprises have no relation to the vocational education and training centers.

Question: It is reported that Darren Byler, an anthropologist of George Washington University, and Adrian Zenz, a scholar on China, alleged that Xinjiang had interned over 1 million Uygurs, Kazaks and other Muslim minorities who all are subject to persecution in internment. What's your answer to such allegations?

Answer: As far as I know, Darren Byler and Adrian Zenz are the hardcore members of the "research group on Xinjiang's education and training centers," an academic body allegedly set up and controlled by US intelligence agencies. They coordinated with anti-China forces within the US to spread false and purely fabricated remarks on Xinjiang in the capacity of alleged experts. They would do anything they could to defame and smear Xinjiang with groundless academic findings as support, which are, of course, the typical tricks used by some Americans.

These centers are education and training institutions in nature. They employ a residential-education model which allows trainees to go back home on a regular basis and ask for leave to attend to personal affairs. Trainees also enjoy the freedom of correspondence. The centers guarantee that trainees' personal dignity is inviolable, and prevent insults or abuses in any manner. A report from Turkey's DHA on May 15, 2019, said, "The centers provide human-based management and services for the trainees. There is no maltreatment or restrictions on personal freedom. The trainees are happy to study and live there. What I saw and felt during the visit was very different from the negative propaganda of the US and other Western countries, and

I felt their double standards were simply rude and unreasonable."

The number of trainees in the education and training program is not fixed; some are coming in while others are going out. As education and training work is effectively advanced, the vast majority of trainees have attained the training criteria and completed their courses, and they are working and living well. The "1 million people" claim is totally baseless, complete distortion and fabrication.

Question: What is the composition of students like in the education and training centers? What is the legal basis of the program? Is it directed against specific minorities?

Answer: In accordance with the *Counter-Terrorism Law of the People's Republic of China*, the *Measures of the Xinjiang Uygur Autonomous Region on Implementing the Counter-Terrorism Law of the People's Republic of China*, the *Regulations of the Xinjiang Uygur Autonomous Region on De-radicalization*, and other laws and regulations, vocational education and training centers have been established in Xinjiang. Trainees at the centers fall into three categories. First, people who were incited, coerced or induced into participating in terrorist or extremist activities, or people who participated in terrorist or extremist activities in circumstances that were not serious enough to constitute a crime. Second, people who were incited, coerced or induced into participating in terrorist or extremist activities, or people who participated in terrorist or extremist activities that posed a real danger but did not cause actual harm, whose subjective culpability was not deep, who acknowledged their offences and thus did not need to be sentenced or could be exempted from punishment, and who have demonstrated a willingness to receive training. Third, people who were convicted and received prison sentences for terrorist or extremist crimes and have been assessed as still posing a potential threat to society after serving their sentences, and who have been ordered by people's courts in accordance with the law to receive education at the centers.

The specific procedures for carrying out education and training in Xinjiang require that relevant authorities determine the nature and circumstances of acts and deal with the above three categories of trainees in accordance with laws and regulations such as the Criminal Law, Criminal Procedure Law and Counter-Terrorism Law. The first category should be initially handled by public security organs, and then given assistance and education by vocational education and training centers. The second category should first be investigated by public security organs; if the procuratorial body, after reviewing a case, makes the decision not to institute legal proceedings, the trainee in question should then be given assistance and education by the education and training centers. The third category, when found to pose an ongoing risk to society after being assessed prior to their release from prison, shall be placed at such centers to receive education to help them reintegrate into society in accordance with the decision of people's courts.

The education and training work in Xinjiang is always based on facts and laws, without targeting any specific region, ethnic group or religion.

Since their initiation, there has never been a foreigner in Xinjiang's vocational education and training centers. Recently, the Australian Broadcasting Corporation falsely claimed that Xinjiang had captured 23 Australian citizens, and that 15 adults and 6 children from the Uygur community in Australia had been detained. This is pure fabrication and denigration, which violates press ethics.

China urged to take "stronger countermeasures" against US' Xinjiang bill

By Xie Wenting and Fan Lingzhi | Dec 4, 2019

China will take strong countermeasures against the US, including releasing an "unreliable entity list" that includes relevant US entities, and imposing sanctions on relevant US officials, experts said, after the US House passed an act filled with groundless accusations against China's Xinjiang on December 3, 2019, local time.

The *Uygur Human Rights Policy Act of 2019* smeared China's counter-terrorism efforts in Xinjiang Uygur Autonomous Region and used fabricated information to slander the vocational education and training centers and religious freedom in the region, analysts said.

A look at the act shows it sticks to the old US rhetoric that uses double standards to distort China's policies on Xinjiang, and it never mentioned the

Xinjiang residents (Photo: Cui Meng / GT)

impressive social and economic development that Xinjiang has achieved.

Chinese government institutions have voiced strong opposition on December 4, 2019 against the US move of pushing forward the act, condemning the US of interfering in China's domestic issues.

Lü Xiang, a research fellow on US studies at the Chinese Academy of Social Sciences in Beijing, told the Global Times that this act doesn't have any review process. The sources of the act are loose and unreliable.

Diao Daming, an associate professor at the Renmin University of China in Beijing, told the Global Times that in addition to conveying the truth to the international community, China can adopt the unreliable entity list to list "those companies that dance to the act."

"China will hit back with stronger countermeasures," Wei Jianguo, a former Chinese vice minister of commerce and executive deputy director of the China Center for International Economic Exchanges, told the Global Times. He hinted that the countermeasures could be even stronger than what China had taken after the US passed the so-called *Hong Kong Human Rights and Democracy Act*.

Wei said China can sanction certain US entities and personnel in the unreliable entity list and restrict their entry to and activities in China. "Chinese people are never afraid of a threat or the US. We will fight back with tough measures," he said.

Erkin Öncan, a Turkish journalist who has followed Xinjiang issues for many years, slammed the act for its sinister intentions. "What China is trying to achieve, the US is trying hard to destroy," Öncan said.

Origins of the act

The act was initially submitted to the US Senate by notorious anti-China Senator Marco Rubio on January 17, 2019. Ironically, the act, which tarnished the counter-terrorism efforts in Xinjiang, was passed at the Senate on September 11, 2019, the 18th anniversary of the 9/11 terrorist attacks.

According to the document that Global Times reporters saw on the US House website, the act is divided into nine chapters, and its core parts include findings, sense of congress and chapters requiring sanctions targeting China. It claimed the act aims to "direct United States resources to address human rights violations and abuses, including gross violations of human rights, by the People's Republic of China's mass surveillance and internment of over 1,000,000 Uighurs and other predominantly Turkic Muslim ethnic minorities in China's Xinjiang Uighur Autonomous Region."

Compared with the previous version that got passed in the Senate, this amended act took out the "specific cases" and added an updated statement of US policy toward China. The act states that US policy toward China should be explicitly linked with the situation in Xinjiang. It also proposes sanctions on certain senior Chinese officials and restrictions on exports.

Before the act was discussed in Congress, the US government had already issued a series of administrative orders against China on Xinjiang-related issues. On October 7, 2019, the US Department of Commerce announced that it would include 20 Chinese government agencies and eight companies in the list of entities which they claimed are related to the suppression of ethnic minorities in Xinjiang. The Chinese government agencies in the list of entities include the Public Security Department of Xinjiang and the Public Security Bureau of the Xinjiang Production and Construction Corps. On October 8, 2019, the US State Department announced that it would impose visa restrictions on Chinese government officials.

Addressing the differences between the administrative order and act, Yuan Zheng, senior fellow of the Institute of American Studies at Chinese Academy of Social Sciences, told the Global Times that the administrative order issued by the government can be cancelled anytime based on the real situation. But for the act, it's extremely difficult to abolish it once it is signed by the president and becomes law. It needs adequate reasons and a whole process to abolish it, which is even harder than legislating.

Once the act is passed, it means a new phase for the US in interfering in Xinjiang affairs begins, Yuan said. He pointed out that this interference will become "law-based" for the administrative departments and Congress. And it will also tarnish China's international image, giving the US enormous influence.

Diao told the Global Times the US hastily pushed the act shortly after Trump signed the *Hong Kong Human Rights and Democracy Act* because congressmen believe it would be easier to get the new act passed.

Generally speaking, the US House was quite busy in the first half of the year. If they don't push it now, they may need to wait until April 2020. "So they want to fight a quick battle. Some congressmen also think the act is easy to get passed under the current situation of pressuring China," Diao said.

"The act shows how US government grossly interfered into China's internal affairs. It's a serious violation of international law and fundamental principles of international relations. It is also a provocation against the Chinese people," Wei said. He added that China is no longer the lamb to be slaughtered and won't tolerate finger pointing by the US at its internal affairs.

Fabrication and double standards

The amended act deleted specific cases in the findings. The Global Times checked these specific cases in the previous version with relevant agencies and found that they were fabricated. Some of them have been clarified in China's white paper, titled *The Fight Against Terrorism and Extremism and Human Rights Protection in Xinjiang.*

Diao noted that American politicians are becoming increasingly sophisticated in their attacks against China.

"The cases they listed in the previous version were not credible and could spark criticism regarding its authenticity. Therefore, they didn't bother to include these unreliable 'cases' that could be attacked," Diao said.

"Pressuring China has become a bipartisan consensus. They don't need many excuses to pass the act," he said.

The act criticized medical facilities at the vocational education and training centers in Xinjiang. Global Times reporters who have visited the centers many times since 2018 saw that they are equipped with complete medical devices, with doctors who can provide free medical services to the trainees around the clock. Seriously ill trainees can be transferred to the local hospital.

It's noticeable that many of the "facts" listed in the act do not have an exact time, location or sources.

"This is self-circulation. I believe that the anti-China lawmakers did not spend any time to study what happened in Xinjiang. They made the so-called investigative findings based on some of the media's unreliable reports and the so-called 'testimonies' of the hearings. The legislators referred to Free Asia Radio and Voice of America to make some unwarranted reports. Then they used these media outlets again to say 'further confirmation' [with their reports]. This is a game that the United States has played for many years," Lü said.

Lü said that the US Congress does not care if the cases are true or not. "They are prejudiced. As long as this mistake does not affect the perception of Xinjiang in the West led by the United States, they won't care," he said.

Aside from factual errors, the act is also full of double standards. It accused China of using advanced technology for surveillance across the region. But the adoption of modern technology and big data to improve social governance is common in the international community.

"I think the US is the last country that has the right to criticize China in tech security. US itself uses high technology to monitor people, and the US commits very serious crimes by doing it illegally," Öncan told the Global Times.

"China's surveillance system is based on security, but the US version is based on the citizens' privacy. They [the US] watch secretly, categorize them and even sell them to companies which are working on matters like the elections."

He noted that it's absurd for the US to criticize China because China uses its surveillance system to prevent crime and make life easier.

"China is not doing it secretly, unlike the US. The US uses the biggest data collection app in the world: Facebook!" he said.

Another example of the double standards is that the US totally ignores the achievements Xinjiang has made.

Öncan said as a country with a base in Guantanamo Bay, the US represents double standards. "The US repeatedly uses the same arguments, which have already been explained by the Chinese government. And they purposely use a 'human rights' discourse which has the wrong context. China secures the beliefs, language and culture by blocking radical Islam and terrorism."

According to public data, from 2014 to 2018, Xinjiang lifted over 2.31 million people out of poverty and the incidence of rural poverty fell to 6.1 percent. More than 70 percent of the general public budget expenditures in the region are used to improve people's livelihood, ensuring that all ethnic groups share the development achievements.

"The accusations against China reflect a 'political tradition' of the US," Lü said. According to him, the US has never stopped such practices ever since the normalization of ties between China and the US. Almost every 10 years, the US comes up with a new issue against China.

"The Xinjiang issue is not new. It was brought up 10 years ago. But at that time, because the terrorist activities were so intense, they could not support it directly. But now when China has made great achievements in Xinjiang and no terrorist activities have happened in nearly three years, they bring up Xinjiang again," Lü said.

Countermeasures

China can adopt countermeasures at the judiciary level. "We should make our stance clear through the anti-secession law and counter-terrorism law. We are a sovereign country and have our own laws. We can conduct a counter-investigation into the US," Wei said.

He suggested China not only restrict the entry of congressmen who endorsed the laws, but also conduct countermeasures, in Wei's words "a precise strike" against the states these lawmakers represent, including restricting the states' trade activities with China.

"We can also restrict and prohibit [the export] of some special commodities that the US needs, including rare earths as far as the WTO permits. We can also impose restrictions on the US in terms of China's current opening-up policies, especially in the financial, service, agriculture, insurance and manufacturing industries," Wei said.

While the act threatens to sanction certain Chinese senior officials and restrict exports of certain items, Diao told the Global Times that they cannot be realistically implemented, and any rational government will not implement it.

"But the act will be like a sword hanging over China's head. In the future, any US president can use it. In this sense, the act will have a very negative influence," Diao said.

Diao suggested China should also impose sanctions on US politicians who pushed the act, and the NGOs behind it. "The US tactic is to place national law above international law. We should also think about coming up with our own agenda," he said.

Yuan said China should give a timely response. He suggests a "precise strike" and that the strike should hit where it hurts the other side most without hurting ourselves.

Lü suggested that if the act damages China, we can consider sanctioning the states represented by those legislators.

Documentary with rare footage chronicles China's arduous fight against terrorism in Xinjiang

By Liu Xin and Fan Lingzhi | Dec 5, 2019

China showed overall counter-terrorism work in its northwestern Xinjiang Uygur Autonomous Region and released rare video and audio evidence of previous terrorist attacks that happened in the region in an English-language documentary on December 5, 2019.

The nearly one-hour-long documentary, *Fighting Terrorism in Xinjiang*, which was streamed on CGTN, China's state broadcaster, has four parts. It begins with explicating the formative years when extremism began evolving in Xinjiang, followed by the grueling fight against terrorism. It also illustrated the interactions of terrorists with overseas forces accompanied by audio and video evidence. The documentary winds up highlighting international cooperation on anti-terrorism.

Zheng Liang, a research fellow at Guangdong-based Ji'nan University, who studied Xinjiang for more than 10 years, told the Global Times that he felt "shocked" after viewing the documentary.

Zheng said that previous videos on Xinjiang's anti-terrorism are not specific and well-edited as the one on December 5, 2019. "This newly-released documentary uses quite different visual languages adopted by mainstream media."

Severe terrorism threat

The beginning of the documentary features the splendid landscape of Xinjiang, its culture and the different ethnic groups in China, including the prosperous markets and people's peaceful and happy life. Then the scene shifts to depicting the threat of terrorism that is wreaking havoc in the region.

Xinjiang has long been the main battlefield of countering terrorism. According to incomplete data, from 1990 to 2016, Xinjiang endured thousands of terrorist attacks that killed large numbers of innocent people and hundreds of police officers.

The documentary features many video footages of terrorist attacks in Xinjiang, including one in Yining of Ili Kazak Autonomous Prefecture in 1997, which left seven dead and 198 injured; Urumqi riots on July 5, 2009, which caused 197 deaths and over 1,700 injuries; the 2013 Seriqbuya attack in Kashi, which left 15 dead and two wounded.

Terrorists also orchestrated attacks in other cities of China — they once ramped a car into a crowd in Tiananmen Square in 2013, and another attack that struck the Kunming railway station on March 1, 2014, left 31 dead and 141 wounded.

"Some Western countries spread the idea that the 2009 Urumqi Riots were ethnic clashes triggered by repression. Chinese experts say that's illogical, given the 9-11 attacks. The anti-China interpretation shows the double-standard approach adopted by some countries," narrated the documentary.

Video footage in the documentary clearly captured rioters torching buses and cars on the roads, vandalizing shops and attacking passengers.

Group Captain Sultan Hali from Pakistan Air Force said in the documentary, "What happened in 2009 definitely was not an isolated [incident], because the whole world was gripped by terrorism, especially following the attack on neighboring Afghanistan by the Soviet Union."

Victims of extremism

For extremists, anyone can be a target. The documentary chronicles the story of Dilqemer, who liked dancing but lost her right leg in a terrorist attack that took place in Luntai County of the Bayingolin Mongolian Autonomous Prefecture on September 21, 2014.

Razye, who was one of the perpetrators of the attack, was also stranded at the spot when the explosion occurred. She lost her right leg and an arm. She and

Dilqemer were in the same hospital.

In an interview with the CCTV, she admitted believing "jihad martyrdom is a path to paradise," but now she knows that violence and killing innocents cannot lead one to the paradise.

"I hope others who are tempted to take this path would not succumb like me. My actions left a lovely girl crippled and I lost limbs, too," Razye said.

The documentary also features videos of terrorists killing their peers and assassinating religious figures. On July 30, 2014, Juma Tayier, the chief imam at Kashi's main mosque, was stabbed to death. He was also the deputy president of the Xinjiang Islamic Association.

Adudulrekep Tumniaz, President of Xinjiang Islamic Institute was cited in the documentary as saying the terrorists' plan "is to eliminate the prestigious and enlightened members of the religious community. Then they would have no opposition and they would be able to further their conspiracy and achieve their

A boy plays snow tubing at the Baicheng hot springs skiing venue. (Photo: Shan Jie / GT)

ends."

Most of the terrorists though claim to be loyal followers of Islam, but in reality, they have very little knowledge of the *Koran*, the holy religious scripture of Muslims.

Murat, who is one of the main perpetrators of the terrorist attack in Hotan on June 16, 2014, could not answer any questions concerning the beginning of Islam, the definition of "jihad" or about the five pillars of Islam.

Li Wei, a counter-terrorism expert at the China Institute of Contemporary International Relations in Beijing told the Global Times that religious and ethnic identities were used by terrorists to advocate extremist views. Under the guise of extremism, terrorism becomes deceptive and seditious, which helps draw young people toward terrorist activities.

On June 6, 2012, Hotan authorities rescued 53 children who were confined in an 80-square-meter room and taught distorted doctrines. Terrorists triggered explosives to hinder police operations. And a suspect jumped off the fifth floor with a 4-year-old child.

The documentary also illustrates the interactions between terrorists in Xinjiang and their overseas accomplices.

The recording reveals that foreign extremists were remotely controlling the actions of the domestic extremists, teaching them how to evade reconnaissance and attack helicopters. Numerous sources have confirmed that the "East Turkistan Islamic Movement" has close contact with terrorist groups.

Working together

Experts believe terrorism is a global threat, and no country can win the war against terrorism on its own. In the face of the threat of terrorism and extremism, Xinjiang has taken a series of measures, including framing laws and regulations and launching effective counter-terrorism operations.

Scrutiny by some Western countries has been constant. But according to the white paper released by the Information Office of the State Council, no terrorism-related incidents have taken place in Xinjiang for nearly three years since the start of the vocational education and training centers.

The complexity of extremism and terrorism makes it hard to tell Xinjiang stories. What is happening there is a test of China's counter-terrorism measures. It's also a way to showcase China's commitment to long-term stability and security in Xinjiang, according to the documentary.

According to media reports reviewed by the Global Times, a special counter-terrorism campaign has been in place in the Xinjiang region since May 2014.

In total, there has been a crackdown on 1,588 terrorist groups, 12,995 terrorists arrested and 2,052 explosives seized in Xinjiang since 2014, stated a white paper on regional work on counter-terrorism, de-radicalization and human rights protection, released in March 2019.

China has also enhanced international cooperation to crack down on terrorist forces in Xinjiang. China has joined 12 global counter-terrorism conventions and played an active role in international multilateral mechanisms, including the international criminal police organization, Shanghai Cooperation Organization (SCO) and Association of Southeast Asian Nations (ASEAN) Regional Forum.

No violent terrorist attacks have happened in Xinjiang in three years. Publishing these videos would let more people and some Western media know more about China's current counter-terrorism efforts in Xinjiang, Zheng said.

"It seems impossible to correct the wrong opinions of the West toward China's Xinjiang counter-terrorism policies. But the documentary would open a window for those who want to know the truth," Zheng said.

Scan QR code to watch the video

China releases English documentary on ETIM terror group's dark hand in Xinjiang

By Liu Xin and Zhao Juecheng | Dec 7, 2019

China released on December 7, 2019 an English-language documentary illustrating in detail that the source of terrorist attacks in Northwest China's Xinjiang Uygur Autonomous Region is the "East Turkistan Islamic Movement (ETIM)" terrorist group and its interactions with other international terrorist groups.

Titled *The Black Hand — ETIM and Terrorism in Xinjiang*, the documentary aired on CGTN on December 7, one day after the state broadcaster aired a documentary on the overall counter-terrorism work in Xinjiang with many exclusive videos disclosed on December 5, 2019.

The previous documentary attracted public attention once it was released. It has been viewed nearly 30 million times and has sparked debate as of press time.

Many netizens commented how the two documentaries showed the severe threat of terrorism in Xinjiang and suggested that Western media, which always groundlessly criticizes China's Xinjiang policies and hype the issue in their reports, should watch them instead of deliberately choosing to be silent on the two documentaries.

Chinese experts said Western media only choose to report what fits their interests and ideological correctness and always neglect the truth about Xinjiang. Their silence on the documentaries also demonstrates their double standards in regards to China's counter-terrorism efforts.

Hiding behind

The documentary released on December 7, 2019 has three parts on telling China's most direct security threat of terrorism, ETIM's separatist strategy and the long-term fight against terrorism.

The documentary begins with the narration of violent attacks targeting civilians of all ethnic groups that frequently happened in Xinjiang and how the region became a battlefield in China's fighting against terrorism.

The background of development of the ETIM is "Pan-Turkism" and "Pan-Islamism," which were introduced into Xinjiang in the late 19th century. Separatist forces attempted to create an independent state, the so-called "East Turkistan" to split Xinjiang from China.

The ETIM was reportedly founded by Hesen Mexsum, a man from Xinjiang's Kashi, in 1997. It has claimed responsibilities for a series of attacks in several Chinese cities, including the Tiananmen Square car bombing in 2013 in Beijing, and the terrorist attacks at the Kunming Railway Station in Yunnan Province in 2014.

Li Wei, a counter-terrorism expert at the China Institute of Contemporary International Relations in Beijing told the Global Times that ETIM is one of the four "East Turkistan" terrorist groups identified by China's Ministry of Public Security. The World Uygur Congress has also got involved with terrorist attacks that happened in China and it is the main organization to defend other terrorist groups.

In 2002, the UN Security Council designated the ETIM as a terrorist organization. Bank accounts of ETIM members were frozen and assets were seized.

In December 2003, China's Ministry of Public Security outlawed the ETIM. It was the first time the Chinese government formally recognized that a terrorist group was operating inside the country, the documentary showed.

In response to some Western countries' allegations on China exaggerating ETIM's threat, the Chinese government refuted them by releasing many videos of terrorist attacks conducted by ETIM.

Since its establishment, the ETIM has maintained close ties with other international terrorist organizations.

Chinese police have found evidence that the ETIM has received significant support from al-Qaeda, and previously from Osama bin Laden, according to the documentary.

ETIM has sent its members to al-Qaeda training camps. Upon completion of training, some of the members have returned to China to conduct terrorist acts.

According to incomplete data, about 20,000 Chinese have illegally snuck out to join the ISIS in Syria and some experts believe the number is about 5,000 to 10,000, Li said.

The documentary also tells a case which illustrates that ETIM colluded with overseas forces, responsible for many terrorist attacks that happened in Xinjiang.

Rashid, the main suspect of the terrorist attack at Urumqi South Railway Station in April 2014, was cited in the documentary as saying that he learned how to make improvised explosive devices (IEDs) from an online video produced by the ETIM.

Before conducting the terrorist attack, he took a selfie video of him making explosive devices.

Rashid said he planned to send the video to a "friend" Ismayil Yusup, who was outside China and a member of the ETIM.

According to the police, Ismayil Yusup was the mastermind of the April 30th attacks at Urumqi Railway Station. He used religion as a cover to recruit members and take spiritual control over them. He then asked them to carry out violent activities while he hid outside the country.

China's police say the April 30th attacks were typical in Xinjiang. Terrorists outside China plot attacks, give orders, spread information online and remotely command attacks in China.

Young victims

Police found the ETIM has produced a large number of online terrorism videos, which cost little and spread quickly. There are lessons on making bombs and training manuals for terrorist attacks.

Li Wei said that the terrorist audio and video materials have led many young people on the road of being obsessed with violence and terrorism. Such materials have served as a catalyst in inciting young people.

"Counter-terrorism efforts do not merely involve military operations. More importantly, they should aim to stop the spread of extremist ideas among young people," said Li.

Some of the videos seized by police could prove that terrorists indoctrinated children as young as 4 years old with extremist ideas and taught them how to use guns. Terrorists give no choice for these children to have a normal life, except for sacrifice themselves with suicide bombings, Li told the Global Times.

Li said that ETIM terrorists used all methods to brainwash young people, children and women into supporting extremism.

Police found a video clip from ETIM member Rozalahong's phone, which shows he teaches his two sons how to use guns. The boy who pulls the trigger is only 6 years old and he cries after hearing the gunshot, the documentary showed.

Nurdun, an ETIM member was cited in the documentary as saying that they teach no knowledge or ethics to these children and raise them in a horrible environment.

"They are bound to become mindless robots, doing whatever they're told, without regard to the consequences," he said.

China is concerned about the spread of ETIM's online videos and calls for the international community to work together to halt their proliferation.

In 2013, the UN Security Council unanimously adopted a resolution calling on members to take specific measures to counter online platforms of terrorist groups.

ETIM and other terrorist groups usually take religious extremism as a banner and use terrorism as a means to foment ethnic division and attempt to separate Xinjiang from China forever, said Shu Hongshui, a professor from Northwest University of Political Science and Law.

International threat

The ETIM is part of an international terrorist system that does not only threaten China. Experts say terrorists are learning from each other.

The April 30th attacks in Urumqi share similarity with the March 22nd terrorist bombing in Brussels in 2016, where coordinated suicide bombings occurred at transport hubs, killing over 30 people. ISIL claimed responsibility.

Western media reports claimed that tensions in Xinjiang are caused by economic and cultural factors. Many focus on ethnic clashes and religious issues but neglect a historical perspective.

Li said that terrorists, who conducted attacks in China or in Western countries, usually wanted to incite clashes between different ethnic groups, religions and cultures.

Some Western media's reports or analysis on the causes of terrorism do not reflect the truth and hinder global efforts to curb terrorism.

Li Sheng, a professor from the Chinese Academy of Social Sciences, said that the first step of countering terrorism is to curb terrorism and thwart the terrorists' attempts and the second step is eliminating the ideas and ideology that underpin terrorism, which will take a long time.

Li Wei told the Global Times that for a long time, China has faced a severe challenge in countering terrorism as domestic terrorists collude with forces from abroad, which get support from anti-China forces in some Western countries.

"China's counter-terrorism work is part of the global effort and its fight against terrorism is not only for China's stability but also makes contribution to the global counter-terrorism work," Li Wei said.

Scan QR code to watch the video

Xinjiang trainees graduate as flexible, regular courses become available to all

By Liu Xin and Zhang Hui | Dec 10, 2019

Trainees who used to be influenced by extremism have graduated from the vocational education and training centers in Northwest China's Xinjiang Uygur Autonomous Region, and the training centers will open to officials, herdsmen and people willing to gain vocational skills, a senior Xinjiang official said at a press conference on December 9, 2019.

Experts said Xinjiang could draw on its experience from training centers on de-radicalization to develop more flexible ways, including offering de-radicalization education to individuals in residential community, considering the complexity of fighting terrorism and extremism in the region.

"Trainees who took courses in standard spoken and written Chinese language, law, vocational skills and courses on the eradication of extremism have graduated from the training centers. With the help of the local government, they have acquired stable jobs, improved their livelihood and lived a happy life," Shohrat Zakir, chairman of the Xinjiang regional government, told a press conference held by the Information Office of the State Council in Beijing on December 9, 2019.

Shohrat said some foreign media's reports of over a million or even 2 million trainees in the centers are "slanderous and groundless."

On *Uygur Human Rights Policy Act of 2019* passed by the US House recently, the chairman said the bill has violated international laws and interfered in China's internal affairs, and stands on the opposite side of the Chinese people and international morality.

The US bill aims to provoke relations between different ethnic groups in China and undermine stability and development, but Xinjiang residents are best qualified to speak on Xinjiang affairs, and the US action will not disturb Xinjiang's development, the chairman said.

Long-term, complex work

Xinjiang has gained useful experience from its series of counter-terrorism and de-radicalization measures in the past three years, especially from the training centers. Trainees who had been influenced by extremism have greatly changed for the better and local security situation has been improved, said Zhang Yonghe, executive dean of the Human Rights Institution of Southwest University of Political Science and Law in Chongqing.

Fighting terrorism and extremism is a long-term and complex work and no country can accomplish it swiftly. Xinjiang could develop de-radicalization work into more flexible ways and offer de-radicalization education in residential communities to individuals who have been influenced by extremism, Zhang said.

Zhang told the Global Times that "people of all ethnic groups in Xinjiang have a deep understanding of the importance of counter-terrorism and de-radicalization work during the past years and it is highly unlikely that Xinjiang would see the spread of extremism and outbreak of terrorism again."

At the press conference on December 9, 2019, Xu Hairong, Communist Party of China secretary of Urumqi, shared three stories of the trainees to show their changes after studying in the training centers.

A trainee named Dilixiati used to run an agritainment and live a good life. But she was being influenced by extremist ideas and thought having a "heretic" for dinner under the apricot tree "made her farmhouse dirty." So she cut the tree and closed her agritainment business. Without a stable income, the family struggled.

Another trainee named Buzuola Rouzi, who learned embroidering, is now opening a workshop on hand-made embroidery products. He is helping more than 30 villagers in his workshop shake off poverty.

"Many similar stories happened in Xinjiang. People in Xinjiang know that if it was not for the training centers, there would be no peaceful life," Xu said.

Li Wei, a counter-terrorism expert at the China Institutes of Contemporary International Relations in Beijing, said Xinjiang's achievements on fighting terrorism and eradicating extremism also strike a blow to overseas "East Turkistan" terrorist groups, international terrorist organizations and anti-China forces.

"These forces are not resigned to their failure in Xinjiang. They will keep sending terrorists back to Xinjiang and try other ways to make trouble in Xinjiang. The US' recent passing of the *Uygur Human Rights Policy Act of 2019* also offers support to terrorist groups outside China," Li said.

"We should always be alert to these overseas terrorists," Li said, noting that if terrorism and extremism surface again in Xinjiang, effective measures, including the training centers, would be taken by the regional government.

Under the principle of personal willingness and choices, the training centers in Xinjiang are now offering daily and open training to village officials, members of the Communist Party of China, farmers and herdsmen, and people who did not graduate from middle or high school. The courses are on laws, vocational skills and standard Chinese language, Shohrat noted.

"The role of the training centers is not based on pressure from some Western countries and media, but in line with improving the counter-terrorism situation in Xinjiang. Xinjiang now aims to cement the previous achievement of eradicating extremism and also pays close attention to the new rise in extremism," Xu Jianying, a research fellow at the Chinese Academy of Social Sciences' Research Center for Chinese Borderland History and Geography, told the Global Times.

Choose to ignore

The two documentaries of Xinjiang's counter-terrorism work, aired on CGTN on December 5 and December 7 last year, were also streamed at the press conference on December 9, 2019. They showed videos of the Urumqi riots on July 5, 2009 and the Tiananmen Square terror attack on October 28, 2013.

Muhammad Asghar, a correspondent from the Associated Press of Pakistan, who visited the training centers in Xinjiang in January 2019, told the Global Times that the videos of horrible terror attacks were "hard to see" and showed the severe threat of terrorism in Xinjiang.

Asghar said Xinjiang's counter-terrorism and de-radicalization work, especially the training centers, was successful. The training centers also successfully decreased the incidence of extremism in Xinjiang. Countries which face the threat of terrorism and extremism could learn from Xinjiang's experience.

Not many foreign reporters paid attention to the documentaries like Asghar did.

Chinese Foreign Ministry spokesperson Hua Chunying asked foreign reporters who attended the press conference how many of them watched the documentaries on December 9, 2019. None said yes.

Hua said that while the documentaries have been widely discussed by netizens in China and overseas, the mainstream Western media chose to remain silent.

"You are very concerned about Xinjiang topics. When people made malicious lies, you are keen on reporting them; but when the truth and facts about Xinjiang are unveiled, you deliberately avoid these. Why? What are you worried about? What are you afraid of? Aren't you going to reflect on this?" Hua asked. Regardless of whether some Western media report it or not, the truth about Xinjiang will not change. "Lies will not cover the truth forever. As media, you have the responsibility to offer the basic facts and truth, not to pretend to be blind or deaf and mislead the public," Hua said.

Senior Xinjiang officials also refuted some fake news and rumors on Xinjiang at the State Council Information Office's press conference on December 9, 2019.

In response to questions in some foreign media reports that Xinjiang violated Muslims' religious freedom and destroyed mosques, Erkin Tuniyaz, vice-chairman of the Xinjiang regional government, said Xinjiang fully respects and protects people's religious freedom.

Erkin said religious and non-religious people in Xinjiang enjoy the same rights and no citizen has been discriminated on or unjustly treated. Xinjiang has more than 20,000 mosques and 29,000 Islam religious faculty and staff. There are 103 Islamic associations and 10 religious institutions in Xinjiang. Xinjiang has also organized chartered flights for more than 50,000 religious people for their pilgrimage to Mecca.

"Xinjiang has never removed mosques, but improved the facilities in mosques," Erkin said, noting that the mosques in Xinjiang have been equipped with electronic screens, flush toilets, air conditioners and firefighting equipment.

"Religious freedom policies have been fully implemented in Xinjiang and the rights of religious people, including Muslims, have been guaranteed. We hope that some Western politicians and media that adopt double standards and bear bias toward China's religious policies could take a correct attitude with regard to China's religious situation and stop interfering in the domestic affairs by hyping religious topics," Erkin said.

Xu Hairong, Party secretary of Urumqi, refuted reports of The New York Times and the International Consortium of Investigative Journalists on Xinjiang, saying their reports were slanderous and smeared Xinjiang's training centers and counter-terrorism work. "The great efforts made by officials and people of all ethnic groups to restore the stability and peace of Xinjiang should be viewed justly and fairly," Xu said.

One sentence repeatedly mentioned by the officials attending the conference on December 9, 2019 was that "Xinjiang people have the final say on whether Xinjiang's policies are good," and they invited more people to come to Xinjiang to witness the prosperity of the region.

Allegedly "missing" Uygurs found living normally, debunks "StillNoInfo" rumors

By Shan Jie and Zhao Juecheng in Xinjiang | Dec 23, 2019

Some overseas organizations and media have been hyping China's policy in Northwest China's Xinjiang Uygur Autonomous Region by initiating an online campaign to "find missing Uygurs in China."

They posted online that some Uygurs are missing after China on December 9, 2019 announced the graduation from vocational education and training centers of trainees once influenced by extreme thoughts.

After digging into the online information released by some individuals and organizations on the alleged missing Uygurs, confirming from the authorities in Xinjiang and visiting some of the "missing people" in different places in Xinjiang, the Global Times (GT) reporters found that they are living normal lives.

The allegedly "missing" people met by the GT reporters slammed those who have taken advantage of their identities and sought to interfere with China's internal affairs, and told those who posted about them to stop disturbing their peaceful life.

The hashtag "StillNoInfo" has been used on social media platforms Twitter and Facebook in December 2019.

With the hashtag, some overseas Uygur people posted photos and names, claiming their relatives or friends can't be contacted and have gone missing.

Some online organizations have also posted photos and names of allegedly "missing" Uygur people in China.

The Global Times found that many figures who were engaged in starting the activity to find "missing Uygurs" on overseas social media are members of "East Turkistan" separatist groups and this is their latest attempt to smear China's Xinjiang policies.

For example, Rushan Abbas, leader of the so-called Campaign for Uygurs, and Halmurat Harri, who started the "MeTooUygur" activity, are found to be members of "East Turkistan" separatist groups. They first stole some Uygurs' photos and information, claimed these people to be "missing" relatives in Xinjiang, spread rumors on overseas media and had interactions with some certain media. Some overseas nongovernmental organizations, especially the Human Rights Watch, are also taking an active role in promoting these rumors.

Rumors busted

Trainees who used to be influenced by extremism have graduated from the vocational education and training centers in Xinjiang, and the training centers will be open to officials, herdsmen and other people willing to gain vocational skills, a senior Xinjiang official said at a press conference on December 9, 2019.

The "StillNoInfo" campaign was launched at the same time on Twitter and Facebook, with people charging that the Uygur people they know in China are still missing.

However, the GT reporters met several people on the "StillNoInfo" list and found that they have been home for months and are living a regular life on the right path after graduating from the training center.

Ruzi Memet Atawulla, 23, works in a shoe factory in Hotan. In 2017, he went to a vocational education and training center after being influenced by extreme thoughts. He graduated in April 2018 and began to work in the factory.

Ruzi Memet told the Global Times that all his classmates in the training center have graduated and been employed.

Now every morning he takes a bus with some neighbors to the factory, working eight hours a day and earning 2,500 yuan ($350) a month.

"I should have made more effort, so that I could earn 3,000 yuan a month," he said.

Ruzi Memet lives with his family in an 80-square-meter house built with the help of the local governments.

The family grows tomatoes, tulips, Chinese cabbages and grapes, which have brought them an income of 16,000 yuan this year. They also keep sheep and cows.

The day before the Global Times visited, Ruzi Memet just got married. "I bought a suite for the wedding," he said with shyness.

However, for this family, Memet Tohti Atawulla, the elder brother, is an unspeakable scar. The Global Times learned that he was suspected of having joined the "East Turkistan" separatist group and has been attacking China's Xinjiang policy. Recently, the elder brother claimed his brother Ruzi Memet was missing.

On December 10, 2019, Memet Tohti posted on Twitter with the hashtag

"StillNoInfo," claiming that his mother and brothers are suffering in "Chinese camps."

Ruzi Memet could not hide his sadness talking about his elder brother. "Brother, you said you went abroad to study, but now you are with the separatist force and attack our [country's] policy," he said.

"Our life is getting better and we have a new house. I hope you stop colluding with the separatists. Our father is getting old and we all miss you a lot," he said, choking with sobs.

"I am not missing"

In addition to those who graduated from the vocational education and training centers, the normal lives of many others living in Xinjiang are also disturbed by online rumors saying those people are afflicted and missing.

Tayir Ablat, 26 and from Urumqi, is now working at Liangxing restaurant in his hometown of Alali Town, Shule County of Kashi. The young man has been working in the restaurant for seven months and was promoted to manager for his good performance.

On December 10, 2019, Twitter user "HusenjanObul" posted three photos, including a selfie of Tayir. The words on the photo read "Where's my cousin."

Tayir said that he does not know of any relatives or friends living overseas. He felt that some overseas separatist forces have taken advantage of his information to smear China.

"I am not missing," he said.

"I live a good life here. I have made money, about 20,000 or 30,000 yuan so far," he noted.

In July 2019, under Tayir's suggestion, the restaurant opened the second floor to sell local villagers other kinds of food — pizzas, hamburgers and hotpot — which attract many young people and children to have a try.

Tayir Ablat now works at a restaurant in his hometown of Alali Town, Shule County of Kashi. (Photo: Shan Jie/GT)

He said that in the future he plans to open a Xinjiang restaurant in Xi'an, more than 2,000 kilometers away from Urumqi, because his younger brother is studying at Xi'an University of Science and Technology.

"I could take care of him and make money," he said.

Abudkerim Abdureyim is 47 years old. He retired from a bus company in Urumqi due to problems with his eyesight. He can get a pension of more than 2,000 yuan a month and is currently working in an industrial park nearby, earning additional 3,800 yuan per month.

Abudkerim lives a quiet life with his wife and two sons in the residential community of the bus company in northern Urumqi. His 75-square-meter apartment is in a typical Uygur decoration with elegant wallpapers and carpets. In his spare time, Abudkerim likes to take care of his plants on the balcony.

His eldest son, 19, will graduate from a technical secondary school next year,

The 47-year-old Abudkerim Abdureyim waters flowers in his home at Urumqi. (Photo: Shan Jie/GT)

majoring in computer science. Employees from the community have promised to help find a job for the young man. Abudkerim's younger son, in grade 5, is also a top student in his class.

Twitter user "Mustapa0991" posted "I #StillNoInfo with my family." In the photo the Twitter user posted, a man holds a board with pictures of people. Abudkerim's photo is at the top right of the board.

Abudkerim wonders who posted his photo and name.

"I am living at home. Please do not share lies and affect our good lives," he said.

Identities

The GT reporters also met some Uygur people in Xinjiang whose identities have been used to hype by their own relatives, even their own children.

Aziz Niyaz and Meryam Gayit, an old couple in Kuqa County, Aksu Prefecture, were also described as "missing" on overseas social networks.

Aziz retired in July 2019 from the county's water conservancy authority in Kuqa. He and his wife now enjoy the life of taking care of their three-year-old grandson at home. When the GT reporters arrived at Aziz's home, he was playing with a toy car with his grandson.

After retirement, Aziz lives a routine life. "My pension is 5,300 yuan. Now the country promotes many kinds of favorable policies, such as medical care for senior citizens. Our grandchild enjoys 15 years of free compulsory education; we do not need to worry," he said.

Aziz's three children all studied medicine. His son Yusup works in the People's Hospital of Kuqa. His two daughters are both abroad, but they have not contacted the family for two years.

"We miss them. We do not know what their life is like now and hope they will come back soon," Yusup told the Global Times. However, what the couple does not

Aziz Niyaz watches TV with his grandson. He retired in July 2019 from the county's water conservancy authority in Kuqa County, Aksu Prefecture. (Photo: Zhao Juecheng / GT)

know is that their younger daughter Buwajar posted the couple's picture online and said they were missing.

On December 9, 2019, Twitter account "mahire" posted some photos of the old couple, saying "this is my family" and that they went missing with many other Uygurs.

"Sister, our father and mother are with me now. I do not know where this rumor came from," Yusup said. "I hope you do not listen to the rumor, study well and come back safely."

Scan QR code to watch the video

New research reveals absurd rumor sources of Uygur detentions in Xinjiang endeared by Western media

By Xie Wenting | Dec 27, 2019

The allegations that China has detained millions of Uygur people in Xinjiang Uygur Autonomous Region came from unreliable studies and sources backed by US government, based on shoddy methodologies and works of a far-right anti-China and anti-communist researcher, a recently published essay in the Grayzone revealed.

"The claim that China has detained millions of ethnic Uygurs in its Xinjiang

A Uygur woman dances at a restaurant in Awati County, Aksu Prefecture of Xinjiang. (Photo: Shan Jie/GT)

region is repeated with increasing frequency, but little scrutiny is ever applied. Yet a closer look at the figure and how it was obtained reveals a serious deficiency in data," said the Grayzone article published on December 20, 2019.

While the "million" figure is widely cited in the West as authentic, an in-depth research shows it is only based on two highly dubious "studies."

The first study was done by the Network of Chinese Human Rights Defenders (CHRD), a Washington DC-based NGO backed by the US government. The "millions detained" figure was first popularized by the CHRD in a 2018 report submitted to the UN Committee on the Elimination of Racial Discrimination, which is often misrepresented in Western media as a report penned by the UN, according to the article.

Grayzone was founded in 2015 as an independent news website dedicated to original investigative journalism and political analysis.

Dubious calculation

While CHRD states it interviewed dozens of Uygur people during the course of its study, their inflated estimate was ultimately based on interviews with eight Uygur individuals, Canada-based writer and lawyer Ajit Singh and Grayzone editor Max Blumenthal wrote in the Grayzone article.

"Based on this small sample of research subjects in an area whose total population is 20 million, CHRD 'extrapolated estimates' that 'at least 10 percent of villagers [...] are being detained in re-education detention camps, and 20 percent are being forced to attend day/evening re-education camps in the villages or townships, totaling 30 percent in both types of camps,'" the article said.

Applying these estimated rates to the entirety of Xinjiang, CHRD arrived at the figures it submitted to the UN claiming that one million ethnic Uygur people have been "detained in re-education detention camps" and two million more have been "forced to attend day/evening re-education sessions," the article added.

The "camps" the CHRD claims are actually vocational education and training centers which employ a boarding school model that allows trainees to go back home on a regular basis and grants leave to attend personal affairs.

Grayzone has previously reported that CHRD receives significant financial support from National Endowment for Democracy (NED). NED is a CIA-backed US foundation which is believed to have played a critical role in innumerable regime changes across the world.

Far-right researcher

The second study, as Grayzone found out, relied on flimsy media reports and speculation. This study was authored by Adrian Zenz, a senior fellow in China studies at the far-right Victims of Communism Memorial Foundation, which was established by the US government in 1983.

"Like the CHRD, Zenz arrived at his estimated 'over 1 million' figure using a dubious methodology. He based it on a single report by Istiqlal TV, a Uygur exile media organization based in Turkey, which was republished by Newsweek Japan," Singh and Blumenthal said.

"Far from an impartial journalistic organization, Istiqlal TV advances the separatist cause while playing host to an assortment of extremist figures." A frequent guest on Istiqlal TV is Abdulkadir Yapuquan, a reported leader of the "East Turkistan Islamic Movement (ETIM)" terrorist group.

Zenz also tries to justify his estimates by citing reports from Radio Free Asia, a US-funded news agency created by the CIA during the Cold War to spew propaganda against China, according to Grayzone's research.

In a November 2019 interview with Radio Free Asia, Zenz even inflated the 1 million figure by claiming China was detaining 1.8 million people.

In an exclusive interview with the Global Times, the spokesperson of Northwest China's Xinjiang Uygur Autonomous Region said the so-called scholars including Zenz actually work for the US intelligence agency, and they cooperate with anti-China forces in the US to smear China's Xinjiang policies.

"Disguised as experts, they made baseless remarks and slandered China's Xinjiang policies as much as possible, aiming to galvanize anti-China forces in the US. What they did was beyond the academic scope — using academic research as a cover, they slandered and smeared China, which are also the old tricks used by the US," added the spokesperson. "The 1 million detention claim is a nonsense and was derived out of nothing."

Grayzone also found that Zenz is a far-right fundamentalist Christian who opposes homosexuality and gender equality, supports "scriptural spanking" of children, and believes he is "led by God" on a "mission" against China.

A search of Zenz's Twitter profile returns no tweets concerning the rise of Islamophobia in the West, nor US wars and drone strikes against Muslim-majority

A woman plays with her granddaughter at a skiing resort in Baicheng County, Xinjiang. (Photo: Shan Jie / GT)

countries. The only Tweet by Zenz concerning Muslims that is unrelated to China is a denial of the double-standard in judging violence when perpetrated by whites instead of Muslims.

In a separate August 2018 report by Blumenthal, he said Washington wants to pressurize China and push the US to spark a conflict with China. He spoke with World Uygur Congress (WUC) chairman Omer Kanat, who took credit for furnishing many of the reports about alleged internment camps in the Western media.

In the report, Blumenthal noted Kanat telling him over "1 million people" were in the camps in Xinjiang and that the figure was offered by some Western media. Kanat also stated that WUC offered more information on the training centers in Xinjiang to the US government and Western media

In an interview with Süddeutsche Zeitung, Dolkun Isa, leader of WUC, admitted they aimed to inflict more pressure on China and force Western companies to withdraw from Xinjiang.

"What is happening in Xinjiang today must be seen in the context of what has been happening throughout Central Asia," read a Workers World report on December 18, 2019.

Xinjiang is a major logistics center for China's ambitious Belt and Road Initiative. Xinjiang is the gateway to Central and West Asia, as well as to European markets. "The US government is deeply hostile to this vast economic development project and is doing all it can to sabotage China's plans. This campaign is part of the US military's 'Pivot to Asia,' along with naval threats in the South China Sea and support for separatist movements in Hong Kong, Taiwan and Tibet," read the article.

Xinjiang refutes latest set of lies from Western media

By Liu Xin and Fan Lingzhi in Urumqi | Jan 3, 2020

Senior officials from Northwest China's Xinjiang Uygur Autonomous Region on January 3, 2020 refuted the latest rumors from Western media, including a New York Times report that the Xinjiang government sends children to boarding schools to "brainwash" them with patriotic education.

The officials said such reports were "baseless" and "packaged with fakery."

Chinese analysts said that certain Western media have ramped up efforts in making baseless news and spreading rumors about Xinjiang without considering the work ethics or their reputations.

More people around the world deserve to know the truth about Xinjiang, experts and officials said.

The Information Office of the People's Government of the Xinjiang Uygur Autonomous Region held the press conference on January 3, 2020.

"[Such reports are] completely subjective fabrication," Parhati Rouzi, an official from Kashi Prefecture, said during the press conference in Urumqi.

XINJIANG RUMORS DEBUNKED

RUMORS		FACTS
Xinjiang's anti-terrorism work targets Uygur Muslims FAKE		De-radicalization and anti-terrorism work in Xinjiang does not target any ethnic group or religion. All work has been done in accordance with the law.
Xinjiang has banned Uygur people from traveling abroad or contacting relatives living abroad. FAKE		Except for people suspected of violating laws, who have been restricted from going abroad, residents in Xinjiang are free to travel overseas and contact people overseas. Xinjiang never restricts people of different ethnic groups from traveling domestically or abroad.
Some US politicians and media have alleged Xinjiang conducts the "massive surveillance" of ethnic groups. FAKE		Xinjiang has installed cameras in public areas, on main streets and traffic junctions to improve social management, and to prevent and crack down on crime. The move has increased residents' sense of security and has been praised by them. The move does not target any ethnic group, and the technology cannot automatically recognize or target any group.
Some Uygur intellectuals and scholars were "detained" and "persecuted" by the Xinjiang regional government. FAKE		Many scholars and intellectuals rumored to have been "persecuted" now live normal lives. They have not been mistreated or detained. They work as normal and have not lost their rights or freedoms.
Notorious separatists including Rebiya Kadeer and Dolkun Isa have alleged that every family has had people taken away by police in Xinjiang, and that the Xinjiang government conducts the "oppression of Uygurs." FAKE		Relatives of Rebiya and Dolkun are living normal lives in Xinjiang. There is no so-called "massive detention" of Uygurs in Xinjiang. The allegation was intended to make trouble for Xinjiang. People of all ethnic groups are aware of these individuals' malicious purpose, and they will never succeed.

GLOBAL TIMES Editors and graphics: Globaltimes.cn

"Boarding school education has been an effective way to improve educational levels and reduce the burden on students and their parents in China's remote areas," Parhati said.

The New York Times report claims the Xinjiang government sends children to boarding schools, separates them forcefully from their parents, "replaces ethnic languages with Mandarin" and "brainwashes" them with patriotic education.

The officials dismissed the report.

"As Xinjiang is a vast region, there are a significant number of students who live far away from their schools, and therefore many of them choose to live on campus ... It is up to students and their parents to decide whether or not to choose boarding education," Parhati said.

In response to the accusation that the regional government sends children to boarding schools to kill the languages and cultures of ethnic minorities, Parhati said that "Primary and secondary education in Xinjiang utilizes six languages to teach, offering courses in standard national language and ethnic minority languages."

"Learning and using the country's common language is a constitutional right, and no one should be deprived of this right. The US is known for its ethnic and cultural diversity, but how could ethnic minorities succeed in American society if they don't learn English?" Parhati said.

"We'd like to point out that the US has decimated the indigenous culture of the American continent, and some of its media and politicians are now portraying China to be committing the historical sins of their own country," he added.

Parhati said that The New York Times despicably made irresponsible remarks about Xinjiang's patriotic education to primary school students.

"All countries in the world educate their young people to love their country. Don't schools in the US conduct patriotic education? In fact, since the end of 19th century, it has been a tradition of American primary and secondary school students to recite and remember the Pledge of Allegiance," Parhati said.

An 11-year-old American boy was reportedly arrested in February 2019 for refusing to pledge allegiance to the American flag, which showed that the US has also attached great importance to patriotic education, Parhati said.

The senior official also rebuked rumors on China sending officials to stay with ethnic minorities to "ask ethnic people to eat pork."

No good person would fabricate lies such as China "demands Muslims drink alcohol, smoke cigarettes and eat pork," or that "ethnic Han men sleep in the same room as local women," the official said.

Parhati introduced that in November 2019, Zomure Dawut said she "found herself land in a pork meal in her relative's home."

In fact, Parhati said, "The 'relative' Zomure referred to is her fifth elder brother Abudhl Dawut's 'relative.' In October 2017, Abudhl was paired with Zhao Qilin as 'relatives.'"

Zhao Qilin invited Abudhl Dawut, his wife and younger sister Zomure and Zomure's children to Zhao's house.

Zhao's mother prepared and cooked the meal for them. Zhao's mother is an ethnic Hui and only eats Halal food, he explained.

"The pork meal claimed by Zomure was totally nonexistent. It is a lie fabricated by Zomure. During the meal, they also took pictures," Parhati showed the picture at the press conference, in which every dish they had was marked and no pork was spotted.

Certain Western media also reported that the former president of Xinjiang University, Tashpolat Teyip, was sentenced to death for attempting to split the country.

Parhati responded to these reports, saying Tashpolat was arrested for corruption and accepting bribes on May 7, 2018, and the intermediate court of Urumqi held an open trial on June 13, 2019.

Tashpolat's case was conducted in accordance with Chinese laws and regulations, and his rights were "fully protected," he said.

Before the trial, Tashpolat told his family via his lawyer that they should not attend the trial, Parhati noted.

In response to reports of mass mosque demolitions, Parhati said the number of mosques in Xinjiang has increased from 2,000 at the beginning of China's reform and opening-up to more than 24,000, or one mosque for every 530 Muslims in Xinjiang.

The number of religious personnel has increased from 3,000 to 29,000, Parhati said.

"Do these figures exemplify religious freedom or are they the result of the 'large-scale demolition' of mosques?" he said.

The official also refuted rumors about forced labor at Xinjiang vocational education and training centers.

Trainees who were on the education and training program, which consists of learning national common language, law, skills and de-radicalization courses, have all graduated, Shohrat Zakir, chairman of the Xinjiang regional government, said during a press conference on December 9, 2019.

"To remedy a lack of occupational skills and employment difficulties, vocational skills training programs are provided ... The education and training centers combine course learning with practical training to improve the trainees' operational skills ... After graduation, the trainees can choose their own jobs ... There is not any forced labor," Parhati said.

Experts said one-sided and biased Western media reports on Xinjiang have alleged forced labor and forced separation of children from their parents.

Like the reports of alleged leaked internal documents, these reports had no truth but only baseless stories, Chinese analysts said.

Western media use negative words and cherry-picked facts to fabricate a miserable image of Xinjiang in order to slander China, they said.

Tu Lingbo from Communication University of China was cited in a report from Cankaoxiaoxi as saying that "Western media and their reporters have bias and misunderstanding on China. They would bring these stereotypes into their stories on China, which made their stories full of 'speculative facts' instead of proved facts and some simple incidents would be made complicated, ideologicalized and politicalized."

Scan QR code to watch the video

Xinjiang refutes CNN report on "destruction of Uygur tombs"

By Liu Xin and Fan Lingzhi in Urumqi | Jan 4, 2020

Northwest China's Xinjiang Uygur Autonomous Region fully respects the rights of ethnic groups and has taken a series of measures, including allocating specific areas for public cemeteries, to protect their rights, a regional spokesperson told the Global Times in an exclusive interview on December 3, 2019.

CNN reported on December 2, 2019 that "more than 100 Uygur graveyards were demolished by Chinese authorities." The allegation was made based on satellite images and the story told by a Uygur poet Aziz Isa Elkun, who left Xinjiang more than 20 years ago and never came back.

Aziz Isa Elkun claimed he could not find his father's grave, which was located in Xayar County in Aksu Prefecture, from a satellite image on Google. However, instead of checking with his family in Xinjiang, the Uygur poet opted to tell the media of his discovery.

"Xinjiang fully respects the rituals of funerals of ethnic groups and has made a series of regulations to protect their basic rights. The region has also set aside specific areas to be used for ethnic groups' graveyards," the spokesperson told the Global Times.

The traditions of funerals of ethnic groups have also been preserved, the spokesperson said.

With economic development and improving livelihoods for locals in Xinjiang, governments at all levels are also making efforts to build public cemeteries and improve facilities at the cemeteries of different ethnic groups. Some people voluntarily choose to relocate the tombs of their relatives to cemeteries, said the spokesperson.

An anonymous source, familiar with the relocation of graveyards situation in Aksu, told the Global Times that previously there was a lack of public cemeteries in rural areas in the prefecture and some graves were scattered over farmland.

To meet local residents' demands, Aksu has built public cemeteries in line with residents' willingness to help relocate graves, the source said, noting that for graves that could not be traced to families, the local government notified the public that it was relocating them to public cemeteries.

The Xinjiang regional government has also made efforts to protect ethnic graveyards, which have historical, artistic and scientific values, by renovating many ancient graveyards in Kashi, Ili Kazak Autonomous Prefecture and Turpan.

Relocating graves to public cemeteries is not a unique phenomenon in Xinjiang, nor does it target any ethnic groups, experts said.

Experts noted that many third- and fourth-tier cities around China build more public cemeteries for local residents to move the graves of their deceased family members to during urbanization. Many prefectures in the Xinjiang region are experiencing urbanization.

However, the CNN report somehow jumped to the conclusion that China has been destroying traditional Uygur cemeteries for several years as part of a "campaign to control Islamic beliefs and Muslim minority groups within its border."

It seems that certain Western media have fallen into stereotypical reporting of China's Xinjiang issues using sensational claims by individuals without checking the facts, and try to portray the Chinese government as the worst violator of human rights, Chinese observers said.

CNN gave no evidence, other than satellite images, to show that the regional government had demolished Uygur tombs. It claimed it talked to the Uygur community in Xinjiang and has also claimed in other stories that all ethnic groups live under tight surveillance by local governments. It also cited some "experts" on Uygur culture living overseas to prove its allegations.

"Why do the foreign media so surely assume that local government demolished the graveyards of ethnic groups? Why can't these tombs be removed to cemeteries? Why don't these foreign media come to Xinjiang to see where these tombs have been relocated? Their purpose is quite clear by only telling half and one side of the story," the source in Aksu said.

Xinjiang people have the final say on what is really happening in Xinjiang and Western media should stop hyping the situation. For experts and scholars who live in foreign countries and have not visited Xinjiang in recent years, they should stop making groundless claims about the region, analysts said.

Scan QR code to watch the video

Xinjiang multilingual tutoring center rejects Western accusation of "cultural genocide"

By Liu Xin and Fan Lingzhi in Artux | Jan 7, 2020

"There are so many people in China and other countries learning English nowadays. Can this be called genocide of our culture or other countries' cultures?" said Maidingjiang Yilimu, who started a tutorial institute in Artux, Northwest China's Xinjiang Uygur Autonomous Region.

Maidingjiang asked the question in response to some Western media reports that alleged Xinjiang's promotion of residents learning standard Chinese aims to kill their ethnic culture.

Maidingjiang started the tutorial institute in September 2019 together with two friends in Artux, Kizilsu Autonomous Prefecture of Xinjiang. They now have 13 teachers.

The Global Times reporters visited the tutorial institute and saw many students attending an English class. Students of different ethnic groups were reading English sentences by following the teacher.

Slogans counting down to the high school entrance examination were hung on

Students attend English class at Maidingjiang's tutorial institute. (Photo: Fan Lingzhi / GT)

classroom walls. The moments from the tutorial institute were just like that of any other tutorial institute in cities nationwide.

Maidingjiang told the Global Times that they receive about 150 students from primary and middle schools every night after school. Parents want their children to improve on their levels in national standard language and English. They hold that a good understanding of the nation's standard language will improve their performance on other courses.

Real contribution

Maidingjiang graduated from Kashi Normal College in 2012. However, unlike most of his classmates, he refused to take the qualification exam to be a teacher.

"I was deeply influenced by extremism at that time and thought working for the government was not what a true Muslim should do. That's why I refused to take the exam and this has forever become a regret for me," Maidingjiang said.

Maidingjiang noted that he often watched and downloaded videos containing extremism propaganda and claimed that "a true Muslim should keep distance from heretics."

He refused to get a job after graduation since he believed many positions were not "halal."

"I wasted more than four years doing nothing but staying home," before being admitted to a vocational education and training center in Artux, Maidingjiang said.

"A teacher from my vocational training center one day told us that a true man should make some real contributions to the society. His words made me think about my previous life and I realized how ridiculous I was. I decided to make real contributions to society," he said.

"I began to have a plan during my study in the training center. I found that my classmates in the centers came from different backgrounds and most of them could

Students do their homework at the tutorial institute. (Photo: Fan Lingzhi/GT)

not speak or write in the nation's standard language. This is a problem when they want to expand their business nationwide or if they want to surf the internet to get more information," Maidingjiang said.

His education institute now aims to offer tutoring services for students of primary and middle schools.

"Many parents send their children here to improve their level of the national standard language," Maidingjiang said, noting that other courses offered by the institute include English and math.

In response to Western media reports that Xinjiang promotes the study of the nation's standard language aims to kill Uygur culture, Maidingjiang said that the accusation is "bullshit."

"As a Chinese, it is our right to learn the nation's standard language. We are also willing to learn it as language is a bridge. The more languages we master, the wider our world will become," Maidingjiang told the Global Times.

"The hope for the people lies in the next generation. Parents are willing to send their children here and they are glad to see their performances of different courses have been greatly improved," Maidingjiang said.

Scan QR code to watch the video

Xinjiang busts secessionist rumors, shows transparency

By Liu Xin | Jan 10, 2020

The regional government of Northwest China's Xinjiang Uygur Autonomous Region addressed a press conference in Urumqi on January 10, 2020 to bust some latest bunch of rumors, including those peddled by notorious separatists Rebiya Kadeer and Dolkun Isa.

This is the second press conference held within two weeks by the regional government to dismiss rumors. Experts believe the move comes in the wake of ramping up of efforts by some Western media and anti-China forces to slander China's Xinjiang policies while Xinjiang embraces more openness and confidence as it strides on the path of transparency.

Xu Guixiang, a senior official of Xinjiang's publicity department, told the Global Times in an exclusive interview on January 10, 2020 that Xinjiang had held the press conferences consecutively since the US and some other Western countries and anti-China forces had ramped up their efforts to spread rumors, smearing Xinjiang's de-radicalization work.

"It is necessary for us to refute slander from anti-China forces, and tell the outside world that Xinjiang is a stable, prosperous and beautiful region," Xu said, noting that the press conference also shows that China has been transparent, open and confident concerning its policies in Xinjiang.

"The two press conferences showed that Xinjiang has always conducted its work in an open and transparent way, including launching the vocational education and training centers, releasing information about graduation of trainees and the poverty alleviation work," said Zhang Yonghe, executive dean of the Human Rights Institution of Southwest University of Political Science and Law in Chongqing.

During briefing, senior officials of the Xinjiang regional government also revealed the involvement of notorious separatists Rebiya and Dolkun, leaders of the Germany-based secessionist group World Uygur Congress, in the terror attacks that happened in Xinjiang. The press conference also exposed their attempts at severing Xinjiang from China together with the terrorist group, the "East Turkistan Islamic Movement (ETIM)."

Two videos as part of the evidence were also streamed during the conference. Relatives of Rebiya and Dolkun were seen in the videos busting their lies.

Dolkun has been slandering Xinjiang using distorted facts for many years. He also alleged that Xinjiang has perpetrated "mass detention" of Uygur Muslims and razed Uygur culture. He claimed his mother died during her captive in Xinjiang's vocational education and training center.

Azgul Isa, Dolkun's elder sister, said in the video their parents died of old age and illness. "It is really heartless of my younger brother Dolkun Isa to use my

A photo showed a man lying in blood, and it was shown alongside the rumor that Uygur people are being murdered. However, the photo was taken following a car accident in Indonesia, and the "blood" was in reality syrup that had spilled from a truck.

deceased parents to smear Xinjiang from overseas. We are very upset about it," she said. Rebiya often peddled lies like violence against Uygurs is everywhere in Xinjiang and every family has someone who has been nabbed by the police.

However, Rebiya's two granddaughters told the Global Times in an exclusive interview that the family is living a normal life and people in Xinjiang are enjoying

Xinjiang rumors debunked

Rumors

Kids were "brainwashed" at boarding schools

"Becoming family" policy forced Xinjiang Muslims to eat pork

Mosques were demolished

Minority trainees were forced to work

Facts

(1) Students can decide whether to choose boarding education
(2) Primary and secondary education utilizes 6 languages, including ethnic minority languages
(3) Patriotic education is a norm in much of the world

(1) No Muslim was forced to eat pork
(2) The "becoming family" policy has shortened the distance between different ethnic groups

(1)The number of mosques in Xinjiang has increased from 2,000 at the beginning of China's reform and opening-up to more than 24,000
(2)There is now one mosque for every 530 Muslims in Xinjiang

(1)There is no forced labor
(2)Trainees acquire skills in the vocational training center and many are employed and lifted out of poverty after graduation

Rumors

Mihrigul Tursun alleged she was suppressed in a vocational training center

Twitter netizens posted tags claiming China has suppressed Xinjiang Muslims

Uygurs are missing

Former president of Xinjiang University was sentenced to death for attempting to split the country

Facts

(1) Mihrigul Tursun has never been sent to prison or a vocational training center
(2) Mihrigul Tursun's brother is not dead as she claimed

China's anti-terrorism and anti-extremism activities have never targeted any ethnic group or religion

Global Times reporters met some people on the missing list and found that they have been home for months and are living normal lives after graduating from the training centers

(1)Former president of Xinjiang University, Tashpolat Teyip,was arrested for accepting bribes on May 7, 2018
(2)The intermediate court of Urumqi held an open trial on June 13, 2019
(3) His rights have been fully protected

GLOBAL TIMES
Source: Global Times, Xinhua
Editor and Graphic: Globaltimes.cn

every freedom. In another video which was streamed at the conference, the two girls urged Rebiya to stop peddling lies and disturbing their peaceful life.

"In the videos, we can see relatives of Dolkun and Rebiya living free lives. Then, how come there is so-called mass detention of Uygur Muslims in Xinjiang?" Guli Abulm, spokesperson of the Xinjiang regional government, questioned.

She termed such people with sinister motives as "scums of the people" who are trying to brew troubles in Xinjiang. People of all ethnic groups in Xinjiang are aware of their malicious purpose and would not let them succeed.

Ridiculing the ETIM, Xinjiang officials said some members of the ETIM are worried that after floating innumerable lies, they would eventually backfire.

Guli particularly threw light on four rumors that were floated by ETIM members, including bogus videos which claimed "Uygur people are tortured" but were later discovered to be not only fake but also unrelated to Uygurs in Xinjiang.

Zhang Yonghe noted that anti-China forces and overseas separatists are colluding together and ramping up their efforts to smear China. By hyping issues related to China's Xinjiang and Tibet regions, they want to stand on a moral high ground, slander China's human rights records and attack its policies on religion. They are also trying to sow discords between China and the Muslim world.

Success story

Three individuals representing people about whom rumors were spread, mostly by Western media, were invited to attend press conference and share their true stories. They were a scholar from Kashi University, a trainee from a vocational education and training center in Kashi, and a trainee from Hotan.

Gulnal Ubli, an official from Xinjiang agricultural machinery bureau, said during the conference that some foreign media and members of the ETIM slandered Xinjiang by maliciously claiming persecution and detention of Uygur intellectuals, including herself.

"These reports are nonsense!" she said, adding that many scholars that have been rumored as being "detained" are living normal lives.

"We have not been mistreated or detained. We are still working on our positions and did not lose our rights and freedom. I want to stress that China is a country ruled by law … All Chinese citizens, including the Uygur people, will face no custody if they do not violate laws," said Gulnal.

However, there is a very small group of so-called "intellectuals" who incite terrorism and extremism, attempt to split the country, stir hatred among different ethnic groups and assist terrorists. "They are the enemy of the people and must be lawfully punished," Gulnal said.

Alijian Tohti from Kashi shared glimpses of his time in the training center. He stressed the living condition in the center was good and they had free accommodation. Their rituals and eating habits were respected and they had opportunities to attend many interesting classes.

Alijian said he went on to work in a company after graduating from the center and is now satisfied with his current income.

Almujiang Abuduaini is a trainee in the Hotan training center. After being influenced by extremism, he barred his wife from going to work, stopped his children's schooling, and did not consult doctors or visit the hospital when they were sick.

Almujiang said, he has changed a lot after joining the training center. He now cares more about his family members and with the help of the residential community, he opened a small shop selling items of daily necessities.

"I can earn more than 10,000 yuan a month and I hired a helper from a poverty-stricken family. Our life is getting better and I love my family and will provide good education to my children," he said.

Officials from the regional government also unveiled the achievements of Xinjiang's work on countering terrorism and de-radicalization. Not even a single violent attack occurred in Xinjiang in over three years, which was the foremost accomplishment.

The stability and harmony of society have brought an opportunity for economic development. The GDP of Xinjiang in 2018 surpassed 1.2 trillion yuan and the per capita disposable income of urban and rural residents was 32,764 yuan and 11,975 yuan respectively. The GDP in 2019 is expected to reach 1.378 trillion yuan.

In 2019, Xinjiang received 213 million trips, garnering a tourism revenue of more than 360 billion yuan.

More transparent and confident

Despite some Western media's relentless attempts at slandering Xinjiang, more conscious people have reacted positively to Xinjiang's current achievements, Xinjiang regional officials said.

"The truth may be delayed but it will never be denied," said Guli, noting that a US news website, Grayzone released a report on December 12, 2019 which disclosed that the figure of "1 million Uygur detention" in Xinjiang was in fact sourced from a Washington-based nongovernmental organization, the Network of Chinese Human Rights Defenders (CHRD).

Based on interviews with only eight Uygurs in an area with a population of 20 million, CHRD "extrapolated estimates" that "at least 10 percent of villagers ... are being detained in re-education detention camps, and 20 percent are being forced to attend day/evening re-education camps in the villages or townships," according to the Grayzone article.

"Lies cannot cover the truth. Slandering Xinjiang will finally be torn down ... Xinjiang's work on countering terrorism and de-radicalization is above board. The great efforts made by people and officials of all ethnic groups on realizing long-term stability in Xinjiang should get a fair and square evaluation from the international community," said the spokesperson.

Analysts believe with the development of Xinjiang, the region has become more open and confident and it welcomes more visitors to espy the reality with their eyes.

Xinjiang has invited more than 1,000 people from 90 countries and regions to visit the region, said officials during the press conference, adding that Xinjiang's anti-terrorism measures are in accordance with UN regulations on countering terrorism and firmly safeguard human rights.

Scan QR code to watch the video

Chapter III

SUPPORT FROM THE INTERNATIONAL COMMUNITY

In the past two years, Xinjiang issues have become one of the most hyped topics in Western media. Sensational headlines and sentences — China's "sweeping campaign to detain and indoctrinate Muslims," "Chinese camps detain millions of Muslims," "the worst human rights crisis" — are used frequently in Western media outlets including The New York Times and CNN. However, a close look at these articles shows their reports are full of loopholes and lack credible sources. Many deliberately twist and fabricate facts or take quotes out of context.

In fact, many foreign diplomats, journalists and scholars who have visited Xinjiang and saw the region with their own eyes have expressed the real Xinjiang is so different from what they have heard and imagined.

Many foreigners exclaimed how their Xinjiang visit humbled them, "The visit to Xinjiang has completely broken the prejudice we had in the past!"

Diplomatic envoys, foreign journalists praise Xinjiang's stability, economic development

By Xie Wenting and Bai Yunyi | Jan 24, 2019

Editor's note

Foreign diplomatic envoys and journalists hailed the Chinese government's efforts to counter terrorism in Xinjiang Uygur Autonomous Region and recognized the significance of the region's vocational education and training centers after they paid a visit. The Silk Road Celebrity China Tour, which consisted of 12 media representatives from countries including Egypt, Turkey, Bangladesh, Pakistan and Sri Lanka, visited Xinjiang from January 9 to 16, 2019. The trip was made following diplomatic envoys from 12 countries visiting Xinjiang from December 28 to 30, 2018 at the invitation of the regional government. Global Times reporters Xie Wenting and Bai Yunyi talked with diplomats and journalists about their trip and their take on China's administration of the region.

Mumtaz Zahra Baloch, Charge d'affaires, Pakistani Embassy in China

GT: Could you introduce your recent Xinjiang visit? During the trip, what impression did Xinjiang leave on you?

Baloch: I was part of the group of diplomats from 12 countries including ambassadors and charge d'affaires that visited XUAR (Xinjiang Uygur Autonomous Region) from December 28 to 30, 2018. We visited Urumqi, Kashi and Hotan. It was an amazing experience to visit this land of immense beauty, history and culture. This was not my first trip to Xinjiang. Our visit reinforced my perceptions about this region that it has a multicultural and multi-ethnic identity, that it is critical for the development of the western regions of China and that it is an important node for regional connectivity under the Belt and Road Initiative.

GT: What impressed you most during the trip? Does it meet your previous expectation?

Baloch: As I said earlier, I had visited Xinjiang on several occasions in the past. Every time I visited I was impressed with the fast pace of development of the region. This policy of development and poverty alleviation is focused not just on the richer cities but also on the poorer cities and counties. The development efforts at the grass roots especially in southern Xinjiang are remarkable and are aimed at improving the living standards of the people there. I was particularly impressed with village-run factories and SMEs (small and medium-sized enterprises) and the low-cost housing being developed for the villagers. I am confident that with such focused strategies to improve access of people to education, housing, livelihood, healthcare and social security, Xinjiang will be able to meet its developmental targets.

GT: Did you visit the vocational education and training centers during the trip? What's your take on it?

Baloch: Our visit program was quite broad which enabled us to get a glimpse of the situation in Xinjiang. During the visit, we had the opportunity to visit the Xinjiang Islamic Institute, the bazaars, mosques, police stations, economic development and poverty alleviation projects and vocational education and training centers.

We were given full and open access to the three centers that we visited in Kashi and Hotan. The training program includes teaching of national common language (Putonghua), law and constitution and vocational skills. The students also participate in recreational activities like sports, music and dance. We witnessed several skill classes being offered in these centers.

During the visits to these centers, we had the opportunity to interact with both the management and the students. We observed the students to be in good physical health. The living facilities are fairly modern and comfortable with separate dormitories for men and women. They are served halal food.

GT: Have you found the existence of forced labor, cultural or religious oppression?

Baloch: During this visit, I did not find any instance of forced labor or cultural and religious repression.

The imams we met at the mosques and the students and teachers at the Xinjiang Islamic Institute told us that they enjoy freedom in practicing Islam and that the Chinese government extends support for maintenance of mosques all over the Xinjiang. I learned that there are over 30,000 mosques all over the Xinjiang that form part of the religious life of the people there.

Similarly, I did not see any sign of cultural repression. The Uygur culture as demonstrated by their language, music and dance is very much part of the life of the people of Xinjiang. We saw that in official establishments, airports, subway stations, police stations or hotels the Uygur language is being widely used. Even the copies of the *Koran* that we saw in the mosques and the Islamic center were translated into the Uygur language. The most visible sign of protection of Uygur culture by the government is the government-run bilingual kindergarten schools where children learn Putonghua as well as Uygur language and culture from a very young age.

GT: Xinjiang has been a region beset by terrorism. How did you feel about Xinjiang's security situation during this visit?

Baloch: We learned that the recent measures have resulted in improvement of the security situation in Xinjiang and there have been no incidents of terrorism in recent months. The counter-terrorism measures being taken are multidimensional and do not simply focus on law enforcement aspects. Education, poverty alleviation and development are keys to the counter-terrorism strategy of the Chinese government.

GT: Based on your observation, do you think the current methods adopted by the Chinese government benefit Xinjiang's development?

Baloch: I understand that Xinjiang's development is a key to the western development strategy of China. We can witness signs of this development even in remote parts of the region including the less developed areas in the south.

Development of infrastructure, airports, railways and the road network has enhanced connectivity of Xinjiang with the rest of China and with neighboring countries. Xinjiang is thus ready to play a critical role in the development of the Belt and Road Initiative.

Xinjiang is undergoing rapid industrialization through preferential tax policies to attract domestic and international enterprises. The governor of Xinjiang informed us that Xinjiang's pairing with better-developed provinces and municipal cities including Beijing, Shanghai, Guangdong, Shandong and Zhejiang has brought fruitful results. Today Xinjiang's GDP exceeds 1 trillion yuan ($144.2 billion).

The hope is that peace and stability in the region together with policies for socio-economic development will further encourage investment in Xinjiang. This would also increase the prospects of the local population playing an even bigger role in development of the region especially with the growing focus on vocational training and Putonghua skills.

Shiabur Rahman, Executive editor of Bangladesh's *Daily Sun*

GT: Did you visit the vocational education and training center? What did you see there?

Rahman: I visited the Xinjiang vocational education and training center that Western media called "re-education camp." I saw learners there being taught Putonghua and laws and trained in different vocational trades. I also saw many of them playing outdoor games and performing cultural activities. I talked to the head of the center and a number of learners to know how they came to the center, what they were doing there and how they were being treated by the teachers or instructors.

Most of the learners I talked to admitted that they either committed small criminal offences linked to religious fanaticism, extremism and terrorism, or were found to be inclined to fanaticism and extremism. I came to know from them that their families sent them to the center happily as they believe the center will motivate them to shun the wrong path and bring them back to the right path. Many learners said they were ignorant of the laws of China and the punishment for the offenses they were getting involved with.

I categorically asked several learners if they had faced any sort of oppression or torture at the center and they answered in the negative. They said they were happy with the treatment by the authorities, and the food and accommodation offered by the center.

The head of the center told the visiting journalists that every learner was trained in a vocational trade for three months after they passed the Putonghua and law exams. According to him, most of the around 1,000 learners, already graduating from the center, have embarked on their careers with some starting their own businesses and others joining different business entities. The head said the center even arranges jobs for the learners who cannot find jobs by themselves. According to him, there are around 2,000 learners in the center at present.

GT: Xinjiang has been a region beset by terrorism. How did you feel about Xinjiang's security situation? Do you think the counter-terrorism methods used by the Chinese government are necessary?

Rahman: We came to know that for Xinjiang, 2014 and 2015 were the worst years when the region witnessed a sharp rise in incidents of terrorism, religious extremism and separatism, the targets of which were mostly ordinary people. Such incidents started to decline following the government's heightened security measures and installation of a close surveillance system to protect the people.

In any society it is the responsibility of the government to protect its every citizen from any ill and I believe the Chinese government and Xinjiang regional authorities are pursuing the right policy in this regard. I also believe that the government should keep an eye on law enforcement agencies to ensure they cannot go beyond their jurisdiction in discharging their duties.

Abbas (pseudonym), a journalist who joined the Xinjiang trip in January 2019

Abbas asked not to give his real name or nationality as he worried that if he honestly shares the positive things he saw during the trip, some people would slander him claiming that he might have taken money from the Chinese government.

GT: What's your impression of the vocational education and training center? Did you suspect the interviewees were arranged to say words against their will?

Abbas: When you listen to the word "camps," you will imagine some places with chains, tired and depressed people. But this was not the camps I visited during my trip. The centers look like a university campus because they have big classrooms and good dormitories. They also have cafeterias and large playing grounds.

There were 40 students in one classroom, and I picked out interviewees on my own. We were free to ask anybody. And we were not picking students just from one classroom, but from almost all classrooms. I also saw some students in classrooms wearing their traditional caps and traditional dress.

You can see from the photos that I've taken. They're all smiling and look in good condition. A man living under pressure would not have such an expression.

GT: Do you think your country should also adopt the same methods of de-radicalization?

Abbas: My country is also plagued by terrorism. I hope my country can adopt some of these measures, such as setting up a vocational education and training center and carrying out poverty alleviation work, to help de-radicalization. But they don't have so much money to do this.

GT: Some Western countries and media outlets have launched vicious attacks on Xinjiang. What's your take on it?

Abbas: I think the Xinjiang government has the right to take all these measures to push forward the social integration of its own people with the society. And if they make some plans to bring people's living standards up, it's a good thing and should be appreciated.

Xinjiang borders eight countries, and none of these eight countries has complaints. Only Western countries, especially the US, which have nothing to do with Xinjiang, are criticizing the Chinese government. But if the people in Xinjiang were lifted out of poverty, if they were given houses and jobs because factories are set up in the area, is it bad? I don't think so.

GT: What do you think of Uygur people being taught Putonghua?

Abbas: I think the government is very right to make people the useful part of society, because we were told that most of the Uygurs cannot speak standard national common language. But if you cannot speak the main and common language of your country, how can you compete? How can you run a business?

Xinjiang joint letter signatories blast West's bias

By Liu Xin in Urumqi | Jul 26, 2019

Government officials, scholars and religion experts from Northwest China's Xinjiang Uygur Autonomous Region defended the country's counter-terrorism and de-radicalization policies in the region against groundless accusations from the US and other Western countries.

China's State Council Information Office (SCIO) released a white paper on July

Yeerkexi Kuerbanbaike, vice president of Xinjiang Writers Association. (Photo: Liu Xin / GT)

21, 2019, to clarify major historical matters on Xinjiang, like it has never been "East Turkistan" and the Uygurs are not descendants of the Turks.

In response to US State Secretary Mike Pompeo's recent criticism of China's policies in Xinjiang, close to 100 scholars and religious experts released a joint letter on July 19, 2019, to express their discontent.

Two experts who signed the letter spoke with the Global Times, sharing stories behind the public letter and their opinions on the latest white paper.

Wanting to be heard

Yeerkexi Kuerbanbaike, vice president of the Xinjiang Writers Association, said she learned of Pompeo's accusations from the news and her first reaction was, "Why did a country's senior official make such groundless and irresponsible remarks on

China's regional situation and policies in Xinjiang?"

"China is the home of all ethnic groups living here. We have the ability to solve problems that happen within our family, and we are doing quite well on this," Yeerkexi told the Global Times on July 25, 2019.

"Why would anyone eavesdrop on others and spread rumors and criticism based on guesswork? It's like the sound of scratching glass with nails, which is deplorable," she said.

Anger and disappointment with Pompeo inspired a few scholars to pen the letter, and many others echoed their feelings and joined them in the letter's composition.

"We felt it is time to make our voice heard by the outside world. For foreigners who have never been to Xinjiang, the information about this place has mostly come from the media. However, false stories from Western media and their hysteria over the policies will demonize Xinjiang," Yeerkexi said.

"We don't want our home, a place of rich culture and with people from different ethnic groups who live in harmony, to be known or remembered by the outside world that way," she added.

This is not the first time Xinjiang scholars have written an open letter. After the riots in Urumqi in 2009, they wrote several letters condemning the terrorists.

More than 200 writers and poets of the Uygur ethnic group released a letter on June 25, 2014 calling for unity and a fight against terrorism and extremism, chinanews.com reported.

Five terrorists drove two cars into a crowd and detonated a bomb in Urumqi, killing 39 and injuring 94 on May 22, 2014. A few weeks earlier, terrorists carried out a suicide attack at a railway station, killing 3 and injuring 79, according to a white paper released by the SCIO in March 2019.

Abudurekefu Tumuniyazi, head of the Xinjiang Islamic Association and the Xinjiang Islam Institution, was the first religion expert to sign the letter.

"I am also angry with Pompeo's remarks. China has repeatedly explained its policies on religious protection, ethnic groups, and the development of Xinjiang on many occasions, and foreign diplomats and media have been invited to Xinjiang. What Pompeo and other US politicians have done neglects the truth and is nonsense," said Abudurekefu.

In January of 2019, Abudurekefu sent a letter to the US Ambassador to China, expressing his opposition toward the false accusations about the Xinjiang policies.

He also sent the letter to the Organization of Islamic Cooperation (OIC) during their representatives' trip to the region.

"I wanted them to know the US was talking nonsense and what the OIC saw in Xinjiang was the truth," he told the Global Times.

Abudurekefu Tumuniyazi (center), head of the Xinjiang Islamic Association and the Xinjiang Islam Institution, discusses China's religion protection policies to foreign visitors in July 2018. (Photo: Liu Xin / GT)

In response to rumors that they signed the open letter under political pressure, Yeerkexi and Abudurekefu said that was nonsense and slanderous.

"Many scholars reached out to me after the letter was released and offered advice on how to perfect it. They also expressed their willingness to sign it," Yeerkexi said.

Responding to concerns

Yeerkexi said that while writing the letter, a few scholars insisted on mentioning the vocational education and training centers as Western media have distorted such issues.

The training centers play an essential role in Xinjiang's de-radicalization efforts.

"The training centers offer people who have been influenced by extremism a platform to learn national laws, standard Chinese, and some vocational skills, so they can understand their responsibilities within society and not be influenced by terrorists," Yeerkexi told the Global Times.

When discussing extremism, Yeerkexi recalled when she worked in Maigaiti County, and saw how it affected young people and children.

Three children were not allowed to attend school by their parents influenced by extremism. It was not because the government didn't provide educational opportunities; it was because of extremism.

"After recent de-radicalization efforts, children are enjoying their right to education. They are learning various subjects, and their eyes are glowing," Yeerkexi said.

"Look what the US did after 9/11 against terrorism. When it comes to China implementing counter-terrorism and de-radicalization methods, why does the US criticize China for similar purposes? Isn't this a double standard?" Abudurekefu asked.

Not for human rights

In response to Western media accusations over human rights violations, Abudurekefu said, "What is human rights protection? Isn't it protecting human rights to ensure people live a happy life in a stable and safe environment? Isn't it protecting human rights to let people enjoy religious freedom?"

"Does protecting human rights include doing what Western countries tell us to do? For some Western countries and media, they say human rights not out of real care but out of some political purpose, which is to contain China," he said.

Abudurekefu met with reporters from the UK at the Islamic Institute in Urumqi in May. He invited the reporters to watch a student prayer meeting.

The reporters declined and said they had a flight to catch. Ten minutes later they returned because, and as they explained, someone had forgotten a notebook. Instead of searching for the missing notebook, they started taking videos of the praying students.

"Eventually, they said they were going to leave. After noticing my insistence in helping them find their missing notebook, a reporter took a notebook from their car and said he had found it," Abudurekefu recalled, noting how some Western media still remained biased even after witnessing the real situation in Xinjiang.

"Will some Western media and countries think Xinjiang is 'normal' when violent attacks happen in the region now and then, and parents worry about the security of their children at work or school every day?" Yeerkexi asked.

"I hope more people read our letter and hear from those who are living in Xinjiang. I welcome everyone to Xinjiang to see what is happening here. They would gain a new perspective on the policies," Yeerkexi said.

Recently, 37 countries sent a joint letter to the UN Human Rights Council in support of China's Xinjiang policies, in response to 22 Western countries that had sent a joint letter criticizing China on this issue.

"Many of the 37 countries are Muslim majority countries. Their support for

China reveals that they know the country's de-radicalization efforts are to help differentiate extremism from religion and to protect the religious rights of believers," Abudurekefu said.

A true Xinjiang

Alwardawy, a journalist from Egyptian media Algoumhuria Newspaper, who just finished a trip to Xinjiang, told the Global Times that the letter from the scholars and religious personnel is the true voice of people who live in Xinjiang and have a sense of the justice there. The voice comes from people who cannot tolerate lies, and it should receive support from the international community.

The reporter also said that what he saw in Xinjiang fits the descriptions in China's newly released white paper — people of different ethnic groups living in harmony, the security situation in the region is maintained well, the cultures of ethnic groups have been protected and mosques can be seen in many places.

He said he has witnessed the white paper's image of Xinjiang.

Gerhard from Germany works at a motor company and has traveled to the company's branch in Xinjiang several times. He said that he has seen the economic development and improvement of people's lives there in recent years.

Some politicians in Western countries and anti-China groups have intentionally distorted what is happening in Xinjiang. The newly released white paper can give a full picture to foreigners of a true Xinjiang and the policies in the region.

Fifty ambassadors throw weight behind China on Xinjiang

By Xie Wenting and Bai Yunyi | Jul 27, 2019

As of 6 pm on July 26, 2019 (Geneva local time), 50 Ambassadors to the UNOG signed a joint letter to the president of the UN Human Rights Council and the UN High Commissioner for Human Rights, positively evaluating human rights developments in China's Uygur Autonomous Region.

The figure is 13 more than the original 37 countries which sent the letter on July 12, 2019.

Iran, Iraq, Sri Lanka, Djibouti and Palestine are among the countries that newly joined to support China's policies in Xinjiang.

A villager shows her medicine box offered by local government for free in Xinjiang. (Photo: Fan Lingzhi/GT)

Some other countries also expressed support in their separate letters and press releases. Many of them have seen the real situation in Xinjiang on recent visits.

In the joint letter, the ambassadors gave credit to China's counter-terrorism and de-radicalization efforts.

They commend China for its economic and social progress, effective counter-terrorism and de-radicalization measures, and strong guarantee of human rights; appreciate the opportunities provided by China for diplomatic envoys, officials of international organizations, and media professionals to visit Xinjiang. They point to the contrast in the views on Xinjiang between those who have visited it and the one portrayed in Western media, and urge the countries to stop using uncorroborated information to make unfounded accusations against China.

"Faced with the grave challenge of terrorism and extremism, China has undertaken a series of counter-terrorism and de-radicalization measures in Xinjiang, including setting up vocational education and training centers. Now safety and security has returned to Xinjiang and the fundamental human rights of people there have enjoyed stronger senses of fulfillment, happiness and security," they said.

The ambassadors also urged the relevant countries to "refrain from employing unfounded charges against China based on unconfirmed information before they visit Xinjiang."

Reasons for signing joint letter: Xinjiang combines anti-terrorism with protection of human rights.

Venezuelan Embassy in China told the Global Times in an exclusive interview that Venezuela signed the joint letter because they recognize the impressive achievements made by China in the field of human rights, which is in favor of its people.

"Venezuela is fully aware of Chinese government's efforts in Xinjiang Uygur Autonomous Region. Since 2013, it has carried out initiatives every year to improve the livelihoods of its population. These initiatives represent more than 70 percent of their annual public budget expenditure in the region, such as the 15-year free education program in southern Xinjiang as well as a 3-year free bilingual preschool program in rural areas," said the Venezuelan embassy.

"We appreciate China's efforts which are based on their own realities, attach equal importance to the fight and prevention of terrorism. It combines the fight against violence and terrorist crimes with the promotion and protection of human rights," the embassy added.

The embassy stressed that China's leadership in human rights is "indisputable." "China is a party to 26 international human rights treaties and their protocols, and has timely submitted its periodic reports to the respective organization created under the *United Nations Human Rights Treaties*," the embassy noted.

What Chinese government does in Xinjiang is in accordance with its legal system and it protects its citizens from the dangers of terrorism and violence as well as provides assistance and education to prevent people from being victims of

Residents and visitors dance happily in China's Xinjiang Uygur Autonomous Region. (Photo: Cui Meng/GT)

terrorism and extremism, according to the Venezuela embassy.

Pakistani Embassy in China reaffirmed to the Global Times that their position is the same as that stated in the letter to UN.

Counselor Lisbet Quesada Luna, Chargé d'affaires of Cuban Embassy in China, told the Global Times that Xinjiang has a diverse multiethnic culture and different ethnic groups live there with mutual respect.

Under the leadership of the Communist Party of China, local governments have made remarkable achievements in the fight against terrorism and the prevention of terrorism, safeguarding the religious freedom of citizens and the preservation of ethnic traditions and culture, Luna said.

"The vocational education and training center allows the professional preparation of inhabitants of that region, which contributes to the better understanding of their environment and enables them to understand, detect and fight against terrorist actions," said the Cuban diplomat.

Support from Islamic countries

It's worth mentioning that a large number of countries signing the joint letter are the countries where the majority of population is Muslim, including Pakistan, Saudi Arabia and United Arab Emirates (UAE).

Global Policy and Analysis Think Tank Eurasia Future concludes that the fact that China's policies are winning support from so many Islamic countries is a "clear indication that many nations seek to learn from China in respect of how to clamp down on extremism whilst elevating the prosperity and solidifying the social harmony of populations susceptible to terrorist infiltration."

However, their support upsets many Western media outlets, which tried to create conflicts. A recent CNN report said that Muslim countries defending China shatters "any myths of Islamic solidarity."

Muhammad Zamir Assadi, a journalist from Independent News Pakistan, told the Global Times that the CNN report is a "clear bias of Western media." Assadi visited Xinjiang in 2016 which left him with a good memory of the region.

"Muslim countries are well aware of the situation in Xinjiang as their ambassadors have been visiting the country continuously. The recent report of Muslim countries on Xinjiang shows that Islamic nations have confidence in Chinese measures for Muslims in Xinjiang," Assadi told the Global Times.

He noted that Western media misinterpreted the Xinjiang situation to the international community for vested interests. "They just want to pressure China by following their governments' foreign policies," said Assadi.

Ahmed Al-Zahrani, vice director of the institute of consulting and research at Saudi Arabia's Jeddah University, told the Global Times that it's "reasonable" for China to strengthen security control and provide local children bilingual education in Xinjiang.

When Al-Zahrani visited Xinjiang a decade ago, he found many issues there. Many local people were then close-minded and knew barely anything about the society outside their sphere. "These people need help to integrate into normal social life," said Al-Zahrani.

Iran is among the countries that also signed the letter, refuting groundless accusations against China and denouncing Western countries for degrading the international human rights mechanism as a political tool. In an exclusive statement sent by the Iranian Embassy to the Global Times, it said that Iran admires "China's principled position and well stabilized practices against the abuse of the issue of human rights for political objectives, regardless of the challenges."

Iran believes that China's commitment to the promotion and protection of human rights is "inherent, genuine and deeply rooted in the country's cultural and historical backgrounds and requirements," read the statement.

Hujjatullah Zia, a journalist from Afghanistan, told the Global Times that he went through disinformation spread by Western media about Uygur ethnic group and the vocational education and training centers, which are called "educational camps" by Western media.

"I believed those were true stories and I was curious to visit Xinjiang. But my perspective was changed when I visited vocational education and training centers," he said.

In the centers, Zia interviewed students who studied there. "They were happy with the education and their studies. They said they were preached about fundamentalism through unknown WeChat accounts. They also prayed secretly. The government noticed the situation. Then they learned law and received training at the centers so that they could have a job in the future and do not resort to fundamental ideology out of ignorance," said Zia.

Zia told the Global Times that two things surprised him most during his trip to Xinjiang this year: the large number of mosques there, and that students at vocational education and training centers could recite the *Holy Koran* and speak Arabic.

Hua Liming, a former Chinese ambassador to Iran and UAE, told the Global Times that although Saudi Arabia and some Gulf countries have close ties with the US, they have different perspectives on China and Xinjiang.

"Some Western countries including the US view Xinjiang as a tool to contain China. But for Islamic countries, they like to see Xinjiang issue from an anti-terrorism perspective," Hua said.

According to Hua, as Islamic countries' understanding about China is deepening, they are increasingly clear of the extremism challenges that China is facing in Xinjiang. Therefore, they have more trust on China's policies.

Al-Zahrani noted that still some people in Islamic countries harbor misunderstandings about China's Xinjiang and its Muslim policies, which is largely because they are exposed to so many fake reports, many of which are from "East Turkestan" terrorist and separatist groups. But what the government has done for the benefits of Xinjiang is hard to find in media.

After returning to Afghanistan, Zia wrote several articles to introduce a real Xinjiang, which he said is to correct many people's misunderstanding. These reports received good reviews in his home country as many readers said they were amazed by Xinjiang's diverse culture.

US double standards

Zia said that people should "differentiate between what is taught at universities and in educational institutes in the US and US foreign policy."

"The US foreign policy focuses more on its financial interests — be it at the expense of human rights," he said.

The Venezuela embassy noted that "the government of the United States is an expert in invasions and economic blockades and should be held responsible for the death of millions of people in the world. It has no morals to become a defender of human rights."

"This government uses the noble cause of human rights as an instrument to 'demonize' countries that do not bend to their interests. It holds the darkest record of massive human rights violations in the world, openly promoting and financing the destabilization of governments that do not submit to their hegemonic claims," the embassy stressed.

With its so-called preventive wars, the US has invaded sovereign countries, using drones to hit people without warning, leaving thousands of innocent people dead, which it brazenly calls "collateral effects." "Our country has denounced in the international forums the policy of interventionism and aggression of the US government against developing countries," said the Venezuela embassy.

Counselor Luna told the Global Times that Cuba rejects the use of the human rights issues to exert political pressure and the tendency to impose punitive actions. "The aim of it is actually to push forward and disguise its regime change operations."

Turkish reporters recognize Xinjiang's de-radicalization achievement

By Liu Xin and Bai Yunyi | Aug 11, 2019

Some Turkish reporters have recently published stories in Turkish media on their experience visiting Northwest China's Xinjiang Uygur Autonomous Region, clarifying rumors that had hurt China-Turkey ties, and recognizing China's de-radicalization work.

For a long time, influenced by the Western media and the East Turkistan separatists living in Turkey, many Turkish people have misunderstandings on China's Xinjiang policies. They wrongly thought "their Uygur brothers are under oppression

Tunc Akkoç (left), Chairman of the Aydınlık Newspaper meets with Abdurrehim Heyit, a Uygur musician in Urumqi, Xinjiang. (Photo: Courtesy of Tunc Akkoç)

in Xinjiang," despite the fact that China has issued a white paper in July stating Uygurs are "not descendants of Turks."

The Global Times reached three Turkish reporters who shared their experience of visiting Xinjiang and how they changed their previous bias toward Xinjiang after seeing local people's happy lives with their own eyes.

To dispel misunderstandings and fight against biased news on China's policies in Xinjiang, China has ramped up efforts on inviting foreign media and diplomats to visit Xinjiang, analysts said.

They noted that more and more people wanted a full picture of what is happening in Xinjiang and recognize the effectiveness of the current policies on fighting against terrorism and de-radicalization work.

Clarified rumors

Gokhan Karakas, who works for daily Turkish newspaper Milliyet, visited Xinjiang in July 2019 and interviewed Abdurrehim Heyit, a musician from the Uygur ethnic group.

Heyit is one of the most famous Uygur musicians in Xinjiang. However, some Western media and anti-China forces have used him as a tool to attack China's Xinjiang policies. They spread news that the musician, saying he was sentenced to eight years in prison and died there.

Hami Aksoy, spokesperson of the Turkish Foreign Ministry said in a statement on February 9, 2019 that Abdurrehim Heyit had died in the second year after he was detained by Xinjiang regional government. The spokesperson also criticized China's policies in Xinjiang, including setting up vocational education and training centers.

Although China soon published video footage of Heyit, who said he is in good health, anti-China forces kept hyping up Heyit's stories.

During his stay in Xinjiang, Karakas paid a visit to Heyit's house in Urumqi.

"There is much discussion of Heyit in Turkey and I wanted to investigate whether he was tortured to death ... According to my observation, there is no sign of Heyit being mistreated. He is in good health and could answer my questions fluently," Karakas said.

In response to whether he was sentenced to eight years in prison, Heyit told the Turkish reporter that he was once under detention for two weeks and was then released after the investigation.

Karakas said that Heyit showed some hesitation when talking about his experience in prison but "other times I saw happiness in his eyes."

Heyit told Karakas that he was a national-level artist and worked for the national dance troupe of ethnic music since the 1980s. His monthly salary could reach up to 10,000 yuan ($1,400).

"Heyit said he would carry on his musical career. He almost cried when I told him that Turkish people care about him. He sent me a Dutar (a musical instrument of ethnic groups living in Xinjiang) as a gift, which I like very much," Karakas said.

In response to questions on whether Uygurs are happy, Heyit said that he is satisfied with his current life and the Uygur group is one of the 56 ethnic groups in China. All groups are equal and should unite firmly together, Heyit was quoted by Karakas as saying in one of his stories.

Karakas published his interview with Heyit on Milliyet, and the story was widely reposted by many online media in Turkey. "This is a successful news report and I am happy about that," he said.

Effective method

Aside from visiting Heyit, Karakas and the other Turkish reporter, Tunc Akkoç, Chairman of the Aydınlık Newspaper, the oldest newspaper in Turkey, also visited vocational education and training centers during their stay in Xinjiang.

"We visited the training centers freely," Akkoç told the Global Times. "There was no limitation, supervision or any intervention from the officials. I randomly entered all the rooms, went down to each corridor in the buildings, went to every student I wanted to chat with and asked questions to anyone I wanted. I had the chance to have a one-to-one conversation with nearly 50 students."

During their visit to a training center in Wushi County in Aksu Prefecture, Akkoç met a trainee named Patimaguli Yisilamu, whose story was enlightening.

"She was forced to work for an Uygur gang and steal for them when she was 13 years old. Later, she was forced into two religious marriages and was infused with the idea that Uygurs are Muslims and Han people are heretic," Akkoç said.

Reports about Xinjiang on Turkish media

"I learned standard Chinese and Uygur here. And I can tell the difference between what is legal and what is illegal. I learned how to protect my rights based on laws," Patimaguli was quoted as saying.

Akkoç said that the trainees talked to him sincerely and no one seemed under any pressure. "Because I looked into the eyes of young people and talked to them together with other reporters. If they are telling lies, we would have known it," he said.

Akkoç also visited the house of a trainee who graduated from a training center in Moyu.

Abuduwaili Abuduhewaier used to spread extremist videos and banned his wife from working outside.

"I was an admirer of killing every day and imagined killing ... After studying in the training centers, I learned every trainee's story and was shocked. My mind has gradually changed ... I now know religious extremism is so wrong," Abuduwaili was quoted by Akkoç as saying in his story.

Abuduwaili's wife Minawaier told Akkoç that she is happy her husband could learn laws and vocational skills in the center. They both now have jobs, and she wants to thank the local government.

Akkoç said that he learned that before being enrolled in the training centers, young people used to beat their wives, prevented women from working, refused to send their daughters to school and spread hatred among different ethnic groups.

The centers offered hope for these trainees, he believed. "They want to use the vocational skills learned from the training centers to make a living," Akkoç said.

He described the trainees about to graduate as modern people closely connected to their country and laws, respectful of other ethnic groups and with the skills to make a living.

"What happened in Xinjiang in recent years is actually a modernization breakthrough," Akkoç said. "Training centers are an important part of this ... The regional government seeks ways to remove the root of extremism."

"It's not only about getting rid of flies, but also about drying the swamp."

Akkoç said China set an example to the world in fighting terrorism and extremism.

The training centers in Xinjiang have become a typical example of how to motivate people and an energy that drives economic development and employment, Akkoç wrote in his stories, noting that there were 1.4 million new jobs in Xinjiang from 2016 to 2018.

Changed attitude

Aside from clarifying rumors, visits to Xinjiang also helped Turkish reporters to change previous bias toward China's Xinjiang policies.

"I saw Xinjiang as a place with high technology. Walking in the streets in Xinjiang, we can feel local residents live a stable and happy life. What impressed me most is that many Uygurs dance in the streets at night and they were happy as they like," Karakas said.

He noted that there are rumors in Turkey about Uygurs having no freedom and being unable to use their own language.

"Uygurs living in Xinjiang can use their language and no one has been told not to use it. Their life in Xinjiang is opposite to what some Western media described. They can open their shops and do what they like," Karakas said.

Aside from clarifying rumors on "Heyit being tortured to death," Karakas said that his visit to Xinjiang also helped him change his bias toward the region.

Karakas and Akkoç are not the only two Turkish reporters who have come to Xinjiang and recognized the regional government's de-radicalization efforts.

Şerif Egemen Ahmet, an editor with the Star Newspaper in Turkey, came to China from June 11 to 20 in 2019. His visit to Xinjiang has also changed his previous impression of the place.

"Xinjiang was an unknown place for me. I thought that there was massive oppression of Uygurs in Xinjiang and we couldn't be safe when we went to Urumqi ... these false charges came from Western media's fake news," Ahmet said.

Ahmet went to Urumqi and Hami. Instead of seeing any "oppression" of the Uygurs, he saw local people were free to go to mosques. One Uygur man he met said the mosques are crowded for Friday prayers.

During a trip to the Islamic Institute of Xinjiang, Ahmet met "brilliant students" and told the Global Times that China gives religious freedom to its people and sends students to overseas universities to become "well-supported religious imams who know Arabic."

Ahmet was also impressed by Urumqi's social and economic development. The city is well-planned and very clean. What he saw in Xinjiang was quite different from what he had heard.

Akkoç was also optimistic about Xinjiang's future development, more investment coming to Xinjiang and the per capita income increasing.

"China can change this situation by strengthening cooperation with international media outlets. Western hegemony in the field of media can thus be overcome."

Unfortunately, "Turkish people are under the influence of Western media manipulation on the Xinjiang issue ... We know that all negative news in Western media is baseless," Ahmet said.

Ahmet noted that the main sources of fake news about Xinjiang come from separatist groups living in Turkey since 1970s. They have foundations and associations.

Ahmet also mentioned that Turkish President Erdogan's last visit to China was very important to China-Turkey relations, as the president said people in Xinjiang are happy.

"But it's not enough to clear up the misunderstanding of Turkish people," he said, noting that more true stories about China's Xinjiang should be told to change people's impression.

Akkoç said that Turkey and the international community do not have enough information about the historical development of China.

Xinjiang is in a strategic position for the Belt and Road Initiative, which will bring peace to the world, Akkoç said.

True stories about Xinjiang should be told in Turkey as it would benefit the China-Turkey ties, he believed.

Turkey's Foreign Ministry said that a delegation is expected to visit China's Xinjiang, Associated Press reported.

Indonesian Muslim group upholds Xinjiang condition

By Xie Wenting | Aug 23, 2019

China's Xinjiang issue is a separatist one, rather than religious, Said Aqil Siradj, chairman of Nahdlatul Ulama (NU), the largest Muslim organization in Indonesia, told the Global Times in an exclusive interview.

"China's religion policy is more democratic than other Muslim countries, even our country, Indonesia," Siradj told the Global Times. "You can see this from Article 36 in China's Constitution and the white paper of China's policies and practices on protecting freedom of religious belief."

Hoping to inform more Indonesian people about Islam in China as well as the real situation in Northwest China's Xinjiang Uygur Autonomous Region, which has been twisted by some Western countries, NU released a book titled *Indonesian Muslims' China Studies* last month, which details what the organization members have seen and experienced in China.

This is the first book in the world that systematically introduces the development and real situation of Islam in China, Siradj said. He hopes the book will change "the negative perceptions of a small group of Indonesian Muslims."

NU, which enjoys more than 90 years of history, has about 40 million members. Former Indonesian president Abdurrahman Wahid once was chairman of NU.

According to Siradj, 23 members from NU wrote this book together which includes their personal experiences and research. He noted that the idea of penning this book came naturally as they wanted to share the truth they have seen.

The organization's members have frequently paid visits to China over the past few years, particularly to places that boast a rich Islamic culture and heritage. They also met with Chinese Islamic scholars to share their experiences during the trips. "We found they are treated by the [Chinese] government very well," he said.

He noted that, after visiting China, he found the Western narrative that "Islam is suppressed in China" could not hold water. "Our finding is Islam is growing in China. They live in peace with other Chinese people and they receive support from the government, such as building mosques, schools and offices."

He added that it's easy for Muslims in China to practice their religion.

During their stay in China, they once joined the Friday prayers in an old mosque with a capacity of 20,000 people. As too many people participated in the prayers that day, some even went outside to pray, according to Siradj.

Western media have said that the government of Indonesia, the country that hosts the largest Muslim population in the world, remains silent on the issue of China's Xinjiang policies. Siradj believes the opinions of the NU can represent the majority of Indonesian Muslims. Siradj has said in previous media reports that Xinjiang is very good and safe, and there is no need for the Indonesian government to interfere.

Geneva-based envoys get clearer picture of China's policy in Xinjiang during visit

By Song Shengxia and Bai Yunyi in Urumqi and Liu Xin in Beijing | Sep 3, 2019

Shaking hands firmly with Maihemutijiang Musha, a graduate of a vocational education and training center in Xinjiang, Ali Mohamed Saeed Majawar, a Yemen envoy to the UN in Geneva, said, "I am so happy to see you back on the right path. I hope you could be a role model for other young people, and that they could learn from you."

Maihemutijiang smiled as he thanked the visiting envoy, who recently headed a delegation of diplomats from eight countries to the United Nations Office at Geneva (UNOG) to Northwest China's Xinjiang Uygur Autonomous Region at the invitation of the Chinese Foreign Ministry.

Geneva-based envoys from Yemen, Equatorial Guinea, Mozambique, Zambia, Côte d'Ivoire, South Africa, Ethiopia and Zimbabwe wrapped up their five-day tour to Xinjiang on September 1, 2019, visiting a counter-terrorism exhibition, training centers, communities, mosques, bazaars, kindergartens, cultural heritage sites and

Foreign envoys to the United Nations Office at Geneva dance with local residents at a square in Urumqi, Northwest China's Xinjiang Uygur Autonomous Region on August 28, 2019. (Photo: Song Shengxia / GT)

industrial parks in Urumqi, Hotan and Kashi.

They talked to trainees at training centers in Hotan and Kashi and Maihemutijiang, the Kashi center graduate.

The 25-year-old newlywed was trained in the Kashi center in 2018 after he was found visiting illegal websites where he downloaded and spread video and audio which promote extremism and terrorism. Influenced by extremism, he became aggressive, arrogant and ready to pick fights with non-Muslims, forcing them to pray.

His father described him as a "wild horse" who was out of control and used to wander on the streets for a few days, reluctant to go home. He refused to eat food cooked by his mother because he thought it was not halal.

After 10 months of training at the center, where he learned vocational skills such as machine repairing, interior design and sewing, he landed a job at a local plastic steel window and door factory, earning over 3,000 yuan ($419) a month. He met his wife at work and got married two weeks ago.

"The training center reshaped my life. Now I live a new life. It is like being reborn," the young man said to the group of visiting diplomats.

Consensus and awareness

Vocational training is an effective way to help young people get work and help fight poverty and extremism, which breed terrorism. China's experience in the vocational education and training center in Xinjiang has been very successful and is worth learning by countries seeking to de-radicalize and fight terrorism, said Majawar, Permanent Representative of Yemen to the UNOG.

I believe the Chinese government should continue its efforts, and has the full right to conduct vocational training and re-education, Majawar said through an interpreter.

Majawar is not alone among the visiting delegates in this view.

Martha Lungu Mwitumwa, Permanent Representative of Zambia to the UNOG, choked through tears and needed a few minutes before she could gather herself to speak after viewing the exhibition on major terrorist cases in Xinjiang at the Xinjiang International Convention and Exhibition Center in Urumqi.

"I feel heartbroken to see how innocent people were killed for no apparent reason. Even the young ones and children were targeted," she said after seeing the pictures of blood and torn flesh of victims, and displays of weapons that terrorists used to commit terror acts which were once rampant in Xinjiang.

"We are here and have seen for ourselves. I am happy to hear that in the past two years, this has not been happening. The government has taken control of the situation and [prevented the spread of terrorism]," Mwitumwa said.

In July 2019, 50 ambassadors to the UNOG signed a letter to the president of the UN Human Rights Council and the UN High Commissioner for Human Rights, voicing their support for China's position on issues related to Xinjiang. Yemen and Zambia are among the 50 countries that signed the letter.

The letter is believed by observers to be a direct response to a letter from some Western countries criticizing China on the issue.

While some Western countries blinded by ideological biases chose to oppose China for the sake of "opposing China" on Xinjiang-related issues at UN Human Rights Council sessions, other countries, especially those from the developing world free from ideological biases, recognize and understand the practices and initiatives China has implemented in Xinjiang, especially after they visited the region, observers said.

It is those countries that are willing to speak for and defend China on its Xinjiang policy, they noted.

"From what we have seen, the training centers are a good initiative, because they are helping the youth, and even the elderly, settle into society," Mwitumwa said.

"Instead of getting involved in evil practices such as terrorism, they will concentrate on business rather than go to the street to kill people. After graduating, they can set up businesses, which will empower their families as well," Mwitumwa said.

Mwitumwa added that she will bring back to Geneva what she saw in Xinjiang and all the stories she heard.

Nelia Barnard, Deputy Permanent Representative of South Africa to the UNOG, who had never been to Xinjiang, told the Global Times, "What I have been exposed to and have witnessed [in this trip] are quite positive. You can see genuine efforts to improve the social, economic and cultural environment of the people here."

Amadeu Paulo Samuel Da Conceicao, Permanent Representative of Mozambique to the UNOG, said in Mozambique, people are aware of what violence

Foreign envoys talk to Maihemutijiang Musha, a vocational education and training center graduate in Xinjiang, and his family at his home on August 31, 2019. (Photo: Song Shengxia / GT)

has brought to innocent people. The visit to the counter-terrorism exhibition in Urumqi reminded him of similar incidents in his country.

At the UN Human Rights Council sessions, he noticed that some Western countries had no clear idea of China's efforts and achievements in Xinjiang. Perhaps they may have some vague idea of what is happening in Xinjiang, but they don't want to speak out and are unwilling to recognize China's efforts, Conceicao said.

Petty tricks in Geneva

The UN Human Rights Council Universal Periodic Review (UPR) mechanism aims to review how well UN member states fulfill their duties and commitments on human rights on a regular basis. In March, China completed its 3rd UN Human Rights Council UPR process, which started in November 2018.

"The impression I got from [what I heard] about Xinjiang in Geneva was Xinjiang was a prison, and people were being manipulated. After seeing the situation, I don't believe what I heard in Geneva," Mwitumwa said.

The information Mwitumwa received about Xinjiang in Geneva only mirrors part of the smear tactics of some Western countries to impose their ideological biases against China's policy in Xinjiang, observers said.

Zuliyati Simayi, a professor at Xinjiang University and a member of the China Society for Human Rights Studies, who attended the review process in Geneva in November, told the Global Times that Western countries usually push NGOs to confront China.

"Given China's international influence, some countries do not want to openly offend China by slandering China's policy in Xinjiang at the UN review sessions. But they would do petty things behind your back, such as using some NGO as their mouthpiece against China," Zuliyati said.

"These NGOs use harsh rhetoric to criticize China under the guise of human rights protection. They appear to value independence but their rhetoric is full of speculations and sentimental judgment," Zuliyati said.

Zhang Yonghe, executive dean of the Human Rights Institute of Southwest University of Political Science and Law in Chongqing, who also attended the November review sessions in 2018, told the Global Times that the US backs many NGOs.

Although the US withdrew from the UN Human Rights Council, it still attempts to turn the UN Human Rights Council sessions into an international stage to confront and antagonize China through either its Western allies or various organizations.

Another trick that the West uses against China during the review sessions is to instigate "East Turkistan" terrorist groups to gather outside the meeting venue to exert pressure on review meetings.

Zhang recalled that in a November session meeting, some "East Turkistan" terrorist groups staged a rally outside the Palace of Nations Square and caused a commotion outside to influence the meeting. Some deliberately approached the Chinese delegates or scholars, took photos of them, attempting to trap them and to make a big scene if the Chinese side prevented them from doing so.

To deal with these dirty tricks, China is neither humble nor pushy but uses detailed data and evidence to convince and win over more countries and organizations, Zhang said.

"During our exchanges with the Jeddah-based Organization of Islamic Cooperation, they finally prolonged the scheduled 40-minute meeting to two hours. Later, they admitted that the source they previously relied on to get information about Xinjiang was one-sided, mainly from Western media," Zhang said.

Seeing is believing

Back at Kashi's training center, the foreign envoys and reporters talked freely to the trainees through their interpreter.

Mairiyemuguli Aili, a female trainee, said coming to the center was the "best choice" in her life. Her eyes became misty when she said this.

She came to the center because she read and spread books that contain content inciting extremism.

Affected by extremism, Mairiyemuguli smashed the TV and radio at home and even swore at her mother because she thought her mother was a heretic. But she is a changed woman after receiving training at the center. Mairiyemuguli wanted to become an electrician after graduating to help her father with his repair shop.

"Xinjiang is still a hot topic in Geneva. But vicious speculations and misleading reports on China's Xinjiang policy are waning, as some countries are convinced the vocational education and training centers in Xinjiang are a feasible and effective way to de-radicalize," Zuliyati said.

That's also because China is more open and willing to invite foreign envoys and media to Xinjiang, Zuliyati said.

"We have seen no problems in Xinjiang, no violation of human rights or freedom of religious belief. I believe officials from any country who have come here must admit it," said Lazaro Ekua Avomo, Permanent Representative of Equatorial Guinea to the UNOG.

"Seeing is believing. For us, we believe what we saw. The Chinese government should continue to inform people of what is happening in Xinjiang. It should continue to talk and let its voice be heard until everyone hears and understands," Mwitumwa said.

International community visits Xinjiang to dispel Western bias against region

By Xie Wenting and Bai Yunyi in Urumqi | Sep 6, 2019

Xinjiang, as a core area of the Silk Road Economic Belt, is enjoying the best period of prosperity and development in its history under the Belt and Road Initiative, which is undoubtedly the biggest achievement in the region's fight against terrorism as well as the best answer to the protection of human rights in China, a senior Chinese official said.

Jiang Jianguo, vice minister of the Publicity Department of the Central Committee of the Communist Party of China (CPC), said that in the fight against terrorism and extremism, Northwest China's Xinjiang Uygur Autonomous Region had set up vocational education and training centers in accordance with the law to eliminate terrorism and religious extremism, and that these centers are a "useful experience," all about the "protection of human rights." These comments were made at the opening ceremony of the International Seminar on Counter-Terrorism, De-radicalization and Human Rights Protection on September 6, 2019.

Jiang noted that the fight against terrorism and extremism is a shared responsibility of the international community. He called on the international community to build consensus and make greater efforts to this process.

Scholars and experts from 17 countries, including China, Serbia, Sri Lanka, France, Italy and Pakistan as well as a representative from UN Human Rights Council participated in the seminar on September 6, 2019, where they shared thoughts and experiences concerning the fight against terrorism and religious extremism, as the threat of terrorism and extremism intensifies worldwide.

Christian Mestre, a professor at the University of Strasbourg in France, told the Global Times that his visit to Xinjiang to attend the seminar was a "discovery" trip.

After seeing what the government has done in Xinjiang to counter terrorism, Mestre hoped that "France and other European countries could take the answers given by Xinjiang."

Opposing double standards

Shohrat Zakir, Chairman of the Xinjiang Uygur Autonomous Region, said on December 6, 2019 that for nearly three years there has not been a single case of terrorist crime, nor have there been underground preaching activities that illegally spread religious-extremist ideas. Criminal and public security cases have also dropped significantly in number.

Statistics showed that at least 1,127 terrorist attacks occurred worldwide in 2018 alone, causing the deaths of more than 13,000 people and incalculable property damage.

Before the seminar on September 6, 2019, experts and scholars visited a counter-terrorism exhibition in Urumqi and a vocational education and training center in Kashi, southern Xinjiang, where they were able to receive first-hand knowledge about the counter-terrorism efforts in Xinjiang.

Predrag Markovic, director of the Institute for Contemporary History in Serbia and vice president of the Socialist Party of Serbia, told the Global Times that "Some Western countries criticize China for the counter-terrorism policies in Xinjiang, but let us ask what the US would do if hundreds of Americans die in terrorist attacks? We already have the answer: they scorched two or three countries."

He noted that China has a peaceful policy of educating and employing people. "They are building a new society (to counter terrorism), said Markovic.

Markovic stressed at the seminar that the US has coercively introduced "human rights" in many countries.

"The noble concept of human rights is often misused as a tool for an imperialist struggle for global domination. In the West, many scholars and politicians have tried to monopolize the concept of human rights," he said.

"Whenever the human rights concept clashed with some American interests, they tended to forget this praiseworthy principle," he said.

"In the struggle for human rights and against terrorism we do not need commands from a single headquarter in Washington DC. We need a mutual support from equal brothers in arms," he said at the seminar.

An example for the world

Jiang listed four principles in the global fight against terrorism and extremism. The first is to uphold common standards and oppose double standards; the second is to take measures according to local conditions on the basis of international law; the third is to protect human rights; and the fourth is to uphold unity and cooperation.

Shu Hongshui, deputy dean of Anti-terrorism Law Department at the Northwest University of Political Science and Law, told the Global Times that China had chosen to host a seminar at this time partly because China has made outstanding achievements in the counter-terrorism and de-radicalization efforts in Xinjiang. "Also, it's a response to some misunderstandings and attacks from abroad. This move could win more support from the international community as we are providing 'China lessons' for the global counter-terrorism and de-radicalization work," Shu said.

Yalini Saranya, program officer at Bandaranaike Center for International Studies in Sri Lanka, told the Global Times that the vocational education and training center is a good model and mechanism to combat terrorism. "It can be a good lesson for Sri Lanka to learn from China, as we have [been struggling for] so many years to counter terrorism, but it doesn't work perfectly," she said.

After visiting a vocational education and training center in Kashi, Saranya told the Global Times that, "I don't think there is any violation of human rights here, because I see all the students enjoying themselves; they are not upset at all."

"And when they graduate from the center, they will be offered jobs by many companies. I think it's also a good thing for the economic growth," she added.

Compared with other countries, "China's counter-terrorism act is set as the best example," she said.

French professor praises China's de-radicalization measures in Xinjiang

By Xie Wenting | Sep 10, 2019

Christian Mestre closely examined every site he visited in Xinjiang, listening carefully to the guide's explanations so that he could catch every piece of useful information about counter-terrorism measures.

It was the first time that Mestre, a professor at the University of Strasbourg in

The director of Xinjiang Islamic Institute in Urumqi, Northwest China's Xinjiang Uygur Autonomous Region, briefs foreign experts on the general situation of the institute on September 4, 2019. (Photo: Xie Wenting / GT)

France, visited Northwest China's Xinjiang Uygur Autonomous Region. However, he was not in Xinjiang as a tourist, but to participate in the International Seminar on Counter-Terrorism, De-radicalization and Human Rights Protection with experts from other countries in September 2019.

Mestre told the Global Times that the threat of terrorism is "very serious" in his own country and an extremely urgent issue. After spending several days in Xinjiang to visit the counter-terrorism exhibition, Xinjiang Islamic Institute in Urumqi and a vocational education and training center in Kashi, southern Xinjiang, Mestre said he hoped some methods taken by China in counter-terrorism and de-radicalization can be adopted by France and other European countries haunted by terrorism.

"We have many issues concerning the treatment of terrorism and the fight against terrorists. And I think there are some answers given by the Xinjiang government for education and avoiding the strengthening of terrorism," he told the Global Times. "I hope that France and other European countries (haunted by terrorism) could take the answers given by Xinjiang."

He also called for cooperation between European countries and China to stop terrorism.

Journey of discovery

According to Mestre, his trip to Xinjiang was more like a "discovery." After visiting Xinjiang Islamic Institute where imams are trained, he was full of high praise.

"There is a large debate in France concerning the [training] formation of imams. You gave a very good answer concerning it because its formation is organized by the state and with some courses concerning the law, the Constitution and many things. And I think it's a very good example and I hope that in France we could take the pattern of your model of formation," he told the Global Times.

"It's a very fine and very clever answer concerning all the matters of religious extremism," he added.

After visiting the imam's school in Urumqi, Mestre later visited the vocational education and training center in Kashi, where he got a chance to have close interactions with the trainees there.

"It's better to give education and the training for all people who are near terrorism and are victims of terrorism and help them get out from this very dreadful situation," he said, sharing his thoughts on the vocational education and training center.

According to Mestre, the measures used to bring these people back into society are very good and can serve as "a source of inspiration" for France or other European countries. "I think (this is) the right and good solution for this kind of religious extremism and terrorism," he noted.

Residents and visitors dance happily in China's Xinjiang Uygur Autonomous Region. (Photo: Cui Meng/GT)

Mestre also pays close attention to the issue of internet terrorism, as many young people watch a great deal of online videos.

In the Kashi center, many young people confessed that they had been misguided by videos spreading religious extremism and terrorism. In the center, they are taught to avoid these poisonous videos, which Mestre believed is both important and useful.

Effective methods

Mestre noted to the Global Times that French people who are suffering from terrorism want effective measures. "They want to be protected and to have the feeling that they are protected."

"I think we have need for security," he said, dismissing the accusation that China's methods violate human rights.

"I think in this kind of period, it's more important to ensure the protection of all citizens than to defend individual freedom," he stressed.

According to Mestre, there is a balance being maintained, as these people are not in jail, but being put through compulsory training. "In France, we have no such education program," he said, adding that France should learn from this model.

"The education for all people including young people and elderly people is a very good thing," he said.

Mestre told the Global Times that it's essential for a country to protect its people when there is a terrorist problem.

"You could take some measures, some rules for ensuring this protection. And for that, I think it's necessary to restrict in a short period, not definitively, some freedom, not all the freedom," he said.

In France, he said some special rules and laws are put in place when an emergency situation arises. "But I think it is not sufficient. I think it's necessary to increase some control against part of the population, because we know that some part of the population is very receptive to some kind of ideas and are very interested by the war [in the Middle East]. And they are very interested in the messages of jihad. I think for these people, some measures are necessary."

He said that France is generally very reluctant to propose these kinds of restrictive measures.

Mestre hoped that more French politicians can find out and understand how China fights against terrorism and religious extremism in Xinjiang.

Mestre summarized at the seminar that the fight against terrorism and religious extremism is focused on six main targets: combating the financing of terrorism by tracking the suspicious movements of funds; fighting terrorist propaganda, particularly on the internet; the implementation of de-radicalization programs in certain areas like prisons; the implementation of de-radicalization and rehabilitation programs; the creation of general structures for training police; and finally the implementation of State education programs to prevent radicalization, mainly by rallying young people to share the State's values and society's principles.

"On all of them, the State put in force many actions and ran several programs, so we had to acknowledge the Chinese policy to be one of the most developed and efficient, particularly in preventative actions," he said.

EDITORIALS

Chapter IV

UNMASKING SOME WESTERN MEDIA'S LIES

When Western people attack Xinjiang's governance, do they really care about human rights? People like US Senator Marco Rubio don't. For such politicians, it's their routine to attack China. They eagerly want to interfere in Xinjiang. Other Westerners don't understand Xinjiang. Their opinions are shallow and misled by the Western media.

Practice is the sole criterion for testing truth. The fact that Xinjiang is getting better speaks louder than all the West's preaching. Criticism from Western public opinion cannot overwhelm governance in Xinjiang. Today's governance in Xinjiang is correct, and has brought tangible benefits to local people. In the name of justice, the West has attacked the training centers which have made significant contributions to reversing the situation in Xinjiang. West's attacks can only prove their dogmatism and hypocrisy.

Turkey in no position to judge Xinjiang

Global Times | Feb 11, 2019

A Turkish foreign ministry spokesperson released a statement on February 9, 2019, accusing China of reintroducing "internment camps" into the Xinjiang Uygur Autonomous Region. The statement took the Western media's exaggerated reports for granted, declaring that Uygur people "incurring arbitrary arrests are subjected to torture." Turkey is capricious and shallow on the Xinjiang question and many Chinese people again feel disappointed at Turkey.

Xinjiang's situation is extremely complicated. The region used to be haunted by violence and terrorism which was almost out of control. Thus Xinjiang was forced to adopt severer governance practices. Officials and the ordinary people of all of Xinjiang's ethnic groups have made great efforts and brought about a fundamental turn for the better. Xinjiang has avoided the fate of becoming a second Chechnya.

Xinjiang's education and training centers, as effective temporary measures, can help eliminate extremism. The centers are the least costly way to make the region stable and avoid war and upheaval. People can have various opinions on Xinjiang's governance, but maliciously attacking China's efforts is not honorable.

As Western people are attacking Xinjiang's governance, do they really care about human rights? At least people like US Senator Marco Rubio don't. For such politicians, it's their routine to attack China. They eagerly want to disturb Xinjiang's condition. Other Westerners don't understand Xinjiang. Their opinions are shallow and misled by the Western media.

Developing countries understand that the affairs of each country and region are complicated in their own ways. Thus they refuse to follow the West on the Xinjiang question. Turkey has a Pan-Turkism complex and always makes irresponsible remarks on Xinjiang. But since Turkey's failed coup in 2016, the country's relations with the West have become estranged. Turkey's attitude on the Xinjiang question has been more restrained.

The statement by the Turkish foreign ministry can be seen as Turkey's sway in Xinjiang-related matters. It may also be viewed as a move by the Turkish government to win right-wing voters in the local elections scheduled in March 2019. It is too early to say that there is a major shift in Turkey's China policy. Ankara needs Beijing's support strategically, and this trend has not changed.

Turkey has no grounds to point an accusing finger at China's domestic affairs. Ankara is no saint toward the Kurds or in the purge following the 2016 coup attempt if judged by Western standards of human rights. It should not follow the Western tune to intervene in China's Xinjiang affairs.

It is worth pointing out that it was the Turkish foreign ministry spokesperson that made the statement. The one who accused China after the July 5 incident in Xinjiang was once a Turkish leader. If Turkey makes no more interference after this statement, China does not need to pay too much attention to it.

After all, a statement by the Turkish foreign ministry will not have any real impact on China's Xinjiang governance. The sway of Turkey will only make the Chinese public feel that the country's diplomacy is immature. If Turkey wants to develop long-term cooperation with China, it needs the support of the Chinese public.

To stabilize Xinjiang is the core matter of Xinjiang governance, no matter what the outside world says. A prosperous and dynamic Xinjiang is the best answer to external accusations.

Western pressure has no effect on China's governance in Xinjiang

Global Times | Mar 21, 2019

Northwest China's Xinjiang Uygur Autonomous Region has always been a hot topic in the West. US media outlet *The Atlantic* even dug out a past incident of 22 Uygur prisoners in detention at Guantanamo Bay and speculated about the reason. Interestingly, Sweden announced it would grant refugee status to Uygur Muslim asylum-seekers from China. Police officers in this very country dumped two Chinese seniors in a chilly suburb late at night in September 2018, but now the nation is showing its sympathy.

Western society's rightist tendency in dealing with Muslims and immigrants is increasingly apparent, made manifest in the rise of white supremacy. New Zealand's mosque shooting is an example. Meanwhile, the West is eyeing China's Xinjiang governance, portraying anti-extremist governance activities as persecution of Muslims.

Western media claimed some innocent Uygur Muslims were persecuted to death at the vocational training centers in Xinjiang, or "concentration camps" in Western rhetoric. However no evidence has been provided to support their allegation. But 50 Muslims were truly gunned down by a white supremacist in New Zealand mosques. Although the gunman is from Australia, he represents the ultra-right ideology spreading fast in the West.

The West is good at argument. While it squeezes out Muslim immigrants, it hypocritically supports Muslims in China protesting against the government. Western elites never admit their values are confusing, but are narcissistic in their behavior.

Despite loud noises from the Western propaganda machine, the accusations have had little real effect. The stories fabricated by Western media and claims they made have amounted to nothing more than a bubble.

This round of media attacks by Western public opinion has not affected governance in Xinjiang. Officials and ordinary people in Xinjiang won't let Western voices influence their judgment or predict the future situation.

Western opinion has a limited influence in the Islamic world. Only Turkey under Pan-Turkism has made statements that intervene in the situation of Xinjiang. No other Muslim countries have followed the lead of the West. The Xinjiang problem is largely an issue created by a few Western countries with their media organizations and a small number of lawmakers that hold an aggressive anti-China stance.

The West failed in pressuring China through the UN Human Rights Council. The West has suffered repeated defeats regarding Xinjiang but still keeps trying. The foreign media has reported that China has invited Western diplomats to visit Xinjiang. At least two Western reporter delegations have visited the vocational education and training centers. China has not refused communication with the West, a reflection of China's magnanimity and self-confidence.

Most importantly, China's governance in Xinjiang is practical and realistic. The country is sincere in helping people influenced by extremism. By contrast, some Western forces, driven by geopolitical factors, attacked China's governance in Xinjiang.

But good prevails over evil. These forces can do nothing about Xinjiang even if they play all their cards.

China on the right track in tackling terrorism and extremism

Global Times | Jul 14, 2019

The government of 37 countries, including Saudi Arabia and Russia, sent a joint letter to the UN showing their clear-cut support to China's policy in its Xinjiang Uygur Autonomous Region. This is a direct response to the 22 developed countries' open letter in which they criticized China's policy in Xinjiang. In comparison to the 22 countries' governments, which only represent the West, these 37 countries are much more representative.

According to reports, the 37 countries opposed politicizing human rights in their joint letter to the UN Human Rights Council, saying that China has made "remarkable achievements in the field of human rights." "Faced with the grave challenge of terrorism and extremism, China has undertaken a series of counter-terrorism and de-radicalization measures in Xinjiang, including setting up vocational education and training centers," the letter said. "The past three consecutive years have seen not a single terrorist attack in Xinjiang and people there enjoy a stronger sense of happiness, fulfillment, and security," the letter stated.

Besides Saudi Arabia and Russia, the envoys of many African countries, North Korea, Venezuela, Cuba, Belarus, Myanmar, the Philippines, Syria, Pakistan, Oman, Kuwait, and other countries also signed the joint letter.

As we can see, these countries belong to different regions including Asia, Africa, Europe, and South America; they belong to different religious cultures including Islam, Christianity, Buddhism; they are all developing countries with different situation of economic development. The population of these 37 countries in total is almost three times of the 22 countries' total population. These 37 countries represent a wider part of the world no matter in the territorial area, population scale or cultural diversity.

Accordingly, their voices are more objective and fair. But due to the suppression of the West's dominant discourse power, their voices have not managed to grab enough attention in the world.

What's worth mentioning is that many are Islamic countries out of those 37. If they do not believe China's efforts in anti-terrorism are sincere, and if they are not aware that the so-called persecution does not exist in Xinjiang, these Islamic countries won't step forward and support China's Xinjiang policy.

Many developing countries, including these Islamic nations, clearly know the consequence of terrorism, extremism, and separatism. That's why they can think from China's position, really understand Chinese governance in Xinjiang and support China's policies. Some Western elites, full of moral arrogance, are far from understanding reality in Xinjiang. Their moral superiority is ridiculous.

The West has played a role in the spread of extremism worldwide, but currently, non-Western countries are the main victims. Extremism and terrorism are the whole world's enemies. China's governance in Xinjiang is of great value to anti-terrorism and de-extremism, and it has been proven effective. This should be praised instead of being criticized.

The West can't ignore the diversity of the world just because it is more developed economically. In face of thc open letter signed by 37 countries, those 22 governments that criticized policies in Xinjiang should be aware that they are only a small part of the world.

White paper sets Xinjiang facts straight

Global Times | Jul 21, 2019

The State Council Information Office published on July 21, 2019 a white paper, clarifying certain misunderstandings about Xinjiang's ethnic, religious, cultural and historical issues in the international community. With the paper, kind-hearted people can distinguish between right and wrong. It is hoped malicious agitators will zip their lip.

Xinjiang has officially been a part of the Chinese territory since the Han Dynasty (206 BC–AD 220). Xinjiang has never been the so-called "East Turkistan." And Uygur people, although speaking Turkic, are not descendants of the Turks.

Economic ties between Xinjiang and the inland region had existed in the Shang Dynasty (1600 BC–1046 BC). After the Qing Dynasty (1644–1911) crushed the rebellion by the Junggar tribe in Xinjiang in 1758, China's boundary in northwest has been demarcated. As for the region's economic achievements 70 years after its peaceful liberation in 1949, anyone without prejudice will understand it if they visit the region.

Some people in the US and the West have launched systematic attacks on China's governance in Xinjiang in recent years. Some have invented an absurd logic: China is "persecuting" the entire Uygur ethnic group simply because the terrorists we are fighting against are Uygurs; China is "cracking down" on the entire Islamic religion because those extremists have such a religious belief. They have even hyped that China is going to wipe out the Uygur culture.

The Xinjiang Uygur Autonomous Region and the whole country have tried their best to dilute ethnic and religious factors in their fight against terrorism and de-radicalization efforts. Media reports in China have always avoided mentioning relevant ethnic group and religion

Our firm policy at the grass-roots level is to isolate a few terrorists and extremists who are determined to confront the country's rule of law, to unite the people of all ethnic groups, and to treat the believers of all legitimate religions well.

However, some in the West have attempted to put vicious labels on the above-mentioned policy in Xinjiang, distorting the fights against terrorism and extremism as "persecution" on certain ethnic group and religion.

The white paper helps people clearly see the development of Xinjiang as a multi-ethnic region and understand the significance of upholding ethnic unity and religious harmony for the well-being of all ethnic groups in the region. Extremism, the common enemy of Xinjiang's people of all ethnic groups, must be stripped out and resolutely eradicated. This is where their common interests lie.

Openness, diversity and beauty have flowed in Uygur people's veins after long-term migration and integration. Supported by some Western forces, a handful of terrorists and extremists in exile have attempted to kidnap the Uygur ethnic group, risking the entire ethnic group as a bargaining chip for certain forces in the US and the West, in a bid to achieve their own crazy goals. The vast majority of Uygur people will never respond to such conspiracy, and the entire Chinese nation will never allow such a plot to have its way.

Some in the US and the West believe it can disarrange Xinjiang by supporting the terrorists and can put pressure on China's efforts to counter terrorism and extremism. But the situation has let them down. Xinjiang is getting better. Its economic and social development is back on track. Extremism has been hit hard and is hated by everyone.

China's governance in Xinjiang has re-established peace and tranquility and benefitted people of all ethnic groups. Islamic countries worldwide understand Xinjiang and thus show their support. With strong discourse power, the West has passed their opposition off as the world's voice. In fact, they have already fallen into isolation on the Xinjiang question.

The US and the West are the true instigators of many disputes within the Islamic world. This is the consensus of over one billion Muslims around the world. US wars against terrorism have vented hostility towards Muslims. The Muslim travel ban issued by the US in 2017 strongly discriminates against Muslims. Despite a few elites on the fringes of mainstream American and Western societies, the vast majority of Muslim immigrants are subject to discrimination in Western societies. The most prominent religious and racial contradiction in the world is undoubtedly between the West and the vast majority of the Islamic world.

Some people in the West are trying to hype the Xinjiang question. One of their vicious intentions is to divert and dilute the contradiction between the US and the Islamic world. Their plots are doomed to fail.

Human rights concept needs to be redefined

Global Times | Jul 27, 2019

As of 6 pm on July 26, 2019, 50 ambassadors to the UN at Geneva (UNOG) had signed a letter written to the president of the UN Human Rights Council (HRC) and the Office of UN High Commissioner for Human Rights (OHCHR) to voice their support for China's governance in its northwest Xinjiang Uygur Autonomous Region.

Compared to the 22 developed countries that accused China's policy in Xinjiang, the ratio of 50 to 22 has shown what real human rights are about and the consensus of the international society on the issue. In the sphere of human rights affairs where the Western voices are echoed, the "silent majority" finally has voiced its opinion. The collectively signed letter has brought down the West from the position of so-called "human rights adjudicator."

China has pragmatically developed economy, improved living standard and social stability. In recent years, the Chinese government has taken measures to fight terrorism and extremism that haunted Xinjiang and restored order and stability in the region at the lowest cost. Hence, growth and prosperity reappear in Xinjiang. But the West has launched the most unscrupulous human rights attacks on China in recent years, aiming at its governance in Xinjiang.

Is China's governance in Xinjiang right? Is it protecting or jeopardizing human rights by striving for peace and stability in Xinjiang? Which is more important: the rights of vast majority of a people of a region and a country or the so-called rights of a very few extremist people who brazenly violate laws and launch terrorist attacks to achieve their extreme goal?

Two different values clash on Xinjiang question. Some Western politicians arrogantly regard their stances universal and they can represent the world in attacking China's governance in Xinjiang.

The first reason for the 50 countries to support China is that they understand Chinese government's goal and resolve in fighting terrorism and extremism in Xinjiang. These developing countries are aware of what they need most to develop human rights and of the severe damage extremism causes to their peaceful growth. They agree with China's idea of human rights and are optimistic about China's rapidly developing economy while simultaneously preventing the situation in Xinjiang from going out of control with firm measures.

Many developing countries have been interfered by Western countries in the name of protecting human rights. The suppression from the West has made it more difficult for these countries to govern and has complicated many issues. They have suffered due to the Western concept of human rights, which actually serves the West's political interests but doesn't fit local conditions.

When the US is cracking down on China and the Western forces are lying about

China violating human rights in Xinjiang, 50 countries stood up voicing their support for China. Some may thus face pressures from the West but this reflects that justice cannot be ignored and it is time for the world to see through the lies on human rights. The letter by 50 ambassadors to the UNOG shows that the vast international society denies the domination of the minority West in the rights sphere.

Saudi Arabia, Iran and many other Islamic countries take China's side on issues related to Xinjiang, which has torn to shreds the West's slander of "suppressing Islam." The terrorism and extremism that are under attack in Xinjiang are something that cannot be tolerated in Islamic countries. Some Western politicians try to incite opposition in the Islamic world by using Islam, but those countries are clearheaded. They know the West is the real source of discrimination and crackdown on Islam.

We wish the letter signed by 50 countries could be a turning point for the international society to redefine so many important human rights issues and a milestone for developing countries to regain the right of speech over human rights issues.

The world should no longer be fooled by some Western forces. The truth behind human rights needs to be uncovered and not left to be freely manipulated by the West. Every country has the right to make its own roadmap for economic and social development that includes plan of human rights progress according to its own domestic milieu.

US moves concerning Xinjiang doomed to fail

Global Times | Oct 10, 2019

US Secretary of State Mike Pompeo on October 8, 2019 announced visa restrictions on Chinese government officials "believed to be responsible for so-called suppression of Muslim ethnic minority groups" in Northwest China's Xinjiang Uygur Autonomous Region. Family members of those officials could also be subject to the restrictions.

Also using Xinjiang as an excuse, the US Department of Commerce on October 7, 2019 blacklisted 28 Chinese entities.

Pompeo has veneered US moves with beautiful rhetoric, portraying the US as sparing no efforts in protecting the human rights of Muslims in China's Xinjiang. This is the most shameful performance in the world.

Almost everybody knows that US policy always regards Muslims as heretics — US President Donald Trump issued the infamous Muslim travel ban soon after he took office. The border wall that the Trump administration promotes has showcased the country's real attitude toward minority groups. How could they really care about the rights of Muslims living far away in Xinjiang?

US government's moves concerning Xinjiang are going against the betterment of the situation in Xinjiang as well as vital development and prosperity in the region. This shows that adding more Chinese entities to the blacklist and visa restrictions on Chinese officials are obviously geopolitical moves by the US.

Xinjiang has made remarkable progress, with people enjoying human rights based on peace and stability. Having been through severe terrorist and extremist activities, Xinjiang has successfully protected the lives of numerous people and peace has returned to the region. It has avoided the fate of becoming another Chechnya.

Xinjiang is part of China. The interests of 1.4 billion Chinese people, including those living in Xinjiang, are the overriding standard to judge right and wrong in Xinjiang. The US standpoint is too twisted and ideological, but US elites like Pompeo are passing it off as the central idea on the Xinjiang issue. The Chinese people won't allow them to judge Xinjiang affairs with American interests.

To undermine Xinjiang's stability, certain US politicians like Pompeo even take terrorism and extremism as political resources that they can use. They make efforts to deny the goal of China's battle against terrorism and extremism in Xinjiang, and label governance in the region as a "crackdown on Muslims' rights." They, joining hands with other Western public opinion elites, are launching public opinion warfare against Xinjiang and are confusing right and wrong.

Most Westerners have never been to Xinjiang. They are prone to misguidance by public opinion and are likely to misunderstand Xinjiang. In addition, with powerful propaganda machines, the US and the West have established a closed public opinion sphere, misleading some people to believe that it is the mainstream opinion of the international community.

But the world has already changed. A huge world is emerging outside the US and the West. It is way bigger than the West and has diverse and urgent development missions. Its governance has received wide support.

The US is keen on promoting Western political system across the world. It might have the calculation that many developing countries are unable to manage Western politics and will stand at the edge of the US-centered world forever.

Xinjiang has taken on an entirely new look. Its socio-economic development, including the tourism industry is growing. It's not hard for every single person to understand how important it is for human rights and welfare to make a turbulent place become peaceful and prosperous. Only malice and prejudice can make people turn a blind eye to such a powerful fact.

The so-called sanctions imposed by the US on the entities and personnel concerning Xinjiang will have little effect. This is because the US cannot manipulate the entire world, and because its acts run counter to justice and human rights.

Western media report on Xinjiang lacks morality

Global Times | Nov 17, 2019

The New York Times on November 16, 2019 disclosed more than 400 pages of "leaked files" from Northwest China's Xinjiang Uygur Autonomous Region and maliciously attacked China's governance in Xinjiang. Western public opinion used their value system to criticize the vocational education and training centers in Xinjiang. Some Western elites are eager to see Xinjiang engulfed in extreme violence and chaos, but they hate it when the situation in Xinjiang has fundamentally improved.

The dispute over Xinjiang is a clash between not only two value systems, but also two interest systems. All Chinese people, including people of all ethnic groups in Xinjiang, hope for peace and prosperity in the region. Measures that help reach this goal are in line with morality and justice. The vocational education and training centers have actualized the goal with the minimum social cost.

Terrorism in Xinjiang has gradually been eliminated since these centers were set up. No more ordinary people are killed by rioters. The lives of those that already committed crimes as well as potential rioters have been saved. Many have returned to their normal lives through de-extremism education.

It is understandable that gaps exist between the Western value system and the situation in Xinjiang. But the terrible thing is the malevolence some Western elites have toward Xinjiang. Do they really care about innocent lives lost to terrorism? Did they feel excited about the repeated terrorist attacks in Xinjiang several years ago, especially the incidents that dragged down the entire China?

They should examine their consciences: Would they prefer to see Xinjiang continue to be chaotic, rather than the region regaining peace and prosperity?

Xinjiang has undergone tremendous changes in recent years. Peace, economic development and prosperous tourism have been regained. Residents of Xinjiang who have long been on tenterhooks and afraid to go out at night are no longer concerned about terrorist attacks. Such changes are significant to ordinary people in Xinjiang.

How many people in the world will oppose such changes in their own cities and prefer to live in a so-called democratic and free society where extremism prevails and terrorism is rampant?

Some areas which were sensitive in the past in southern Xinjiang are bordered by Pakistan and Afghanistan. But thanks to some decisive measures taken in Xinjiang, the region has moved completely away from the chaos of neighboring countries. Moreover, Xinjiang has not become another Republic of Chechnya.

Practice is the sole criterion for testing truth. The fact that Xinjiang is getting better speaks louder than all the West's preaching. Criticism from Western public opinion cannot overwhelm governance in Xinjiang. Today's governance in Xinjiang is correct, and has brought tangible benefits to local people. In the name of justice, the West has attacked the training centers which have made significant contributions to reversing the situation in Xinjiang. It can only prove their dogmatism and hypocrisy.

More than 50 countries have expressed their support for governance in Xinjiang, which from another perspective demonstrates how narrow-minded and self-righteous the West is.

Xinjiang should keep following the current successful governance model, further stabilize the situation, continuously release positive energy in society, and promote peace, stability and economic prosperity. History will evaluate the governance in Xinjiang, and the standard will never be determined by Western public opinion. It will only depend on what the people of all ethnic groups in Xinjiang have gained, and whether their lives have become better.

Geopolitics drives Western media's attack on China's governance in Xinjiang

Global Times | Nov 27, 2019

Recently, BBC and several other Western media outlets claimed to have seen the "leaked documents" on Xinjiang Uygur Autonomous Region and slandered vocational education and training centers there. For quite some time, the centers have been the target of certain Western media to attack China's human rights record, and they are probably going to create more "leak" in order to keep up the heat.

Attacking China on human rights is what the US and Western public opinion institutions are good at. This is not because their accusations are correct, but because they can use their ridiculous rhetoric to instigate the Western public against China. The US and Western media do not actually care about whether doing so benefits China's human rights development. What they want is to drive a wedge between China and Western public opinion by presenting a distorted description of China's situation, especially the condition of Xinjiang vocational education and training centers.

Western elites who have been attacking China's human rights record always evade very basic questions. For example, China's political system has greatly promoted economic development. Better living conditions and increased modernization in metropolitan areas, aren't those the development of human rights? Western media neglect all of these and just take the side of a few dissidents, always attacking China for the same thing.

On Xinjiang, they cannot face up to one question: Is having a safe and peaceful living environment a prerequisite for human rights? Xinjiang suffered terrorist attacks for quite a long time, and the situation had almost gone out of control. Wouldn't opening vocational education and training centers be a much more peaceful way to restore stability than going through a war like that in Chechnya?

China and the West have different standpoints on the issue of Xinjiang. What China really wants is to bring peaceful life back to the people there, and this is what real human rights are about. The reason the West likes to get involved in this issue is to a large extent out of hypocrisy. The West's intention of heating up the issue of Xinjiang is purely driven by geopolitics.

Chinese people do not need to be upset by the nonsense Western elites dish out. The world is complicated, and most importantly, China's detractors cannot have any real impact on the issue of Xinjiang. Their attacks may seem bustling, but actually turn out to be a bunch of bubbles.

First, they cannot have any impact on governance in Xinjiang. It has been three years since Xinjiang last saw a terror attack. Today's Xinjiang is on its way to rapid recovery, and its booming tourism is the best evidence. Western media blast China nonstop, but they cannot have any actual influence on Xinjiang. They just cannot do anything about it.

Besides, even with all these efforts that Western media put into, most countries do not follow them at all. Many Muslim countries publicly support China, backing China's policy in Xinjiang. The whole "leaked documents" drama shows how unwilling Western media outlets are to accept their failure in attacking China.

Western media outlets take themselves too seriously to even regard their own voices as an expression of the entire world. All they do is just repost among themselves and asking some NGOs, which have been manipulated by certain intelligence agencies to create a circus. All their tricks have been exposed.

Xinjiang has been free of the haze of terrorism and extremism. The people in

Xinjiang are on their way to a safer and more peaceful life. No one can speak for the people of Xinjiang. They are enjoying the same rights as other places in China. The future of Xinjiang is in their own hands.

Xinjiang's peace and prosperity unnerve US

Global Times | Dec 4, 2019

The US House of Representatives passed the so-called *Uygur Human Rights Policy Act of 2019* on December 4, 2019 (Beijing time). The bill requires the Trump administration to publicly denounce China's policy toward the Xinjiang Uygur Autonomous Region, impose sanctions on Xinjiang officials under the *Global Magnitsky Human Rights Accountability Act*, and restrict exports of technologies to Xinjiang, unscrupulously attempting to exercise long-arm jurisdiction over Xinjiang.

This is an intervention bill, but only a paper tiger without one particular lever that can actually impact the governance in Xinjiang. The US Congress is becoming a machine, producing sleazy China-related bills which can only entertain themselves.

China's governance in Xinjiang is effective, which has immensely curbed terrorism and made great progress in de-radicalization. Xinjiang is getting increasingly better day by day; peace and prosperity are reappearing in the vast region. We should maintain such a stable situation and ignore those anti-China politicians in the US Congress. They need to know how powerless they are. Yes, they are despised like clowns by the Chinese people.

Regarding China-related issues, the US Congress is turning itself into an ideological institution, and a show field that cooperates with Western media to discredit China. US lawmakers are grabbing the job of some commentators to discuss China issues to raise ratings.

US political elites are increasingly enchanted by launching public opinion wars against China, as this is what they are best at, and its cost is quite low. It can also help release their anti-China sentiment and produce a "sense of accomplishment."

China should be prepared for a long-term battle with the US. Faced with the force of US opinion machines toward an anti-China direction, we must pinpoint the parts that may cause actual harm, and despise those full of bubbles. We must deal with them seriously, but not be overly devoted. Robustness is golden.

The most fundamental way to defeat slander against Xinjiang affairs by certain US and Western forces is to govern the region well, maintain the current trend of stability and development, strengthen protections of the rights and interests of the people of all ethnic groups. If Xinjiang is indeed getting better, all sorts of defamation will lose their foundation.

China should take strong countermeasures on US interference in Xinjiang. On one hand, the real facts and true information about Xinjiang need to be spread to the world. By doing so, more people will understand the necessity and rationale behind the work of de-extremism in Xinjiang. On the other hand, we must fight back at the US. Even though it might not change what the US has done, it can still be a warning to other countries, making them think twice about the price they will pay by following the US.

The US has run out of cards against China. As long as China analyses the impact that the US has caused wisely and adopts countermeasures properly, it will be easy to get around this unfavorable situation. The most important thing for China is not to let the US get under its skin, and secure the strong momentum for its development. In a few decades, when China's economy is as powerful as that of the US, the US will not and cannot sanction China anymore. To fight its way out, China can only do so by its own strength.

Enduring the hardships to revive is a lesson that the Chinese already learned thousands of years ago. China's prosperity in the future will be the best response to US provocation.

Why do Western media ignore China's documentary on Xinjiang?

Global Times | Dec 7, 2019

An English language documentary, *Fighting Terrorism in Xinjiang*, which was aired on China's state broadcaster CGTN on December 5, 2019 unprecedentedly exposed the trauma that violent terrorism and religious extremism have brought about to the region. It has garnered extensive attention on overseas social media platforms. Some netizens from abroad commented that it uncovers the fact that Western media outlets are telling lies about Xinjiang and that Western journalists who have hyped Xinjiang issue by fabricating stories should carefully watch the documentary.

However, a strange phenomenon is that contrary to the heated discussion among netizens, no established Western media outlets have reported on the documentary so far. Western media and Western politicians who always scrutinize the Xinjiang issue have collectively gone silent. Is there anything that more aptly shows the hypocrisy and double standards of these media and politicians over the Xinjiang issue?

Western media and politicians have expressed particular "concerns" about Xinjiang recently. They fabricated an image of Xinjiang based on their imagination and used it to slander China.

The documentary tells of a Xinjiang different from what they imagined, citing indisputable factual material. This is probably why it has been snubbed by

Western media. They have neither the courage nor the will to acknowledge they contrive stories about Xinjiang. They may never expect China, which used to keep a low profile over the Xinjiang issue, would have made such an English language documentary and are feeling lost about how to respond to it.

One certain thing is that when it comes to the Xinjiang issue, the Western media don't report about facts and instead report selectively. Their reports are ideologically driven, subjective, partial and don't care about facts. What they have done is an insult to media professionalism, having degraded themselves to "political thugs" against China.

It's noticeable that the documentary made public many rare video footages of terrorist attacks including the Urumqi riots on July 5, 2009, the Tiananmen Square terror attack on October 28, 2013 and the Kunming train station assault on March 1, 2014. Incomplete statistics show that from 1990 to 2016, thousands of violent terrorist attacks were launched in Xinjiang, killing large numbers of innocent people and hundreds of police officers. A total of 197 people died in the "7/5" Urumqi riots alone.

Those Westerners who point an accusing finger at the Xinjiang issue don't live in Xinjiang. The grim anti-terrorism situation there is merely a topic of discussion for them, but for more than 24 million Xinjiang people, it means a horrible threat to their life and property. It is reassuring that no terrorist attacks have occurred in Xinjiang over the past three years. This is a big victory for Xinjiang in the global war on terror and extremism. The region's counter-terrorism measures are appropriate.

Mainstream Western media refuse to recognize Xinjiang's achievements in combating terrorism. Instead, they are using their politicized human rights criteria to find fault with the region. They have become the accomplice of the terrorists and extremists.

We can't count on outsiders to report truth about China. We should tell our own stories. There are many touching and commendable stories concerning

Xinjiang's anti-terrorism efforts. The documentary is a start, and we should produce more works of this kind in the future. The facts about Xinjiang are indisputable and Western propagandists can't shun them eventually.

Abdulaheb should be wary of risks from West

Global Times | Dec 9, 2019

According to Western media reports, a Uygur woman named Asiye Abdulaheb, currently a Dutch citizen, said she had helped with the release of "secret Chinese government documents" on Xinjiang. She claimed that she and her ex-husband "received death threats," and thus hoped to "protect herself and her family from retaliation" by speaking out.

This story sounds so vivid in the Western context. It's very much in line with the Western public opinion's imagination of an "authoritarian China," but it cannot hold up to closer inspection. Abdulaheb asserted that she had "received death threats" on Facebook Messenger. Even if it's true, how can it be concluded that the threats were sent by Chinese related agencies and were serious? The internet houses all sorts of people and forces. They may send such a message for various purposes.

It was reported that she posted a tweet in June 2019 "with the excerpt from the documents" on her own initiative. The move was apparently with the intention of drawing attention. The woman's way of doing things shows that she is not afraid of creating trouble. She didn't intend to be an "anonymous whistle-blower" from the very beginning. But she told reporters that she was scared when receiving an online threat. Her behavior was inconsistent.

Abdulaheb's profile photo has been spread all over the Western media, a result of her interaction with Western public opinion. And it seems that both Western media outlets and Abdulaheb herself are willing to see such an outcome.

As a Chinese media outlet, the Global Times has no way of weighing the authenticity of Abdulaheb's story. We can only draw the conclusion from her story that she knows what the Western media wants, and has the guts and solutions to provide a story they need.

As for the death threat she mentioned, we would like to tell her and the Western public that the Chinese government has never had a record of endangering personal safety to dissidents living abroad.

Since the end of the 1980s, a large number of dissidents went into exile in Western countries. Many of them continued to engage in acts that jeopardized China's national interests, but none received life threats from the Chinese mainland.

If Abdulaheb is worried about her safety, we advise her to guard against US intelligence agencies and extreme Xinjiang secessionist forces. They may exploit her to stir up extreme incidents in order to frame the Chinese government.

By making public her identity, Abdulaheb has attracted more attention in the West. Some Western forces are further exploiting her to smear the Chinese government. Abdulaheb might be happy to be used since it fits her interests and those of Western forces.

The problem is Abdulaheb thinks the more her identity is made known, the safer she will be. But this logic doesn't hold water and could endanger her, because as she gains greater recognition in the West, Western public opinion will be made to believe that the Chinese government wants to harm her. To some dark forces, it is tempting to threaten her personal safety and frame the Chinese government.

No matter what she has done, we wish that she is safe in the Netherlands. She already jeopardized China's national interests, and any harm to her safety will not undo the damage. China has no incentive to do any harm to her. But it's different for US intelligent agencies and Xinjiang secessionist forces. Even in Western media, there may be people who wish to see something happen to her. This is the real risk that Abdulaheb should seriously watch.

Dirty public opinion war won't deter China's governance in Xinjiang

Global Times | Dec 23, 2019

After Turkish-German soccer star Mesut Özil took to Twitter to criticize the governance of China's Xinjiang Uygur Autonomous Region, some other sports and cultural celebrities have followed suit, putting pressure on Xinjiang through social media.

Some others used social media to post "missing person" posts to question Chinese authorities' claim that all trainees at the vocational education and training centers have graduated. Most of those posts are cheap spam.

Both incidents are clearly being planned and pushed by some anti-China forces. In the first case, some sports and cultural celebrities are mobilized; although most of them believe in Islam, some of them live in the West and are deeply influenced by Western public opinion. And they choose Western social media to send political message, which is worth noting itself. Strictly speaking, these posts are more echoes of Western opinion, rather than attitude of the Islamic world.

When commenting on Özil's post, a spokesperson of the Chinese Ministry of Foreign Affairs said that he is welcome to visit China's Xinjiang.

Western public opinion has overwhelmingly slandered and labeled Xinjiang's governance, but a handful of celebrities following suit on Western social media have never been to Xinjiang. They just blindly followed what Western media described.

They should be encouraged to visit Xinjiang to see if it is true that mosques have been destroyed and Muslim women have been forced to marry Han people.

Seeing is believing. Özil and others should take responsibility for their remarks on Xinjiang. They should come to Xinjiang to see if the Muslim community has smooth communication network, and compared with chaotic ethnic regions of other countries, if Muslims in Xinjiang have better life or not.

Those Xinjiang-related posts, in general, are a wave of organized or coordinated pranks. First, according to authorities in Xinjiang, more than half of those missing person posts are vague and they don't know who the proclaimed missing person is and the individual cannot be found in Xinjiang. Some are indeed trainees who have graduated from the vocational education and training centers. Some others are not trainees but criminals who have already been sentenced for crimes they committed, and quite a few of them have been listed in the previous "missing people" posts abroad. Xinjiang has long publicized their crimes, but this time these cases have been hyped again.

As we all know, social media is often not the place to be reasonable. It is more suitable for slogans, troubles and demonstration of public opinion. The organizers of those missing person's posts are catering to Western public opinion and creating a new wave of public opinion to smear Xinjiang. The truth doesn't matter to them at all.

There have been many violent and terrorist incidents in Xinjiang in the past, and of course some criminals need to be brought to justice. There is a clear line between criminal prosecution and the work of vocational education and training centers whose mission is to de-radicalize. Some of the dark forces outside the country have deliberately mixed them, questioning a legitimate campaign.

These are not new to people who understand the internet. Those posts are not the pursuit of justice, but a dirty war of public opinion.

In the end, what happened in Xinjiang is not a debate about values, but a movement to restore peace and prosperity, a movement to defend and save the lives of countless people. Human rights in the slogan cannot replace the rights that more than 20 million people of all ethnic groups in Xinjiang cannot live without every day. Misunderstandings will eventually melt, while lies will be deflated or laid bare with facts.

Chapter V

XINJIANG KEY WORDS: PROSPERITY, STABILITY, CONFIDENCE

Over the past 10 years, the situation in Xinjiang has remained under control, as a fundamental turnaround has been achieved after a turbulent journey. This is the joint result of China's institutional and national strengths. China can accomplish any task under the leadership of the Party, including the eradication of the influence of the "three evil forces" in Xinjiang of separatism, extremism and terrorism. Chinese society as a whole should thank Xinjiang officials and people for their hard work and sacrifice over the years. The world should respect and understand the fundamental improvement of Xinjiang's situation at minimum social cost. Xinjiang has not become an "ulcer" in Central Asia, but has become a permanent contributor to regional prosperity. Those Western forces who have long accused Xinjiang of improper governance should re-examine their consciences.

Governance in Xinjiang deserves respect

Global Times | Oct 15, 2018

Xinjiang's situation has been improving in recent years. Its flourishing tourism shows Chinese societal confidence in Xinjiang security is recovering rapidly. The Xinjiang Uygur Autonomous Region revised its anti-extremism regulation on October 9, 2018, which will further promote the fight against the three evil forces of separatism, extremism and terrorism in Xinjiang.

The regulation stipulates that government above county level can set up vocational training centers. This has attracted wide attention. Since the beginning of 2018, some Western media and politicians have been viciously attacking actions adopted by Xinjiang to help those affected by extremism to return to their families and society through educational transformation, accusing Xinjiang of "violating human rights." Trainees learn the national language, laws and job skills in the institutes. Western forces accuse the authorities of religious persecution. Radical Western politicians and media have set off a wave of anti-China rhetoric and Xinjiang has become their new target.

When terrorism was spreading in Xinjiang a few years ago, the local authorities took firm action and successfully prevented the situation from worsening. Xinjiang miraculously realized a soft landing toward peace and stability. The turmoil was avoided and tranquility was restored.

Thanks to the incredible hard work of people and officials in the region, the success has contributed to Northwest China and even the whole country. By strengthening governance, Xinjiang has avoided extreme situations which happened in other parts of the world. It should be seen as a rare positive example of governing high-risk situations.

From Bosnia and Herzegovina to Kosovo, Libya and Syria, the tragic stories are different but also similar. Many people died and a large number of refugees fled those regions. The West intervened in those regions' turmoil, but the price was high. Does the West really want to see shocking humanitarian disasters in Xinjiang and watch Xinjiang create hundreds of thousands even millions of refugees?

Officials in Xinjiang and Western forces have different goals. The governance in Xinjiang is to restore peace and stability, wipe out extremism and benefit people of all ethnicities in the region. But Western forces only want to find fault with China, suppress China internationally on the one hand and mess up governance in Xinjiang on the other.

Those Western forces don't care about the welfare of the Xinjiang people. They would rather sacrifice stability in Xinjiang and the lives of hundreds of thousands for a single geopolitical victory over China.

Vocational training centers in Xinjiang and internment in the West are fundamentally different. An increasing number of trainees reintegrated into society and found employment after finishing training at the vocational training centers. Obviously, vocational training is a periodic and temporary plan aimed at eradicating extremism. It has been proven effective with the least cost to Xinjiang stability.

Some Westerners who know nothing about Xinjiang interpret the region with their stereotypes and political prejudice. In the West-led opinion sphere, they make up a set of narratives against governance in the region. These narratives are detached from the reality in Xinjiang and full of their own values, geopolitics and sentiments.

Even Chinese authorities find Xinjiang governance a thorny issue, so how can Westerners have the sincerity and patience to rack their brains to offer suggestions? They are just messing up the whole thing and creating a narrative against China.

China needs to strengthen communication with the world over Xinjiang governance, but the purpose is not to persuade Western political and opinion elites who hold a hostile attitude toward China. They don't plan to understand Xinjiang.

They more hope to see a turbulent Xinjiang. They are only interested in finding a new perspective to mount an offensive against China and add a fresh angle to their outdated rhetoric.

Governance in Xinjiang stands on righteous side

Global Times | Oct 17, 2018

Some governments above county level in the Xinjiang Uygur Autonomous Region have set up vocational training centers, where people who are brainwashed by extreme thoughts and have committed misdemeanors learn Putonghua, China's national language, laws and job skills. These training centers, helping to enable these people to return to normal life, have played a key role in stabilizing Xinjiang. The anti-extremism regulation released by the region provides the legal basis for it.

Western opinion has launched a stinging attack on governance in Xinjiang. Who is standing on the righteous side, the Xinjiang government or Western forces? The Xinjiang government has been aiming to stabilize Xinjiang and wipe out violent terrorist attacks. After a terror attack on July 5, 2009, local government exerted enormous efforts to achieve this goal. But after another terror attack in 2013, the situation in Xinjiang deteriorated and was about to spiral out of control.

Since the vocational training centers were set up, the situation in Xinjiang has changed for the better. They may not operate flawlessly, but aim to stop impetuous killings and comfort people frightened by violent terrorist activities. These are the core of human rights.

What do those Westerners who denounce governance in Xinjiang want? They seem to show a tolerant attitude toward people who are brainwashed by extremism and commit acts that damage peace and order in Xinjiang.

Extreme thoughts used to spread recklessly in Xinjiang and radicals acted wantonly, leading to more violent terror attacks. More than 20 million people of all ethnicities in Xinjiang lost their peaceful lives. People from other parts of China didn't dare travel there and young people from Xinjiang were leaving their homeland. The basic conditions of human rights in Xinjiang were being destroyed bit by bit. Is this what Westerners want?

It's believed most Westerners do not want Xinjiang to become chaotic. They just don't understand the real situation in Xinjiang and are misled by ideologically frantic opinion elites. But there are some Western political and opinion elites who are not only arrogant, but also malicious against China. They just want to see a turbulent Xinjiang. They hope China's governance model fails in Xinjiang and makes Xinjiang a mishap amid China's rise. But they don't need to shoulder responsibility for the welfare of Xinjiang people. They are only interested in messing with local governance and embarrassing the central government. Governance in Xinjiang stands on the high moral ground, as the objective of governance is happiness and benefit for the Xinjiang people. In the West-led opinion context, this objective may meet with temporary grievances, but people's peaceful life is the eventual criteria of this objective.

China understands the difference between its own condition and that of the West's. It also understands the differences in values. China will try to communicate more with the West about controversial topics. But whatever China does prioritizes the interests of the Chinese people. The objective and practice of governance in Xinjiang is justified and our belief will not be shaken due to external misjudgment and accusations.

Xinjiang's stability more important than pleasing the West

Global Times | Nov 16, 2018

Reuters reported on November 15, 2018, that a group of 15 Western ambassadors in Beijing, including those from Canada, Australia and some EU member states, wrote a joint letter seeking a meeting with the top official of China's Xinjiang Uygur Autonomous Region over vocational training centers, which they called "re-education camps."

Intervention in Xinjiang affairs by Western countries has gradually intensified. Some Western politicians and media have shown a strong willingness to exert greater pressure on China.

But in doing so, they must be aware of the link between their behavior and the attitude of international society, the wish of people in Xinjiang and the entire China, as well as their own capabilities.

The voices of some Western nations have lately been concentrated, but they represent the minority in the world. On Xinjiang affairs, China has been maintaining good communication with Islamic countries and the developing world. Those who tend to stir up trouble are always the minority among Western countries, which hardly represents the world. To be more specific, they can only represent one voice on earth.

The kind-hearted Chinese people do not wish to be caught up in any conflicts over human rights with any nation. If we can balance the feelings of Westerners and Chinese interests, Beijing is willing to meet them halfway. But the Xinjiang issue touched the bottom line of the interests of local ethnic groups and all other Chinese people.

Those Westerners should think about it. For people in Xinjiang and the entire

China, which task is more important? Restoring social stability to avoid the spread of violence which could lead to a humanitarian disaster, or accept Western principles in exchange for a cease-fire on human rights conflicts between China and some Western countries?

The vocational training centers have already had an immediate effect on the de-radicalization of Xinjiang society, which has been playing a decisive role in restoring peace and tranquility in the region. Why would Xinjiang listen to the fault-finding of the West, which contradicts reality?

Over the past few years, many violent terrorist incidents have erupted in the region. Fortunately, the efforts of officials and people of all ethnic groups have turned the table. We don't mind if those Westerners do not help or give them their blessings. But it is, indeed, irritating to see them stand on the opposite end of the fundamental interests of Xinjiang people.

Regardless of how much pressure the West places on China, Xinjiang will stick to its own path. Will far fewer lives be lost? Has stability been established? Has Xinjiang's comprehensive development been achieved? When history judges Xinjiang's governance, these will be the criteria.

Xinjiang must maintain long-term stability

Global Times | May 6, 2019

The US Assistant Secretary of Defense Randall G. Schriver recently labeled the vocational education and training centers in several places in China's Xinjiang Uygur Autonomous Region as "concentration camps."

This is the craziest attack by a US official on the governance of Xinjiang.

Washington's growing smear campaign on China's Xinjiang affairs is clearly part of a broader US policy of suppressing China. But the US does not have the ability to mess up the situation in Xinjiang. Even in the international arena, it is very difficult for the US to open up a diplomatic front specifically for Xinjiang.

So, we don't have to be swayed by the whining of some US officials. China has the capital to advance its work in accordance with the established policy on the governance of Xinjiang.

How to effectively manage Xinjiang well should be the first consideration in the long-term affairs of the region. It is worthwhile to pay attention to the reaction of international public opinion and try to increase the understanding of the Western world, but it should be placed in a secondary position.

At present, the situation in Xinjiang has shown an obvious trend of stabilization, which shows that various measures, including the establishment of vocational education and training centers, have played a role.

New Zealand and Sri Lanka have recently suffered religious massacres. Xinjiang, in turn, has been shielded from the flow of international terrorism and extremism. International opinion will gradually turn in the favor of Xinjiang governance.

As long as Xinjiang can maintain basic stability and avoid the catastrophic resurgence of violent and terrorist activities, the number of education and training centers will gradually reduce after a period of time.

The governance in Xinjiang will gradually return to normal, and in this process Xinjiang will finally bid farewell to large-scale bloody terrorist activities.

All the accusations of so-called ethnic persecution in Xinjiang are historically indefensible and will eventually fade away.

The next challenge for Xinjiang is to maintain the current stability and consolidate the learning outcomes of many trainees of the education and training centers to prevent a new wave of extreme events.

The people of all ethnic groups in Xinjiang, and the whole country, are a community of shared interests. This must be fully understood by the people of all ethnic groups in Xinjiang.

Xinjiang needs to strengthen grass-roots publicity and education work, so that people in sensitive areas can understand the general situation of the game between China and the US, as well as the attempt made by some Western forces to incite extremism within China, which would serve as cannon fodder for their China strategy.

Xinjiang may not need to set the level of social security higher than other parts of the country. But it must stay basically stable and resolutely avoid large-scale terrorist activities that occurred in previous years. This will be the key indicator for a final evaluation of Xinjiang's governance outcomes at this stage.

China's anti-terrorism experience in Xinjiang useful to UN

Global Times | Jun 16, 2019

Under-Secretary-General of the UN Office of Counter-Terrorism Vladimir Voronkov recently paid a visit to Northwest China's Xinjiang Uygur Autonomous Region, despite objections from some Western countries such as the US and the UK. US Deputy Secretary of State John Sullivan on June 14, 2019 spoke by phone with UN Secretary-General Antonio Guterres to "convey deep concerns regarding Voronkov's travel to Xinjiang" and claimed China's counter-terrorism measures in the region amount to a "repression campaign" against Uygur people and other Muslims.

Washington is obviously not playing a simple word game but aims to throw the Xinjiang question into its presupposed human rights–related trap and mislead the world's public opinion on China's efforts in counter-terrorism.

The Xinjiang question is first and foremost about counter-terrorism, otherwise human rights and stable development are like a cynical tale of a tub. For a long time, the West has smeared and attacked China over human rights issues by not only spreading but also creating slanders.

Those who attack China over the Xinjiang question have used the veneer as defenders of human rights, but in fact many of them didn't know what has happened in Xinjiang over the past few years and some didn't even know where Xinjiang is.

Just as diplomats and media correspondents from Muslim countries have seen in Xinjiang, the vocational education and training centers there are a helpful tryout of counter-terrorism and counter-extremism. People brainwashed by extreme thoughts can learn skills to help them return to society.

These measures protect people living in Xinjiang from the dangers of terrorism, safeguard social stability and promote economic development.

Today, Xinjiang is experiencing the best period of development in recent years. Tourists to the autonomous region sharply increased by 75 percent in 2018, while per capita disposable income of Xinjiang residents surpassed 20,000 yuan ($2,888).

Xinjiang has been hard hit by terrorism. But due to timely and effective actions, terrorism has been contained in the region. Counter-terrorism measures in the region are jointly carried out with social governance, which has strongly curbed a resurgence of terrorist activities and put efforts in cracking down on the foundation of terrorism.

The whole process has been effectively carried out on the basis of maintaining people's stable life and making people enjoy the benefits of counter-terrorism. Hence, it is winning more and more support.

Counter-terrorism is a global challenge. The situation in Xinjiang has fundamentally improved with a large amount of work but relatively small social cost. People will realize how precious the Xinjiang experience is if they compare the region to Chechnya, Afghanistan and Syria.

Not everything is perfect in the process of enacting a large-scale fight against terrorism and extremism. When we evaluate counter-terrorism activities, we should consider their effects and costs. The US counter-terrorism tool is to go to war in Afghanistan and the Middle East at cost of a shocking number of innocent lives, which has not produced a solid effect. That's why the US and other Western countries should learn from Xinjiang's experience. Accusing counter-terrorism activities in Xinjiang of harming human rights is disrespecting the lives of people there. They humiliate the lofty concept of human rights.

While the West plays word games and a political game of "go" on the Xinjiang question, the region's governments at all levels are pursuing peace, stability and prosperity for all people living there. Time will prove the achievements of China's governance in Xinjiang.

Xinjiang's prosperity driven by China's strength

Global Times | Jul 5, 2019

What is Xinjiang like today? At the end of June 2019, Xinjiang began to operate special tourist trains connecting major scenic spots in the north and south of the region. Tourism is recovering and developing rapidly throughout the autonomous region, and performance of tourism is a gauge of local social security conditions.

Today, Xinjiang experiences peace and development. The region was one step away from the turmoil triggered by terrorist attacks and ethnic and religious conflicts. It came close to becoming a second Chechnya or a second Syria. Both internal and external forces once launched a raid to turn Xinjiang into the new focus of the "three evil forces" (terrorism, extremism and separatism) in Central Asia. However, the Party and government led people of all ethnic groups in Xinjiang to turn the tide and eventually ease the situation and place the region on the right track.

For people of all ethnic groups in Xinjiang, peace and stability are the starting point of happy lives. Back in the days when violent terrorism was frequent, investment continued to leave, tourists avoided the region, the economy declined and people were haunted by fear. Such a nightmare gave human rights no space. What once happened in Xinjiang was also having an impact outside the region, including Beijing, Kunming and other Chinese cities.

In recent years, the governance measures Xinjiang has taken have brought a miraculous change to the region.

Xinjiang has been free of violent terrorist attacks for nearly 30 consecutive months. This has not only restored peace and tranquility in Xinjiang, but has also rebuilt confidence in its society and reversed Xinjiang's image in the country.

Western public opinion has been carrying out various smears on the governance of Xinjiang. In particular, they have attacked vocational education and training centers in the region. However, the disturbance brought on by these attacks is incomparable with the benefits enjoyed by people of all ethnic groups in Xinjiang and Chinese society as a whole. Real peace and stability in Xinjiang is far more important than what Western public opinion thinks of the situation. Chinese people's understanding of this situation is maturing and gradually becoming an unassailable force.

Those Western powers vocal about the issue do not care about the well-being of Xinjiang's people. The Western forces that attack China's governance in Xinjiang are all the proponents of the "China threat" and "China collapse" theories. Challenging China via the Xinjiang issue is, for them, interchangeable with challenging China via the Hong Kong issue.

As long as Xinjiang remains peaceful and stable, it will be very difficult for those in the West to create a stir about Xinjiang or keep Western public opinion focused on the area in the long run. The hyped topics, such as vocational education and training centers, will gradually become monotonous and will increasingly lose their credibility in Western media.

Over the past 10 years, the situation in Xinjiang has remained under control, but a fundamental turnaround has also been achieved after a turbulent journey. This is the joint result of China's institutional and national strengths. China can accomplish any task under the leadership of the Party, including the eradication of the influence of the "three evil forces" in Xinjiang.

Chinese society as a whole should thank the Xinjiang officials and people for their hard work and sacrifice over the years. The world should respect and understand the fundamental improvement of Xinjiang's situation at minimum social cost. Xinjiang has not become an "ulcer" in Central Asia, but has become a permanent contributor to regional prosperity. Those Western forces who have long accused Xinjiang of improper governance should re-examine their consciences.

Xinjiang situation to realize a soft landing

Global Times | Aug 1, 2019

Officials from Northwest China's Xinjiang Uygur Autonomous Region said at a press conference on July 30, 2019 that most trainees have graduated from the vocational education and training centers in Xinjiang and secured jobs. This has garnered extensive attention both at home and abroad.

The governance in Xinjiang has made great achievements in recent years, fundamentally turning around the situation in the autonomous region. Violent terrorist activities once rampant have been effectively contained. There have been no new violent terrorist activities in the autonomous region for consecutive tens of months. Peace and prosperity have re-emerged throughout Xinjiang. The rapid recovery of tourism is a prominent sign of the turnaround.

However, over the past two years, Western public opinion has been accusing China's governance in Xinjiang, focusing on the vocational education and training centers, which the West slanders as "re-education camps." Western opinion claims the aim of setting up these centers is to "persecute the religion" and "eradicate Uygur culture."

Xinjiang has made these achievements under unfair external pressure, bringing back precious peace and development to people of all ethnic groups. Counter-terrorism and de-radicalization have always been an arduous task. The collective and unreasonable condemnation of Western opinion has created additional challenges. But Xinjiang has not wavered in its determination to defend the fundamental interests of people of all ethnic groups, neither has China's determination.

This time, the autonomous region released a great amount of crucial information on the vocational education and training centers. Information received by the Global Times through other channels also shows that a great number of trainees have indeed graduated and returned to the society.

Although officials have yet to publish detailed figures, the improving situation of Xinjiang is expanding to all spheres. As a powerful interim measure, the vocational education and training centers play a pivotal role in making these achievements possible.

It is worthy of recognition that the situation in Xinjiang has been changed through strengthening social governance that uproots extremism rather than through massive violence. Without an "anti-terror war" or "cultural revolution," Xinjiang has kept its original social structure and cultural tradition, but terrorism and related evil forces have been destroyed.

Xinjiang has not closed its door and completely rejected the views and feelings of the outside world. Over the past year, Xinjiang has invited tens of foreign envoy groups, international observers and journalists to visit the autonomous region, especially the vocational education and training centers. This attitude is a manifestation of Xinjiang's sincerity in combining anti-terrorism and de-radicalization work with respect for human rights.

Xinjiang once suffered from chaos over a period of time. Terrorists were rampant and extremism echoed external forces. Xinjiang carried out counter-terrorism and de-radicalization work under pressure because of the strong leadership of the Communist Party of China Central Committee and support of the whole country, also because the government cares about ordinary people and takes responsibility for the interests of them.

The happy life of people of all ethnic groups in Xinjiang is the supreme judgment on the governance of Xinjiang. History will not draw conclusions based on Western bias.

The international community has a fair view on the governance in Xinjiang. Fifty countries spoke highly of the governance in Xinjiang last week, a milestone in the debate on human rights in Xinjiang. With more trainees of the vocational education and training centers graduating and back to society, the Xinjiang question will realize a soft landing. This is a great victory for the Chinese people, including those of all ethnic peoples in Xinjiang.